AN UNCERTAIN ATTACHMENT

He stretched his long legs out on his bedroll. He was impatient to leave. He wanted to ride away from this ranch with no guilt and no attachments.

But he wanted her—even now, just thinking about the soft swell of her breasts made his body harden.

"Dammit," he ground out, trying to forget about the way his body was reacting to her.

But closing his eyes didn't help because he could see visions of her dancing, her tangled hair swaying about her, her hips moving invitingly. The ache inside him grew deeper, the emptiness blacker. He wanted to be the man to take her hand and dance beside her, if only for a moment in time.

Whit's eyes snapped open. He couldn't allow anything to hinder his search for Drew. Guilt anchored him to the past, and determination dictated his future. His goal was a path he must follow to the end.

Other *Leisure* books by Constance O'Banyon:

HAWK'S PLEDGE

Constance O'Banyon

LEISURE BOOKS NEW YORK CITY

A LEISURE BOOK®

July 2006

Published by

Dorchester Publishing Co., Inc.
200 Madison Avenue
New York, NY 10016

ISBN 0-8439-5635-6

The name "Leisure Books" and the stylized "L" with design are trademarks of Dorchester Publishing Co., Inc.

Printed in the United States of America.

Visit us on the web at www.dorchesterpub.com.

*This one is for you, Glenn Hoyle.
You were my inspiration for this book
because you once walked in the boots
of my hero. With so much love,
from a grateful sister.*

HAWK'S PLEDGE

Prologue

El Paso, Texas—1849

"Stand up straight, boy," Nolan Wilkins said harshly as he jabbed his young nephew in the back with a stubby finger.

Drew Hawk tried to comply as he held tightly to his fidgety two-year-old sister, Jena Leigh, who was squirming to get down and investigate her surroundings. "I don't want to see you slouch when the matron comes in—is that clear? If she ever gets here," Wilkins grumbled under his breath.

Ten-year-old Whitford Hawk stepped between Drew and their uncle. "You leave my brother alone," the young boy ordered defiantly, glaring at the man he despised. Little Laura Anne pressed her small body close to Whit, her eyes wide with fright. The young boy placed a soothing hand on her shoulder. "Don't be afraid, Laura Anne," he said gently to his sister. "I won't let anyone hurt you or Jena Leigh or Drew."

Wilkins's eyes blazed with anger and he started

1

toward Whit to retaliate, but the door to the office opened abruptly, and he turned to face the woman who swept into the room.

Mrs. Kingsley's gaze touched lightly on the four Hawk children, and then she focused her attention on the adult in the room. "You must be Mr. Wilkins. I'm sorry to have kept you waiting," she said by way of an apology. "I'm run off my feet—three children coming down with sore throats and two others with earaches. But I mustn't bother you with my problems. Now what was it you wanted to see me about?"

Whit's chin quivered; he knew that if he gave in to the fear that choked him, he'd only upset his sisters. As he was the oldest of the family, it fell to him to be the strong one and to protect his brother and two sisters from whatever bad luck came from the meeting with the matron of the orphanage. He had to hold the family together no matter what happened—they had only one another, and he wasn't about to let anyone separate them. Taking a deep breath, he attempted to gain control of his emotions.

Through the open window a hot blast of wind swept across Whit's face—he hated it here. Not wanting to hear what the adults were talking about, he stared instead at the scenery beyond the fenced yard, at the barren, sunbaked land. To him, El Paso seemed dull and colorless, with the exception of the line of trees that grew along the banks of the Rio Grande. In the distance he saw rugged, desolate mountains that appeared to be bare except for the scraggly scrub brush and cedars that the never-ceasing wind had twisted into unnatural shapes.

This harsh land would never be home to him. His

home had been the seaport town of Galveston, where soft breezes blew off the Gulf of Mexico and bright flowers of every imaginable description competed with the spectacular colors that streaked the western horizon at sundown. Whit longed for the carefree days when his family had been happy living in that city. But that part of his life had been smashed, and his memories were becoming vague and distant. His reality was here in this inhospitable land where the heat scorched his throat with each deep breath he took.

Whit's attention settled on Laura Anne, who was clinging to him. Her hair was snarled, and he ran his fingers through the blond curls, trying to untangle them. His heart throbbed as he listened to his uncle explain that he could no longer feed and clothe the four youngsters who had been dumped on his door- step. Gripping Laura Anne's small hand in his, Whit watched Drew run a comforting hand over Jena Leigh's back as she whimpered softly. Whit saw the uncer- tainty in his brother's eyes, and he knew just what Drew was feeling, because Whit felt the same emo- tions himself: they were humiliated by the circum- stances that had led them to this day. Pride ran deep in the Hawk children—pride was about all they had left now.

Whit flinched in indignation as his uncle continued to speak. Nolan Wilkins was a small, agile man with boundless energy, and always seemed to be in motion. What hair he had left was curly and stuck up in sprigs across the bald spot in the middle of his head. Whit noticed that his uncle was having trouble finding a comfortable position for his hands; he poked them in his pockets, drummed them against the arm of the chair, then finally steepled them on the desk in front of him.

"You see, Mrs. Kingsley, these here kids ain't even my own kin. Their pa was my wife's brother, and he's simply no good. He gambled away a thriving shipping company down to Galveston way, so his wife up and left him and the kids and went off with another man. My brother-in-law, being of weak character, had the gall to dump these kids on me while he went off galli-vanting, free as a bird. I let the kids stay at my place while my wife was alive—she insisted on it. She was good about things like family—I ain't."

Wilkins glanced in irritation at Jena Leigh when she began to whimper again, and he watched critically while Drew soothed her before he continued explain-ing the situation to the matron. "I'm not a rich man— I got me a small spread down near the Rio Pecos, but I don't hardly make enough to keep myself going, much less these here kids. I just can't take care of 'em any longer."

With an unreadable expression on her face, Mrs. Kingsley sat in a stately pose behind the scarred oak desk. "How did you find out about my foundation, Mr. Wilkins?"

"Reverend Stillwater, in Pecos, told me you take in kids who ain't got no family, and that you don't charge for it. The reverend said you'd turned your own house into a place for homeless kids—was he right about that?"

"I do take in children if the circumstances are right." Her gaze shifted quickly to the children, then back to Wilkins. "But keep in mind we can always use donations. We have thirty-five youngsters to feed and clothe."

Wilkins twisted uneasily in his chair. "Don't go looking for me to give you money. I ain't got it to give."

The matron whisked a strand of gray hair back into her snood and patted it into place. She had a chubby face, and her cheeks dimpled when she compressed her thin lips. When her gaze met Whit's, he thought he saw sadness in her light blue eyes, but the knot in his throat didn't go away; it only tightened more. He realized that whatever their fate was to be, from this day forward it lay in her hands.

"I don't think we need discuss any more of the details in front of the children, Mr. Wilkins." She stared at Whit and then her gaze rested briefly on each of the children. "When was their last meal?" she asked emphatically.

The rancher looked taken aback for a moment. "What . . . er . . . huh?"

There was a touch of accusation in Mrs. Kingsley's tone. "It's easy to see these children are skin and bones, and they are exhausted. When did you last feed them?"

"Well," Wilkins replied, as if the question were beyond his comprehension, "they had beans and fatback this morning at the way station."

"That would have been six or seven hours ago," she speculated, her voice turning as cold as winter ice. She reached for the bell that rested on the edge of her desk and rang it with such force it resounded through the room. "I'll have Mary take the children and feed them and find a place for them to rest. The little ones

Constance O'Banyon

look all done in. They are very young to have made the long journey from Pecos on a public stage."

"There weren't no other way to get 'em here," Wilkins said defensively. "I had to use my own money for their coach fare, and I can tell you it set me back quite a bit. Is there any way I can be repaid?"

The frosty blue gaze hardened. "I am certainly not prepared to pay you for your . . . sacrifice."

Wilkins was clearly becoming agitated by Mrs. Kingsley's attitude. "These kids ain't my obligation. I've had them a full year. Will you take them or not?"

"I have never refused to take in a child in need." Her voice softened a bit. "I will certainly not turn away these children."

Whit noticed that Jena Leigh had fallen asleep with her head resting on Drew's shoulder. He pulled Laura Anne to him while anger almost choked him. He felt the need to say something before it was too late. "You aren't going to separate us. We stay together or we don't stay at all." His chin rose a notch in defiance. "Laura Anne is afraid of the dark, and Jena Leigh will cry if you take her away from the rest of us."

Mrs. Kingsley rose from behind her desk and moved toward Whit. She was shorter than he'd thought— just a mere head taller than he was.

She gently touched Laura Anne's cheek, and the child smiled at her. Whit pushed the woman's hand away because Laura Anne had a sweet and trusting nature, and he had to protect her from those who might take advantage of her trust.

The matron smiled in understanding. "Tell me each of your names, and how old you are," she said softly, not in the least offended by Whit's attitude.

6

Whit became the family spokesman. "I'm Whit—I'm ten years old. That's my brother, Drew—he's nine. My sister Laura Anne is three, and Jena Leigh was two last week."

Mrs. Kingsley started to touch Whit's arm but he backed away from her, pulling Laura Anne with him. She sighed softly. "Well, Whit, I'm going to overlook one of my rules just this one time—I'll allow the four of you to stay together for tonight. You and your brother can see your sisters settled in and explain to them that no one here is going to harm them. What they *will* get is three meals a day, a warm place to sleep, and a good education."

Whit's arms circled Laura Anne protectively. "I said we are not going to be separated—not ever!"

"Now look here, boy!" Wilkins said forcefully, getting to his feet and moving with a heavy tread toward Whit. "You'll do—"

Mrs. Kingsley held up her hand to silence the man, and he dropped back into the chair, subdued. "Whit," she said, "I know how you are feeling at this moment, but we have rules here, and though I may stretch them a bit until tomorrow, I can't break them. Our boys occupy one dormitory, and our girls are in another. Can you understand that?"

Whit watched a tall, brown-haired young woman enter and stand with her hands clasped demurely in front of her, waiting for instructions from the matron. He took a big gulp of air and flexed his fingers into fists. "No. I don't understand at all. But you'd better understand this—no one takes my brother and sisters away from me."

"We will talk about this tomorrow," Mrs. Kingsley

said kindly. "For now go with Mary, and she will see that you have something to eat and a place to rest."

Whit had no choice but to do as he was told, because the babies were hungry and tired. He looked at his uncle. "I don't ever want to see you again. You're a mean man. None of us likes you. And none of us will call you uncle—not anymore!"

Wilkins's face reddened, and he ran a finger around his starched collar as if it were suddenly too tight. "Now, boy, you have no call to talk to me that way. Everything you stand in was bought by me."

Mrs. Kingsley nodded at Mary, and the girl guided them out of the room, but not before Whit heard the matron speak to his uncle in a harsh tone.

"Did their father leave no provision for their up-keep?"

Whit watched as his uncle squirmed, tapping his fingers on the edge of the desk. He might be mean-spirited, but he considered himself a God-fearing man and prided himself on being truthful, at least the way he saw the truth. "Well, the man did send money at first, but then it suddenly stopped coming. I ain't heard nothing from him for some time now."

"He has not kept in contact with the children?"

"He did write some, maybe four or five letters. But we ain't heard from him since he said he'd bought him a gold mine and was going to work it. He was in California then. Gold mine indeed," Wilkins said in disgust. "While I was left to put food in his kids' mouths and clothes on their backs."

The door closed, and Whit heard nothing more.

After the Hawk children had eaten, Mary showed them to a small room with four cots. Whit held Laura

Anne in his arms until she fell asleep, and Jena Leigh curled up beside Drew.

Whit was too worried to sleep. He blamed his mother for most of their troubles. He thought about the ache and the yearning he'd felt when she left them; he also recalled how his sisters had cried for their mother for a time, and then, when their memories of her faded, they stopped asking for her. Whit tried not to think about her, but he still had visions of her brushing her long golden hair on the veranda of their home. He'd thought her hair was the prettiest sight he'd ever seen. Both Laura Anne and Jena Leigh had their mother's blond hair, while he and Drew got their dark hair from their father, he supposed. Unbidden, memories of his mother reading to them found their way into his thoughts, and he remembered going to church with her and listening to her sing in the choir, her beautiful voice soaring above all the others.

Whit turned his thoughts away from the mother who had betrayed them all. He didn't know why she had abandoned them, but he did know that if you loved someone, you didn't leave them.

Not ever!

When he looked over at the cot next to him, he noticed that Jena Leigh had fallen asleep with her head resting on Drew's arm. A bright moon illuminated the small room except for the dark corner near the door—that darkness would have scared Laura Anne if she had been awake, and his hold on her tightened. It wasn't right that Drew and the girls had no one but him to protect them. He vowed that he'd one day search for his father, and when he found him, he'd make him do right by the younger ones. He would go looking for him now, but Drew and his sisters depended on him. The girls were young and defenseless; they certainly didn't need anyone else to desert them.

Whit didn't quite know what to make of Mrs. Kingsley. She seemed nice enough, but you could never tell about a grown-up until you really got to know them. Sometimes they only pretended to be nice.

He thought about living on his uncle's ranch. It hadn't been so bad when Aunt Martha was alive; she had been kind and affectionate and had let them play in the mornings and had read to them every afternoon. But the very day after she was buried, their uncle had roused him and Drew out of bed before sunup, put them each on a horse, and told them to work the cattle. In the beginning he and Drew had looked on their new responsibility as an adventure, but as days passed into weeks, and weeks into months, Whit had watched Drew become so exhausted he could hardly stay in the saddle.

The girls had become another worry for Whit; they had been left in the care of Dora, the housekeeper their uncle had hired after Aunt Martha took ill. The woman had been nice enough at first, but then she became sly and mean when their uncle wasn't around. The one good thing Whit could say about his uncle was that he'd never struck them. The same couldn't be said for the housekeeper.

It still made Whit angry when he remembered coming home after working hard all day and finding bruises on Jena Leigh's arm. He'd known immediately who had put them there. He had waited until everyone else had gone to bed before he went into the kitchen to confront Dora. She had been drying dishes, and she glared at him, telling him there was no use looking for food because it had already been put away.

He had stepped close to her, determined to face her down. Angrily he had shaken his fist in her face and warned her that she'd better never hit one of his sisters again, or she would be sorry. She must have believed him, because after that night, as far as he knew, she had never hurt his sisters again.

Whit was old enough to understand that Dora's purpose had always been to get them out of the house so she could become the next Mrs. Wilkins. He hoped his uncle did end up marrying that woman—she was just the kind of person he deserved to spend the rest of his life with. There would be a certain kind of justice in that union for both his uncle and Dora.

Whit was so tired that his eyes drifted shut, but troubled thoughts swirled in his mind, and he lay awake long into the night.

There was only one possession he still had that reminded him of happier times in Galveston. Thinking he might be comforted if he wore the signet ring his father had give him, Whit eased away from his sister and reached under the bed, fumbling in the clothing he'd stashed there. When he found the ring, he slid it onto his finger, but it brought no comfort at all. Designed for him to wear when he was grown, the ring was too big now, but his father had assured him he'd grow into it one day. Taking a deep breath, Whit remembered how honored he had felt the day his father had given him the ring. Proud of his achievements when his shipping business was at its peak, Harold Hawk had designed a family crest. For his sons and himself he had commissioned rings—for his wife and daughters he'd had oval-shaped pendants made with the same crest.

Whit thought Drew had been asleep for hours, so he was startled when he found his brother watching him with a questioning expression.

"Whit, tell me again about our rings."

Whit had patiently explained about the rings many times, but he knew that Drew was comforted by the tangible reminder of their past; he cleared his throat and spoke softly so he wouldn't wake the girls. "They are made of wrought gold and enameled in different colors. The tall ship depicted in the design is the *Sarah Jane,* named for our mother. The hawk flying above the ship represents our last name. The red rising sun depicts Papa's rise in fortune." Whit drew a deep breath. "Of course, that was before Papa lost everything."

Drew's lashes fluttered and he fought to hold sleep at bay. "And below the ship on the banner surrounded by vines and orchids are the Latin words *Quattuor mundum do,* which means, 'To four I give the world,'" Drew said drowsily.

"That's right," Whit concurred. "It means to us four children, Papa gave the world." Whit was just about to explain that the orchids symbolized Jamaica, their father's birthplace, when Drew interrupted him.

"What's going to happen to us now, Whit?" Drew asked in a worried voice.

"We stay together," Whit replied. "We never allow anyone to break us apart." In a short time Whit heard the even breathing that told him Drew had fallen asleep. Whit sighed and surrendered to the sleep that dragged him down into the darkness.

It wasn't until the next afternoon that Mrs. Kingsley called the Hawk children into her office to explain that their uncle had already left. The girls were seated at a small table, where they were given cookies and milk. Laura Anne daintily dipped her cookie in the milk and took small bites, while Jena Leigh had already spilled her milk and had cookie crumbs all down the front of her gown.

Mrs. Kingsley merely laughed and cleaned up the mess. "Don't cry, sweet one," she said to Jena Leigh. "Everyone has accidents, especially when they are as young as you are. Don't let it bother you a bit."

Jena Leigh dried her tears on her small fists and gave the matron a half smile. Whit's heart broke for his sister. She was so hungry for affection that she responded to the least bit of kindness from anyone.

Drew stood beside Whit, ignoring the lure of the cookies, but his gaze kept darting in that direction. Whit planted his feet wide apart and put his body between the matron and his sisters. "What did you want to say to us?"

"Take a chair, Whit, Drew. What I have to say concerns you both." Mrs. Kingsley indicated the two chairs that had been drawn up in front of her desk.

Drew shook his head. "We'll stand, ma'am. We aren't going to be here very long. Papa will be coming for us real soon."

"Yes, of course he will," she said softly. "But in the meantime you will be staying with us; therefore, I

13

want to explain some things to you so you will understand the way things work around here. Why don't you take a chair?"

Whit nodded to his brother, and they both sat down stiffly.

"We aren't here to be adopted out," Whit said with feeling. "No one is going to break up our family."

"You are right about that, Whit. In fact, I have here your father's last known address in California, and I intend to write to him and let him know that I'll keep you safe until he comes for you." She picked up a pen and shuffled through some documents. "I just want to explain some of our rules to you."

Even though Whit didn't want to like Mrs. Kingsley, he found he was softening toward her. Of course, she could be just acting kind to get his trust. He'd keep an eye on her to make sure she wasn't being deceitful.

"If your father doesn't come for you, for whatever reason, I want you to consider this your home. I hope all of you will take advantage of our educational program here. We have three excellent teachers on staff. I myself teach history. I think you would like my class."

"What about my sisters?" Whit asked. "They're too young for school."

"Laura Anne and Jena Leigh will have activities suitable for their ages. They will be with girls their own age and play games that will teach them to count, and others that will help them learn the alphabet. I am of the opinion that fun activities make it easier for a child to learn. I am also of the opinion that a child should be educated from an early age and not be held back if she happens to be female." Her voice was thick with sadness, as if she had made this speech too many times before. "I want my children to have the best education I can provide for them, to arm them for the day they leave me and go out on their own."

Whit met Mrs. Kingsley's gaze. "Me and Drew can read and write some. Laura Anne knows the alphabet, but I'm afraid Jena Leigh can only count up to five."

"You will all learn. I have found that young minds are so ready to absorb knowledge. . . ." She paused. "Ah, but my thoughts wander at times. What do you say, Whit? Will you give us a chance?"

"If we are going to be separated, when will we get to see our sisters?" Drew demanded.

"You will see them every morning at prayer service and at mealtimes. You will be able to spend most of the day with them on Saturday and Sunday. How does that sound to you?"

Looking at her carefully, Whit saw no deceit in her eyes, only open honesty, so he began to relax a bit. He wanted his brother and sisters to experience the education Mrs. Kingsley promised them. "I guess we could stay around for a little while. Just until the babies are older, or until Papa comes to get us."

She stood up and rounded the desk. When she attempted to put her arm around Drew, he was stiff and unyielding, and Whit had taken a step back, his hard gaze warning her that he did not want to be hugged. Having encountered this attitude from numerous other children, the matron merely smiled and shook each of their hands.

"Welcome to your new home. I'm glad to have you

with me—I do so hope each of you will be happy here."

San Francisco, California

Simon Gault walked slowly down the crowded street with a wide smile on his face, barely able to contain his pleasure. He'd been surprised by how easily he'd assumed Harold Hawk's identity and fooled everyone at the assayer's office. The man hadn't been the least bit suspicious. Of course, no one in town knew Hawk, and for that matter, they didn't know Simon either. He had just come into the possession of a great fortune, thanks to Harold Hawk.

Simon had committed murder, and no one would ever find out about it. He had been so clever—it had only taken one stick of dynamite to bring the mountain down, sealing Hawk's dead body in a mine shaft under tons of dirt and rock.

Simon dodged a heavy freight wagon as he darted across the street to the saloon. His mouth was dry, and his hands were shaking with excitement. He had killed once before, and it had bothered him for a while, because his first victim had been a woman. She had been a tarnished woman who'd sung in a saloon back in St. Louis. He couldn't remember her name, or even what she looked like. He hadn't set out to kill her; it was just that his lovemaking got a little rough at times.

But Hawk had deserved to die!

Simon had despised the man from the first moment he'd met him, because something about him had reminded Simon of his own father. Even Hawk's slight accent had been like his father's. He'd found out later that they'd both come from Jamaica.

His jaw settled in a hard line. Hawk had cheated him, but he had gotten even with the man. No one could play Simon Gault for a fool and live to tell about it.

He stepped up to the bar and ordered whiskey, but he didn't drink it right away. He took it to a nearby table, sat down, and propped his feet on one of the chairs. Lowering his eyelids to slits, he remembered selling Hawk what he had thought to be a worthless, played-out gold mine. At first Simon had congratulated himself on his genius in tricking the gullible Hawk. But just two months ago word had filtered into Sacramento, where Simon had been staying, that a man named Harold Hawk had struck it big. It had galled Simon at the time; the more he thought about, the more his hate for the man had turned to rage.

That should have been his gold—his mine, his strike!

Simon took a sip of whiskey, and it burned all the way down his throat. He hadn't bought the good whiskey he preferred because he didn't want people to see him throwing money around. He couldn't afford to draw attention to himself. His thoughts took him back to the day he had confronted Hawk at the mine. The man had been strapping packsaddles on a mule, while six others stood already loaded and tethered together. Hawk was so happy that he'd struck it big. He mentioned that he was going back to claim his children, and then returning to Galveston, Texas. He'd even thanked Simon for selling him the mine, and the fool had admitted to finding a rich vein of gold not ten feet from where Simon had stopped digging.

When the arrogant bastard had turned his head to tighten a tether rope, Simon had picked up a shovel and hit him hard across the back of the head. Hawk had crumpled to his knees. In a fury Simon hit him again and again, continuing to strike him even after he'd known Hawk was dead.

Harold Hawk had been a big man, and it had taken Simon over an hour to drag the lifeless body to the bottom of the mine shaft. He had quickly set off a charge of dynamite, sealing the evidence of his crime forever.

Before Simon had left the site, he'd gone into the tent Hawk had called home while he worked the mine. He felt great satisfaction in going through Hawk's personal belongings. The fool had recorded all his thoughts and dreams in a journal. Simon had tucked the journal into his saddlebag, thinking he might find something useful in it. He'd also discovered a sealed envelope addressed to an orphanage in El Paso, Texas. With a snarl, he ripped open the letter. Apparently Hawk had four children, two boys and two girls. The man had written that they would soon be reunited as a family, and he would try to buy back the Hawk Shipping Company.

Simon smiled—he supposed the kids would just have to stay where they were, because their pa wasn't coming back for them.

The only other thing of value Simon had found at the site was a cedar box full of useless papers and pictures, which were of Hawk's kids, he supposed. His heart had beat faster when he reverently picked up a signet ring he'd found in the bottom of the box. Admiringly, he stared at it for a long moment. His hand had trembled as he'd slipped the ring onto his finger. His shoulders had straightened, and he'd felt the power of respectability that went along with the ownership of that ring. He had taken the ring with him, then burned the tent and everything else in it.

With no guilt and no remorse, Simon had gathered the reins of the pack mules and made his way to San Francisco. He despised men like Harold Hawk, whose manners were so correct, who always seemed to be flaunting their knowledge, looking down their noses at those they thought were beneath them. Well, so much for Hawk's high opinion of himself; Simon had shown him who was the better man.

That night in the hotel room Simon read Harold Hawk's journal. He smiled in gratification when he read the part about how Hawk had left Galveston because he couldn't face the friends who pitied him for his wife's desertion, or the enemies who gloated because he had gambled away his shipping company. The more Simon read of the journal, the more his hatred of the dead man escalated, and Simon knew why: Hawk sounded too much like Simon's own father— the man who had taken all his mother had to give and had given her nothing in return—not even his last name. As a child in Mobile, Alabama, Simon had dwelled with his mother in the shadows of the big mansion where Daniel Gault lived with his wife and their three legitimate sons.

His lip curled in disgust at the memory of his father sneaking into their little house at night so no one would see him. He often heard his father beating his mother, but Simon never dared to intervene, because Daniel Gault hadn't needed an excuse to take out his rage on his illegitimate son. Simon's mother had always gone around looking bruised and battered, her spirit broken. Instead of feeling pity for her, Simon had felt only contempt for her weakness. He never understood why she'd allowed Daniel Gault to mistreat her so brutally.

Simon had almost been relieved when his mother had died the very day of his fourteenth birthday. Even as she'd gasped for breath, his mother's last words had been of the man who had ruined her life.

Daniel Gault hadn't bothered to go to the funeral, probably because he didn't want anyone to see him there. He had stopped by the house later that night with orders for Simon—he'd given him a horse, a saddle, and a hundred dollars, insisting he leave Alabama the next day and never return.

Well, he'd left, all right, and he'd never returned, but he had taken the one thing his father had always denied him—he took the name Gault.

Daniel Gault had died a few years back, after being shot by a jealous husband, cheating Simon of the opportunity to settle the score with him.

He stared at the ring that he wore on his middle finger—it was too big for him, so he removed it and tucked it into his vest pocket. He'd be a fool to wear it where someone might recognize it and force him to answer awkward questions about how it came to be in his possession. Simon flinched, wondering why the ghost of Harold Hawk still haunted him—the memory of the man was like a burning in his gut that just wouldn't go away. He took another drink. In spite of the fact that he had acquired all of Hawk's possessions, the man had still beaten him. The only way Simon could think of to banish the man's ghost was to succeed where Hawk had failed—to be respected where Hawk had been ridiculed. Simon wanted to walk with his head held high, to leave his old life and bad memories behind him.

He was going to Galveston, Texas, to start a new life.

Chapter One

Laredo, Texas—1866

A cloud bank moved across the sky, devouring the crescent moon, darkening the shadows in the streets and alleyways. It was just past midnight, and most of the respectable folks had gone to bed hours ago. But across the street from the Swindon Hotel, the flickering light from the Lucky Seven spilled into the dusty streets, while tinny music filtered through the air. A sudden wind kicked up, the force of it slamming against the bat-wing doors and making them rock back and forth.

The owner and bartender, Victor Palmer, ran a polishing rag over the top of the bar, thinking no amount of rubbing would bring the dull wood back to life. So far it was a night like most others. No trouble yet—not even from the drunk at the end of the bar, who was swaying on his feet. Three men, regulars, were playing cards near the door—they came in every Friday night, placing small wagers, no big pots there.

Palmer looked at the four men at the table at the back of the room; his gaze settled on one man in particular. He knew Whit Hawk only by reputation, and he realized Hawk had positioned himself with his back to the wall so he could watch everyone's comings and goings. Of all the men in his saloon tonight, Hawk was the most interesting, and probably the most dangerous. He wasn't what anyone would call a troublemaker, but more of a trouble settler if it happened to come his way. He was a gambler of the highest reputation. He looked every inch a true gentleman in his black suit and black leather vest. This was the first time Palmer had seen him in person. Palmer was shocked to see that the gambler was somewhere in his twenties, younger than his reputation implied. But his eyes were old, heavy with cynicism.

The word around Texas was that Hawk went from town to town without putting down roots anywhere. As far as anyone knew, he had no family. He'd ridden into town two nights ago and, to Palmer's knowledge, hadn't slept much since then. He'd been playing poker most of that time. The pile of money in front of him told its own story.

A sudden gust of wind rattled the swinging doors again, and the bartender noticed a quick flicker in Hawk's amber gaze. Palmer watched him assess each person in the room thoroughly.

Hawk's gaze slid with bored indifference over Trudy and Sassy, the two women who were there to see that the customers got everything they wanted. Trudy had already offered to sit with Hawk and bring him luck, but he'd given her a gold piece and sent her on her way with a pout on her lips.

After Hawk finished appraising everyone in the room, he casually shuffled the cards, curving them into a perfect arch.

"You gonna shuffle the spots off the cards, or you gonna deal?" Buck Southerland asked in an irritated voice, his hazel eyes flashing with anger, his hands fidgeting nervously on the felt table.

Southerland hadn't won a hand since he'd sat down several hours earlier, and it didn't help his mood any that he was gambling with money he couldn't afford to lose—some of it wasn't his. The money in front of him at the moment belonged to his father-in-law, who owned the freight yard and had given the cash to Southerland so he could make the bank deposit. But Southerland had heard that Whit Hawk was in town, and he'd wanted to see if the gambler was as good as everyone said. He hadn't intended to use his father-in-law's money, but he'd lost all of his own in the first three hands.

Palmer summed Southerland up in two words—reckless and weak. The man was of average height with a stocky build. Although he was only in his late twenties, his hairline was receding at an alarming rate. Yeah, the man was reckless and heading for trouble if he didn't keep his opinions to himself.

Southerland had married the boss's daughter, and he actually loved her. It was her birthday next week, and he had wanted to buy her something special. But he'd already lost the money to do that with.

"Something bothering you, Southerland?" Although Whit Hawk had not raised his voice, there was still the hint of a threat in his tone. "If there is, spit it out so we can get on with the game."

25

Southerland started to say something, but paused when Hawk held the cards out to him. "Cut?"

"Hell, yes!" Cutting the cards deep, he slammed them on the table with such force it caught everyone's attention. The man at the piano stopped playing; the drunk at the end of the bar looked at them blurry eyed; the two women stared in disbelief at Southerland's stupidity; the three regulars watched carefully, as if deciding whether they should stay or leave.

"You've won the last five hands," the man grumbled. "If you're not cheating, you're the luckiest bastard I've ever seen."

Whit said nothing, but his jaw muscles tightened as he dealt the cards, making them sail expertly across the table to land in front of each man's hand.

One of the men, the town barber, Joe Frisco, looked at his hand and threw it in the middle of the table. He then slid his chair back and stood, stepping back a pace. "I ain't going to stay in this game if you're going to make brainless remarks like that, Southerland." He reached for his hat. "And just a little friendly advice—you're a fool to accuse Whit Hawk of cheating."

Southerland glared at the barber. "Is that right? Well, you've got your opinion, and I got mine."

The fourth man, a drifter, Cal Winters, had ridden into town a few hours earlier. He knew Hawk, or at least knew about him; they'd never actually met until tonight. It was said that Hawk had once ridden for Luke Masterson's ranch down near Sonora. Apparently Hawk had been responsible for helping break up an outfit that had been rustling the old man's cattle and driving them across the Rio Grande into Mexico. It was also said that Hawk was cold and deadly, and just looking at him, Cal believed it. He slid his chair back and grinned. "Sounds to me like you are a hothead and itching for a fight, Southerland. If you are, you'd better pick someone besides him." He nodded at Whit. "Word has it that he doesn't suffer insults to his reputation."

Frisco nodded. "I heard the same thing."

Victor Palmer walked around the bar and now stood behind Hawk. "I don't want any trouble here, Southerland. You've had too much to drink. Why don't you just go on home and sleep it off?"

Southerland eased to his feet, a hard gaze fixed on the gambler, his hand slowly easing down to his holster. The gun was his father's and had rarely been used. The amount of whiskey he'd consumed was making him reckless. "I say you're cheating. And I'm gonna get my money back one way or another."

"Ease off, Southerland," Whit warned. "You mentioned earlier that you had a wife and kid waiting at home—I wouldn't want them to have to bury you."

Southerland licked his dry lips as he stared into the coldest, deadliest eyes he had ever seen. If he killed the man, he could take all the money; everyone would agree to that—the man had no friends here, while Southerland had been born and raised in Laredo. His hand twitched and sweat ran down his forehead, pooling in his eyes and making them burn. His gaze settled on the stack of money in front of Hawk, and he remembered that much of it belonged to him. That was the deciding moment—his hand went to his gun, but before he had even touched the handle, the gambler stood and drew his own gun in one smooth motion.

"Are you right-handed or left-handed?" Hawk asked.

Southerland felt his body tremble, and fear clogged his throat. "I . . . What difference does it make?" He figured he was a dead man.

Whit cocked his gun. "I asked if you're right-handed or left-handed. Just answer me."

Southerland didn't know what the gambler meant by his question, but the look in those cold eyes was enough to send him to his knees. "Right-handed," he admitted, his body shaking from fear.

"In that case, put your right hand on your head and unbuckle your gun belt with your left hand."

Southerland didn't hesitate, but it was difficult to unbuckle the belt with his left hand—the more he tried to hurry, the more he fumbled. "Don't shoot me, mister. I take it back what I said about your cheating."

"I don't have to cheat to beat you," Whit said in a deadly, cold voice. "Everything you feel and see is reflected on your face. You shouldn't play cards—you're too easy to read."

Southerland finally unbuckled his gun belt and let it slide to the floor. "What are you going to do to me?"

Whit picked up the man's gun and unloaded it, tossing the shells and the empty gun onto the table. Everyone was waiting tensely to see what Hawk was going to do. "That depends on you."

"I was wrong. I gambled with money that wasn't mine. Now I don't even have money left to buy milk for my baby."

A look of disgust crossed Whit's face. "A man would have to sink pretty low to gamble with money that would feed his child." Whit shoved his own gun back into his holster and proceeded to count out the exact amount of money Southerland had lost to him. He tossed it at the cowering man. "Pick up your money and go home," he said curtly.

Southerland scrambled forward and gathered up the money, cramming it into his pockets. "You aren't going to shoot me when I try to leave, are you?"

Whit's eyes narrowed. "I don't shoot men in the back, but I wouldn't turn my back on a man of your caliber. Take the money and get out. You can pick your gun up tomorrow when you're sober."

Southerland cringed, knowing everyone was watching him in disgust. He had his money back, but he'd paid a high price for it—his own respect. He had no doubt that word of his actions would reach the ears of everyone in Laredo. Even his father-in-law would learn of his disgrace.

"Southerland, I don't want to see you in here again," the bartender said tersely. "Get out of here and stay out."

Whit folded the remaining money and slid it into his vest pocket. He waited until the barber and the drifter moved away before he engaged the bartender in conversation. "I'll be heading out in the morning, but before I leave, I wonder if I could ask you a few questions."

Palmer liked the cut of the man. He liked the way Hawk had handled Southerland and avoided shooting the fool. "Come on up to the bar and I'll buy you a drink."

Once they reached the bar, one of the women started in Hawk's direction, but Palmer shook his head at her, and she veered off to talk to the piano player instead.

He slid a whiskey toward Hawk. "You said you wanted to ask me something?"

Whit stared down at the amber liquid. "Have you ever heard of a man called Drew Hawk?"

Palmer frowned as if he were trying to remember. "No. I can't say as I have. He kin of yours?"

"Yeah. My brother." He reached into his pocket and removed a ring and slid it onto his finger so Palmer could get a closer look at it. "Ever see anyone wearing a ring like this?"

Palmer studied the ring with great interest. "Does the bird represent your family name?"

"That's right."

"No. I can't say that I have ever seen anything like that—if I had, I'd've remembered it."

Whit raised the glass to his lips and downed the whiskey in one swallow. "Thanks for the drink."

Palmer stared after Hawk as he moved toward the door, the muscles across the gambler's shoulders rippling with each step he took. He watched him adjust his hat and step out into the wind, soon to be swallowed up by the night. The bartender shook his head. So Hawk did have some family. A brother—how about that?

Whit had packed everything he owned in his leather saddlebag and hoisted it onto his shoulder. There was no reason to remain in Laredo any longer. If Drew had ever been in the town, the bartender would probably have known about it. Whit had no home, nothing to tie him down, no reason to stay anywhere for very long.

Each town he traveled through was beginning to look very much like the last one. His life was like a restless wind that blew indiscriminately and with little purpose. Only the thought that he might one day find Drew kept him going.

He stepped to the window and stared down on the street below. The wind howled, sand swirled, and grit sifted through the open window, taking him back to another time and place.

Whit's heart ached when he thought about the family he'd lost.

Guilt lay heavily on his shoulders; he blamed himself for everything that had gone wrong. If he had only remained in El Paso, he might have saved Laura Anne and Jena Leigh from the fire that had destroyed the orphanage and taken their lives.

Sorrow was eating him alive.

If he allowed it, anger and frustration would take him down into a darkness so deep he would never recover. He'd spent years searching for his father, and now for Drew. He couldn't give up or admit defeat. If his brother were still alive, he'd find him sooner or later.

Whit battled just to get through each day. The loneliness in his heart was like a dull ache that never healed, never went away. People crossed his path, leaving no lasting impression on him whatsoever. If he died today, there would be no one to mourn his passing. He leaned his head against the window casement and closed his eyes.

His search for his father had gotten him nowhere.

The people he'd questioned at the assayer's office in San Francisco had directed him to the location of a mine that had been registered in his father's name. But when Whit had reached the site, there was nothing left but rubble, and it had been clear that the mine had been deserted for years. He'd found a warped plank where the paint was chipped and faded, but there was enough lettering left so he could make out the name Hawk. No one could tell him where his father had gone. But he did find out that his father had struck a rich vein of gold.

Whit's eyes narrowed. He should have saved himself the trouble of searching for his father—if he was still alive, he'd covered his trail thoroughly. It appeared Harold Hawk had never intended to return for his children.

Whit had been eighteen that Christmas he left El Paso to search for his father. It still cut deep to remember how angry Drew had been when he found out Whit was leaving. His brother had accused him of deserting them, but had relented a bit when Whit convinced him that he was going to make their father provide a home for their sisters.

But when he returned to El Paso, it had been too late to save the girls.

He drew in a shuddering breath, remembering the moment he had dismounted beside the charred ruins of the orphanage.

With a thousand questions whirling through his mind and fear racing through his heart, he had gone directly to the sheriff's office to find some answers. The deputy had dealt him a stunning blow when he explained that it was almost a certainty his two sisters had perished in the fire. The man had gone on to describe how it had been impossible to make a positive identification of anyone, since the bodies had been so badly charred. Several of the children had escaped, but more of them had died than lived. It had torn at Whit's heart to learn that Mrs. Kingsley had also died in the fire.

Whit could still feel the anguish those words had brought him. When he'd left to find his father, Laura Anne had been only eleven. She had so loved life, and everyone had adored her exuberance. Although Laura Anne had been only one year older than Jena Leigh, she had always looked after her younger sister like a mother hen. The last time Whit had seen Laura Anne, her tears had soaked his shirt, and it had been like a knife in his heart to leave her.

Jena Leigh, the baby, had always been such a serious child, with her head often stuck in a book. As young as she'd been then, she'd understood why Whit was forced to leave them to search for their father. If he closed his eyes, he could still see her big amber-colored eyes swimming with tears, begging him to return as quickly as possible.

According to the deputy's accounts, Drew had left El Paso a few months before the fire, telling everyone he was heading out to look for his brother. If only they had found each other.

Whit turned from the window, and with bitter self-recrimination, gripped the bedpost so tight his arms trembled. He had searched long and hard, and he was becoming weary. He had no life, no existence outside his need to find Drew. He took a deep breath and tried in vain to shake off the gloom that haunted him. He'd once had a family—now they were all gone.

Nights were the worst for Whit, because sometimes he'd wake in a cold sweat, dreaming his sisters were crying out for him to save them. It was always the same dream, and it always ended as they were swallowed by fire.

Maybe Drew was still alive—Whit just didn't know anymore.

Maybe he had a mother somewhere, but he certainly didn't intend to search for her. To his way of thinking, she was the reason for all their troubles.

He glanced down at his ring, the only binding tie that would help him find Drew. He removed it and shoved it in his pocket. He didn't like to wear it. It reminded him of the lies his father had told him.

Before he'd left El Paso in search of his father, he'd given Drew the ring their father had made for his brother and fastened his sisters' pendants around their necks. It hurt to think what must have happened to those pendants: they were probably lying beneath the burned-out rubble.

After the fire, only the hope of finding Drew gave him a reason to go on day after day. That one purpose drove him, carrying him from town to town.

For three years he'd worked on a cattle ranch near Sonora, then a ranch near San Angelo. But the pay had been scant, and he'd needed money to continue his search. That was when he discovered that gambling came easy to him. In that way he wasn't so different from his father, but in a more important way they were nothing alike. Harold Hawk's gambling had been a sickness that had finally cost him everything. Whit didn't have the same obsession; he merely found gambling a means that allowed him to travel the length and breadth of Texas in his never-ending quest.

If his father was still alive, Whit hoped their paths never crossed; he had a score to settle with Harold Hawk.

He supposed it was possible that Drew could have fought in the war—it was even possible that he might have fallen in battle, and that he was buried in some unmarked grave hundreds of miles from Texas.

No. Drew couldn't be dead, or he would feel it. Whit had to keep a flicker of hope alive. He just had to. A fire smoldered inside his gut—he blamed his mother and father for destroying so many lives. Whit suddenly smiled, thinking of the one bright spot in his life. He'd learned that his uncle Nolan had, indeed, married his housekeeper, and they had five children— all girls. Someone in Pecos had told him that his uncle stayed drunk most of the time and had finally lost his ranch. Whit had no pity for the man. In fact, he didn't feel anything at all for him.

He watched the tattered curtain ripple in the wind. The years he had spent at the orphanage had not been bad years. Mrs. Kingsley had become important in all their lives with her kindness. She'd been the only purely unselfish woman he'd ever known, and he still grieved over her passing. He knew in his heart that she had died in that fire while trying to rescue her children. Because of her steadfast insistence, Whit now had a well-rounded education, for all the good it did him. A gambler didn't need an education; he only needed to know human nature so he could predict how his opponent would react in any given situation.

He shouldered his saddle and went through the door and down the stairs. Once outside, he crossed the street to the livery stable.

It was time his search took him back home.

Back to Galveston.

Chapter Two

Another town.

Copper Springs.

Whit had risen early, packed his gear, and made his way quietly down the stairs of the small hotel where he'd spent the night. The lonesome wailing of a train whistle shattered the silence as he crossed the street to the livery where his horse was stabled. It had been after midnight when he'd arrived in this place, which looked the same as many others he'd traveled through.

It would be another day's ride before he left behind the green, rolling hill country and reached the sweeping prairies that would eventually level off as he neared the Gulf of Mexico. He was still two days, maybe three, from Galveston, and he swore he could already smell the salt air.

Home.

His one worry was, if he did find Drew in Galveston, would his brother blame him for their sisters' deaths? If he didn't, he should. Whit owned the guilt and lived with it every day of his life. Maybe Drew didn't know that their sisters were dead. Whit had written several letters to all three of them while he'd been in California searching for their father. But since he'd been constantly on the move, he hadn't received any letters from them.

The closer he got to Galveston, the more anxious he became. He hadn't had a restful night's sleep in a long time. If only he could lose the images of his sisters burning to death, maybe he would be able find peace in his soul.

Memories, sharp and tender—Laura Anne's sweetness, Jena Leigh's smile—he carried those with him as well. He also kept score of the mistakes he'd made over the years. And there had been many.

He frowned as he glanced up at the sky. Thunderclouds hung low in the midmorning dreariness, dampening his spirit even more. It had been raining off and on for three days, and he was ready to see the sun.

Whit realized now that he should have gone straight to Galveston after he'd left El Paso. But he'd been broke and had had to work as a cowhand. No excuses—he knew why he had delayed returning home. Galveston would be his last hope. If he didn't find his brother there, he wouldn't find him at all.

He breathed in the thick air, knowing he'd have to make camp at nightfall. Observing his surroundings with a practiced eye, he knew this part of Texas was too rocky for farming, but it had some of the best grazing land in the state and sustained several of the biggest ranches. He gazed worriedly at the darkening sky, hoping the rain would hold off until nightfall.

He was less than an hour out of Copper Springs when his horse suddenly began tossing its head, limp-

ing and favoring its right front leg. With an impatient
curse, Whit dismounted and bent down to inspect the
affected hoof. When he discovered the gelding had
thrown a shoe, probably some time back, he wondered what else could go wrong.

He removed his hat and slapped it against his thigh
in irritation, knowing he couldn't ride the horse. It
might go completely lame if he did.

He'd bought the animal from a rancher near San
Angelo two months ago, and it had been a good,
sturdy mount. Glancing about him, he hoped to find
evidence of a ranch or a homestead nearby, but there
was no sign of cattle for as far as the eye could see.

Whit caught the reins in his hand and led the limping animal forward, taking it slowly, although impatience was eating away at him. He had gone only a
short way when he noticed his horse's limp had become more pronounced. He glanced behind him,
wondering if it would be closer to return to Copper
Springs or take his chances on finding a ranch somewhere ahead. Either way he was probably in for a
long walk, and he wasn't sure his horse was up to it.

The road he had chosen was not well traveled, and
that was the very reason he'd come this way instead of
the direct route through Houston. The only person
he'd seen all morning had been a man driving a freight
wagon just out of Copper Springs, and he doubted
he'd meet any other travelers with the storm brewing.

Whit had been walking for about an hour, and
heat pressed in on him. He stopped, removed his suit
jacket and tossed it across his saddle, then unbuttoned
his shirt and rolled up his sleeves. He was thirsty, but
he decided to save the water in his canteen in case he

couldn't find a river or a pond along the road. He was certain that the Colorado River was somewhere in the vicinity, but he hadn't crossed it yet.

He'd gone only a short way when he spotted the river in the distance. Relief flooded through him as he stared at the sturdy live oaks that grew along the riverbanks.

Whit led the limping animal forward and allowed him to drink while he assessed his surroundings. Judging by the location of the sun that was trying to break through the clouds, it had to be midafternoon. He should be thinking of setting up camp, and this was as good a place as any to spend the night.

Later on, he would hobble his horse while he set out on foot to find someone to help him.

After he had satisfied his own thirst and filled his canteen, he sat beneath the shade of an oak tree, watching a hawk soar in the distance until it became only a tiny speck against the clouds. He tried to curb his agitation. He'd probably lose a day, maybe more, if he didn't find a place to have his horse shod. He leaned back and closed his eyes—he was so weary of traveling, heartsick because he had no hope, nothing but his stubborn determination to keep him going.

After a while he dozed off, his head falling back against the rough tree trunk.

Jackie Douglas felt guilty. She needed to get home. There was so much work to do back at the ranch house, but she halted her Arabian anyway and allowed her gaze to sweep over the land that had been in her family for three generations.

La Posada.

An ache formed in her heart, and tears choked her throat. Within a month her ranch would probably belong to someone else, and there was nothing she could do to prevent the bank from taking it over. She'd received a letter just last week from the Copper Springs bank, informing her that if she didn't pay the five thousand dollars owed on the mortgage, the ranch would go for auction.

She shook her head, wanting to drink in the beauty as long as she could. Dandelions dotted the meadow, and their dried flowers drifted on the soft breeze like flakes of snow.

Unable to ignore her urge to get closer to the strangely beautiful phenomenon, she dismounted. For the moment she wanted to forget about her troubles and think only of a time when life had been good on La Posada. When she'd ridden away from the house, she'd been wearing her green skirt and a white blouse. Her grandmother would be displeased that Jackie hadn't bothered to change into a split skirt or even to saddle her horse. It had felt strangely exhilarating to ride bareback with her skirt flowing about her and her unbound hair rippling in the wind.

When she reached the meadow, Jackie impulsively dropped down on the grass and removed her shoes, laughing as the wind tore more fluffy seed heads from their stems and sent them spiraling around her. It was a hot day, and she considered tucking her skirt into her waistband, but finally decided against it.

Humming softly to herself, she turned around in a circle, holding her hands out, trying to catch the elusive blooms. She dipped and turned, humming an old song her mother had sung to her as a child. Jackie was pretending she was dancing with the man who had just stolen her heart. There was no such man, but she hoped there would be someday.

Jackie closed her eyes, unable to see the face of her imaginary partner. He would be someone she had not yet met. She imagined his arms around her, guiding her into each step. And they would dance together perfectly.

Was he out there somewhere looking for her as she was waiting for him to find her?

She paused to pluck another dandelion and blew on it softly, her breath sending the feathery seed heads scattering. She thought of Hutch Steiner, whose father owned the neighboring ranch. Hutch had asked her several times to be his wife. If she agreed, it would probably solve all her problems, and she could keep her ranch. Hutch had been her brother's best friend, and she liked him well enough, but not enough to spend the rest of her life with him. She didn't understand why she couldn't love a man as fine as Hutch; he was everything a woman could ask for in a husband. He was tall and handsome, and always treated her with respect. But nothing stirred in her heart when she was with him. He had once kissed her, and afterward she'd wanted to wipe her mouth. Somehow she couldn't imagine spending the rest of her life with him. Not even if it was the only way to save La Posada.

She didn't want to think of Hutch today. She lifted the hem of her skirt and danced with her imaginary partner—the one who would someday find her and make her heart pound; the one with whom she'd want to spend the rest of her life.

At first Whit couldn't identify the sound that floated
to him on the wind. It was coming from just over the
next rise. As he listened intently, he finally recognized
it as the sound of a woman's voice. Standing, he
stretched his cramped muscles and adjusted his hat
before making his way up the incline. Whoever she
was, maybe she would agree to help him.

When Whit reached the top of the hill, he stopped
dead in his tracks, transfixed by what he saw. It was
almost as if he had wandered into a dream, a fantasy.
The woman had long red hair that fell below her
waist in ringlets and glistened as it caught the rays of
the sunlight that had finally broken through the
clouds. Barefooted, the woman gathered up the hem
of her simple green skirt, showing a flash of lace petticoat. She gracefully dipped and spun, humming to
herself.

White feathery dandelions floated on the wind and
fell around her like drifting snowflakes. She paused to
pluck another downy bloom, her breath sending the
seed head scattering.

He could only stare as she danced gracefully
through the grass, her laughter like music to his ears.
Each motion of her head sent her long scarlet curls
rippling about her. Whit blinked several times; the
snowlike blossoms surrounded the woman in an ethe-
real world. A sunbeam slanting through a hole in the
clouds bathed her in soft light.

He was stunned. Mesmerized. Something stirred
within him, and there was a tightening around his
heart.

He tore his gaze away from her and quickly

scanned the area. Other than the beautiful Arabian that grazed nearby, the woman was alone. There was no sign of a saddle, so she must have ridden bareback.

His gaze was drawn back to the redhead. She was slender and delicate. The top of her head would come up only to his eyes. He wasn't certain if she was real, or if he had wandered into a dream.

Jackie sensed she was no longer alone, and she stopped. Her gaze searched the hillside. When she saw the stranger watching her, it took her a mere second to react: she dove toward a nearby tree, where she had propped her rifle. Jerking it up and resting the stock against her shoulder, she cocked it and aimed.

"You're on private land, mister. You'd better keep moving on."

He took a step toward her, not wanting to scare her. "I don't mean you any harm, ma'am. My horse threw a shoe, and I watered him at the river. I hope you don't mind."

Jacqueline Douglas shook her head, humiliation flushing her cheeks because a stranger had seen her acting like a complete fool. She wondered how long he'd been watching her dance. "Now that you've helped yourself to my hospitality, you can just leave." Her grip tightened on the rifle. "I suggest you do it pronto!"

"That poses a problem for me, ma'am. You see, I can't ride my horse until he has been shod." He buttoned his shirt, rolled down his sleeves, and buttoned them. "Would it be possible for you to help me? Or maybe you could sell me a horse?"

She laid her cheek on the rifle stock, taking careful aim. "How do I know you're telling the truth?"

For Whit it seemed an opportune moment when his gelding came limping up the hill, dragging its reins.

It took Jackie only a moment to determine that the stranger had been telling the truth. She watched him remove his coat from the saddle and slide his arms into it. He certainly didn't look at all like any of the saddle tramps that had been traveling the road lately; he had the appearance of a gentleman, but, being a woman alone, Jackie had to be careful all the same. Slowly she lowered her rifle but kept it cocked just in case she should need it. "Where were you headed before your horse threw a shoe?"

"To Galveston, ma'am," he said smoothly. "My name is Whitford Hawk."

Suspicion slowly grew in her mind, replacing her fear and embarrassment. "If you are one of those Yankees that occupy Galveston, you can just keep going. I don't want you on my place, and I don't intend to help you."

He smiled and shook his head, deliberately exaggerating his Texas drawl. "Ma'am, do I sound like a Yankee to you?"

Chapter Three

Jackie studied the stranger for a long moment, trying to decide whether or not she should keep her rifle aimed at him. His horse was definitely limping, so Mr. Hawk had been telling her the truth about that. She could never stand to see an animal suffer; she'd have to help him.

When Whit spoke, there was exasperation in the tone of his voice. "Ma'am," he said, as if he'd read her mind, "you can hold your rifle on me all the way to your house if it'll make you feel safer, but I have to get this animal tended to. There is no other alternative."

He was right about that. Jackie wasn't ready to trust him completely, but she certainly didn't want to take him to her grandmother with a gun at his back either. As he gathered his horse's reins and led the animal down the hill, she couldn't help noticing how tall he was, probably six-two or six-three. She couldn't quite make out his features because his hat shadowed his face.

"I guess you can come to the house with me, and we'll see what we can do about your horse," she told him. "I'm sure you're hungry, too?"

"Yes, ma'am. I surely am."

"We'll see you fed after we've looked after your horse."

As he walked toward her he had a long stride and a sure step that exuded confidence. He was a gunfighter, she speculated; she just knew he was. Why else would he be wearing such a fine black suit, unless he'd just come from a wedding or a funeral? The closer he advanced on her, the more tense she became. She was all alone with a man she didn't know.

"I hope your place isn't too far, ma'am. My horse's hoof seems to be getting worse, and he's limping more than he was just a while ago."

Jackie regarded him with a critical air. "What did you do to him, try to ride him into the ground?" Her tone was accusing.

When Whit drew even with the woman, he respectfully touched the brim of his hat. "No, ma'am," he replied. "If I was set on crippling him, I'd have ridden him on to the next town. I've been walking for miles."

Jackie's finger was still on the trigger of her rifle. She wasn't yet ready to relinquish her gun. "Then let's get him some help."

When the woman took a hasty step away from him, it bothered Whit that she didn't trust him. He'd never harm a woman, and he couldn't remember a time when a woman had been afraid of him. He made an attempt at polite conversation, trying to put her at ease.

"Sure is a hot day."

Jackie could only imagine what Mr. Hawk thought of her dancing barefoot and without a partner. Whatever had possessed her to do such a crazy thing? She hid her embarrassment under the guise of indifference. "The ranch house is about a mile in that direction." She pointed her rifle to the south. "It's a good walk," she said tersely. "I hope you are up to it."

He smiled down at her. "I'll try to keep up with you. May I know who I'm indebted to?"

She raised her head, and her gaze collided with amber eyes that were filled with amusement. "I'm Jacqueline Douglas."

Whit stared into midnight blue eyes that were framed by lashes so long they shadowed her delicate cheekbones; their color was so vivid they were almost violet. There was not a freckle on her tanned face, unusual for a redhead. She had a pert little nose and a full mouth. Her hair looked as soft as silk as it blew against her cheek.

He watched her impatiently shove a handful of curls over her shoulder. She was wildly beautiful, and as untamed as the Texas he loved so well.

"And Mr. Douglas?" he asked, wondering if she had a husband.

"My father was Mr. Douglas, and my brother after him." She swallowed several times, thinking about the letter she'd received two years ago informing her of her brother's death in battle somewhere in Pennsylvania. "I'm the owner of La Posada."

He had been so busy watching the curve of her cheek and the fullness of her lips that he thought he might have misunderstood. "Surely you don't run the place by yourself."

Her chin rose proudly, or stubbornly, he couldn't tell which.

"Do you think a woman can't run a ranch as well as a man?" she asked icily. "I know as much about ranching as anyone around here, and maybe more than some people."

"I didn't mean to imply you were incapable of—" Whit broke off, suspecting she would find his stab at an apology shallow and insincere. He had the fixed impression that Jackie Douglas was a proud woman, and she wouldn't stand for any nonsense from anyone, especially a man she didn't know. He smiled to himself. Of course, she was still stinging from the fact that he'd seen her dancing in the meadow, and she would probably never feel comfortable with him.

She ran her hand over the flank of his gelding. "We need to get your horse to the barn so he can be looked after."

He liked the sound of her voice—it was deep and throaty. "I would appreciate anything you can do to help."

She dropped down on the grass, turned her back to him, and slipped into her shoes, lacing them decisively about her ankles.

Whit watched her gain her feet and brush the grass from her skirt. His focus was on the dandelion fluff that still clung to a curl near her cheek. He smiled and untangled it from her hair, holding it on the tip of his finger until his breath sent it floating to the ground.

Her gaze immediately hit the grass. "I don't usually . . . I have never done such . . ." Her face reddened, and she shook her head. "We should head for the house now."

"Your secret is safe with me, little redhead." He sensed a vulnerability in her. He had the feeling that if he said the wrong thing she would shatter into a hundred fragments. "Let us just say, for now, that you owe me a dance, one I intend to collect sometime in the future."

Her eyes snapped with anger. "I don't go to dances."

"That's a pity," he said with a lazy grin touching his lips.

She drew in a deep breath and shaded her eyes against the sun. "Let's go."

Whit's smile was slow and easy when he reached out to take another dandelion bloom nestled on the top of her head. She jerked back and glared at him. "If you touch me again, I'll leave you here to fend for yourself."

"I beg your pardon. I meant no offense." Whit could read something in her eyes that puzzled him— not fear, not anger, but more like bewilderment. She was very troubled about something. But he didn't want to get involved in her difficulties, whatever they were. All he really wanted to do was get to Galveston.

He stood beside the little beauty, acting the polite stranger. A woman like her could get under a man's skin with just the tilt of her head, a toss of the luxuriant red curls framing that beautiful face.

She shouldered her rifle instead of sliding it into her saddle holster. She watched dark brows come together above smoldering amber eyes. His gaze took her breath away, making it difficult for her to speak with any authority. "Just don't get too close to me again. I still have my rifle, and I know how to use it."

Whit laughed in amusement. "I just bet you do. Scares me to think about it."

With indignation she gathered the reins of her horse, deciding there was no proper way she could mount the animal without showing a fair amount of petticoat—not that Mr. Hawk hadn't already caught a fair glimpse of her petticoat while she'd been making a fool of herself.

Whit watched her lower her head, her hair falling around her face like a silken curtain, her lips still trembling. He knew what she was thinking and feeling; it was written on that exquisite face. "Don't fret over a situation that brought me such pleasure." His voice lowered. "Just remember you owe me a dance. One day I expect to collect on that debt."

Her head snapped up, and her sapphire blue gaze flickered over his face. "If you were a gentleman, you would not mention that again. Never. Ever."

He suppressed a grin. "You are right, of course. Once again, I beg your pardon."

Jackie tried to get her emotions under her command so she could return to sanity. Tomorrow would be a full workday. If it didn't rain there was the hay to gather, although the crop was poor this year and hadn't yielded enough to meet their demands. Then there was the fence on the eastern section of the ranch; it needed new posts, because the wire was practically dragging the ground. She would soon have to cut the young bull out of the herd and pen him in the corral. What she needed was money, and a lot of it. Her thoughts returned to the man who walked silently beside her as if he knew she needed to gather

her wits. Politeness dictated that she make a stab at some kind of conversation.

"You did say you were on your way to Galveston."

His gaze brushed across her face, and he noted the adorable blush on her cheeks. There was amusement in his voice. "Yes. I did."

As they walked along, Jackie found herself counting his steps by listening to the sound of his spurs. She could feel his presence, knew each breath he took. When he looked at her she could feel that, too. She found herself wanting to know more about him. "Is Galveston your home, Mr. Hawk?"

When she gazed at him with those wide blue eyes he could hardly remember his name. He'd met many women, some as pretty as Miss Douglas, but none of them had made his heart do a quick somersault as it was doing now. His expression became guarded— he'd scare the hell out of her if she knew what path his thoughts were taking.

It scared the hell out of him.

"Galveston was my home when I was younger; however, I haven't been back there in quite some time."

"Then you haven't had to deal with the wartime blockade of the harbor, or the occupation of Yankees troops now that the war is over."

"No. I haven't. I was in far west Texas for the major part of the war."

She stared at him, realizing he was a man who didn't like to talk about himself. "You are a native Texan, aren't you?"

"Born and bred."

"Are you saying you didn't join the Confederacy and fight in the war to protect Texas?"

"I'm in agreement with Sam Houston—Texas should never have been a part of the South's lunacy. We were never in any danger, unless you count the blockade of Galveston harbor, and that was little more than an irritant. An inconvenience."

"How can you say that? Are you telling me you just sat out the war?"

"Miss Douglas, there are different ways to fight a war. The Confederacy needed beef, and the ranch I rode for supplied a good bit of it for our boys in gray."

She stopped and stared at him. "That could not have been as important as defending Texas. Texas needed all her sons."

"Texas lost too many of her sons in a conflict that was doomed from the beginning." He could tell his views on the war were making her angry.

"All the respectable men I know went to war."

"And how many returned?"

Her chin trembled, and she looked away from him. Her lashes swept downward to hide her eyes. "Far too few."

The Arabian started pulling away from Jackie's grip in a quest to return to the barn, so Jackie yanked firmly on the reins to bring him under control. They walked along silently for a time before she spoke again. "Do you still have family in Galveston?"

He glanced at the ground and watched his shadow merge with hers as they walked side by side, and he had the strangest feeling that more than their shadows had merged. That thought shook him. "Not any-more," he said in a short, clipped tone.

Jackie fell silent, sensing he didn't want to talk about himself.

"You have a nice spread here, Miss Douglas."

"There was a time when La Posada was one of the most respected ranches in all of Texas." She shrugged. "That was before the war and before . . ."

She lapsed into silence, and he could feel her withdrawing from him. He felt unrest stirring within her and instinctively realized she had suffered some kind of loss, and it had affected her deeply—maybe a husband, or the man she loved, probably in the war that she so staunchly defended. He made another stab at polite conversation. "How much land do you have here?"

She squinted her eyes against the sun, which had finally pushed all the way through the clouds. "Over four sections, closer to five."

He whistled through his teeth. "That's a lot of land."

"Yes. And a lot of fence line to ride." She met his gaze with one of expectancy as she asked, "You said you worked on a ranch?"

He paused as his horse stopped and pulled back on the reins. Whit bent down to examine the hoof. With a shake of his head he stood, then ran a soothing hand over the animal's flank. "That's right. Among other things I worked on a ranch in California and three here in Texas."

He sounded like nothing more than a drifter to her. "If you are looking for a job, we could use a good hand. I can't pay much, but my grandmother is a fine cook."

He grinned. "Now that's an inducement that's hard to turn down."

She shrugged. "Well, if you should change your mind, we can always use someone with your experience."

His voice deepened. "I'll remember that."

Whit gazed into the distance, forming his words in his mind before he voiced them. "I have business in Galveston that can't wait." He squinted his eyes toward the sun. "How far is it to Galveston from here?"

"It's a good day and a half by buggy. On horseback you could probably make it in one day."

"Really?"

"If you have a good horse." She couldn't resist the jab. "Which you don't."

He nodded. "You are right about that."

Jackie glanced up at him, her gaze fastening on his beautiful mouth. She was hit by a strong feeling that took her completely by surprise: she didn't want him to just ride out of her life.

What was wrong with her?

How could she have such strong feelings for a complete stranger?

She was bewildered by her reactions to him. Maybe it had something to do with the way she melted inside whenever he looked at her.

Jackie wondered what kind of man Whit Hawk was—she sensed no threat in him, but she imagined he could be a very dangerous man if provoked. He was a troubled man; she somehow knew that. Whatever awaited him in Galveston was important to him. It was probably a woman.

Her gaze swept up his long legs to his leather holster. Her father had once told her that she could recognize the cut of a man by the kind of gun he wore. He'd said that if a man had a fancy, hand-tooled scabbard and a pearl-handled gun, he would be nothing but flash and no fight—a dude, a show-off. Whit Hawk's gun belt was solid black and laced low on his leg. His six-gun was not fancy, and, as far as she could see, there were no notches carved on the handle.

Her gaze rose higher. He was lean, his shoulders broad and muscular. She could see the shadow of a beard, so he hadn't shaved in a couple of days. His hair was obsidian black and hung past the nape of his neck. His face was tanned, his chin strong and stubborn. His features were finely chiseled, and he was handsomer than he had a right to be. She imagined he would be trouble for any woman who tried to tame him. He wasn't married; she knew that for a certainty—he was too arrogant, too sure of himself to share his life with a woman.

Her heart slammed against her breast when Whit turned his golden gaze on her. She had never seen anyone with eyes the color of his, and in that short moment Jackie saw something else in that golden gaze. Something painful flashed there momentarily; then it was gone.

Jackie wondered what his story was, and she wondered why she even cared. It seemed that this man carried the weight of the world on his shoulders. She stared down at the ground with a frown on her face, wondering if he could hear her heart beating.

"It's not far to the ranch now. Just over the next rise."

He nodded, completely absorbed in his own thoughts. Whit knew that wherever life took him, he would never forget this young woman. He could tell she was uncomfortable with him, but it wasn't that she was afraid of him any longer. It was something else he didn't care to examine. His life was a solitary one, and he was always leaving something behind. He had every intention of leaving this place as soon as his horse was well enough to ride.

A disturbing thought echoed through his mind.

Jackie Douglas was going to belong to him.

Chapter Four

Nada Douglas stepped off the porch and raised her hand above her eyes to shade them against the bright sunlight. She'd heard Jackie ride away just after noon. It had been cloudy then and looked like it might rain; now the sun was out, and it was just another hot day.

A worried frown furrowed her brow. Her grand-daughter should have been back by now. Nada had baked an apple pie for Della Grommet, who'd just had her fourth boy, and she'd wanted to take it to her friend while it was still fresh. But it would have to wait until tomorrow, because Nada couldn't go any-where until she knew that Jackie was safe. Jackie's well-being was a constant worry that nagged at Nada every day. Maybe, she thought, Jackie had ridden to the western pasture to see about that young bull that was she was so fond of.

Nada's frown deepened. Jackie wouldn't have stayed away this long, knowing how Nada worried about her. Her granddaughter was always depend-able: if she said she'd be a certain place at a certain time, she was always there. Jackie's brother, Matthew, Nada's only grandson, had been like that, too.

But, of course, Matthew was dead now, and Jackie had to run the whole place with very little help.

Jackie was so determined to do everything herself, and the girl was just plain worn out. She was too young to have such responsibility thrust on her shoulders. Jackie should be having fun with young people her own age, but there was no time for that. Most days Jackie saddled up before sunup and rarely returned home until nearly dark.

Nada's only son, Jackie's father, had died back in 'fifty-nine, almost a year to the day after Jackie's mother had died of the lung sickness. Sadly, Nada's only grandson had died in a battle in a town called Gettysburg, Pennsylvania.

Nada sighed. Matthew was buried among strangers, and she ached because she could never visit his grave.

Jackie had taken her brother's death hard. She'd tried so desperately to keep the ranch going, because she thought her dead brother would expect it of her.

Nada swatted at a gnat that was nagging her. There was no way of saving the ranch now. They were just lucky they'd kept the house in Copper Springs. It had belonged to Jackie's mother's family, and now belonged to Jackie. At least they'd have a place to live when the ranch was lost to them.

Jackie had only two wranglers to help her with the work. Both men had ridden for the La Posada brand when Nada's husband had been boss, and now they worked for Jackie. Mort Jamison and Ortega Sandoval were both getting on in years, and Jackie refused to work them too hard. Mort's eyesight was failing, and he had rheumatism in both his hands. Out of kindness, Jackie had made Mort responsible for the horses and keeping the tack in good condition. He lived in the small house that had always belonged to the foreman of La Posada.

La Posada had once been the pride and the jewel of the Douglas family. It had thrived in Nada's husband's day, and they had gained seven hundred more acres during her son's guardianship. Then it began to crumble when the war came along and her grandson had gone off to join the Confederacy.

Nada's gaze tracked Mort as he led a horse to the corral. She watched him grasp the pump handle to fill the nearly-empty trough. Ortega wasn't much younger than Mort, but he was still sturdy and strong. He and his wife, Luisa, had raised five children on the ranch— all girls. Now those girls had gone off with husbands of their own, four of them moving to San Antonio and one to Houston.

But Jackie's real problem wasn't the lack of hands to help around the place. Her trouble was with the bank in Copper Springs. Two years ago Jackie had mortgaged the ranch, and then last year she'd been forced to add most of the stock to the note. Nada had watched her granddaughter struggle to meet the payments, but no matter how hard Jackie worked, she'd fallen behind on the mortgage.

If it hadn't been for the war, the drought, and a shortage of men to drive the cattle to the railhead in Houston, they might have saved the ranch. Now the future looked bleak. Lately the grazing was so poor they'd been forced to burn the thorns off prickly pear cactus so they could feed it to the stock. The hay crop had done poorly, but what little they had was ready to harvest—if it didn't rain. If that happened, they'd be forced to buy feed for the cattle, using more of their precious money.

Time was running out, and the sooner Jackie realized she couldn't save the ranch, the sooner they could make plans to move into Copper Springs. The only things on the ranch that still belonged to Jackie were her prize bull and her Arabian gelding. Jackie had refused to add either of those animals to the note at the bank: The Arabian had been Matthew's horse, and Jackie would never sell it. The bull Jackie had handfed when its mama had gotten tangled in barbed wire and died of the deep wounds.

Nada sighed. Jackie had hopes of breeding a sturdier herd of cattle using the young bull as a stud. But it was too late for that now. Nada had prayed for a miracle to help them, but land was not worth as much as it had been before the war—it would be again, but not in time to help them.

They were living in hard times. Too many soldiers had returned to Texas to find their ranches already taken over by the banks.

Her gaze swept toward the horizon, and she was suddenly swamped with relief when she saw Jackie.

Then she frowned.

Her granddaughter was not alone, and Nada didn't recognize the man who walked beside her. Since they were two women living by themselves, they had to be on the lookout for the drifters and deserters that now crowded the roads. They had learned to be suspicious of strangers.

Nada quickly moved back onto the porch, wondering if she should get the rifle that hung over the fire-place, loaded and ready to use.

Jackie didn't seem to be distressed in any way, but Nada wondered why they were walking instead of riding. A swift assessment of her granddaughter's gelding told her the animal seemed to be fine, but there was no saddle. She nodded in understanding when she glanced at the stranger's horse and saw that it was limping.

Nada went into the house and untied her apron, hanging it on a hook in the kitchen, then smoothed her hair and went back outside, waiting for them to approach.

Nada heard Jackie's voice as she directed the stranger to the barn; then her granddaughter called out, "Gram, Mr. Hawk's horse threw a shoe."

Whit glanced at the sprawling one-story house that had been constructed of the beautiful white stone that was so prevalent in this part of Texas. They had approached from the back of the house, and from the look of the place he concluded that the Douglas family was quite successful.

Nada hurried down the steps with a healthy gait for a woman approaching her sixty-seventh birthday. "Where did you find this man?" she asked Jackie as the stranger disappeared inside the barn.

"I didn't. He found me."

Nada frowned slightly on her way to the barn. "Honey, all your life you've been bringing strays home. Let's see if we can help this one for you."

Whit unsaddled his horse and threw the saddle over a stall door. He hadn't seen any wranglers around, but he assumed they were out working cattle.

He bent down to examine his horse's hoof, running his finger along the ridges, and sighed inwardly. It didn't look good.

A woman he presumed to be Miss Douglas's grandmother bent down beside him and took the hoof in her blue-veined hand.

She confirmed her identity. "I'm Nada Douglas." Her practiced hand moved over the hoof. "I can see why your horse threw a shoe. This hoof is diseased, and probably infected. Naturally it'll have to heal before the animal can be reshod."

Whit nodded. "That's the way I see it, too." He stood and offered the woman his hand so he could assist her to her feet. "I'm Whit Hawk, ma'am."

"How do, Mr. Hawk. I'm Jackie's grandma. I'll have Mort file the hoof down and apply ointment. I'm thinking it might take a few weeks for it to heal, though. It's bad."

Whit nodded. "It is bad," he agreed solemnly.

Nada lived on a ranch where the health of the animals came before anything else. "This horse has suffered."

Whit felt guilty, because she was right. "I can see that now." He looked into her light blue eyes; something about her reminded him of Mrs. Kingsley. It wasn't her appearance, because Mrs. Douglas was as tall and thin as Mrs. Kingsley had been short and heavyset. It was more the eyes and the soft expression in them, the knowledge that was stored there, and the caring nature of both women. He was a gambler, and he could tell a lot about people just by looking into their eyes. Hers were honest, and he knew she would be straightforward, with a no-nonsense approach to life. She had known hardship, and she had felt heart-break, and yet she held on to her love of life. Her hair was streaked with gray, and he decided, judging by her delicate bone structure, that she must once have been a beauty like her granddaughter. She was still a striking woman.

Nada patted the rump of Whit's horse. "It took the animal a while to get in this condition." There was mild reprimand in her tone. "It seems to me you should have noticed it before now."

"You're right, Mrs. Douglas. I should have taken better care of him. It is not my habit to misuse an animal."

Nada watched him carefully, judging him. "How long have you had this horse?"

"Two months," he confessed, feeling the censure in her tone that reminded him even more of Mrs. Kingsley, who'd had the ability to make him feel guilty when he'd done something she'd disapproved of. "I got him from a rancher in San Angelo. I had a veterinarian examine him at the time; they both assured me the horse was healthy. I took their word."

"Those two must have been in cahoots. Any good veterinarian could have seen the hoof was infected." Her eyes twinkled. "I'd say you were like a lamb to the slaughter."

Whit's mouth curved, and then he laughed out loud. "That's about the right of it, ma'am. They must still be laughing at me back in San Angelo."

Nada looked Whit over carefully. "You don't seem to me to be a man whom anyone could take advantage of."

He shifted uncomfortably under her gaze. "Until now, I would have agreed with you."

She ran her hands over the horse's flanks, stepped forward, and looked inside the animal's mouth. "He's healthy enough otherwise. When he's well, he'll make you a good mount if he's not skittish."

"He takes well to a firm hand on the reins."

Jackie had been watching the exchange between her grandmother and Mr. Hawk. She smiled with a touch of mischief. "Gram is right, Mr. Hawk." For some unknown reason Jackie didn't care to examine too closely, it gave her a great deal of satisfaction to find fault with him. "You got fleeced by those men in San Angelo," she said.

Nada shot her granddaughter a surprised glance and shook her head. It wasn't like Jackie to take such delight in someone else's misfortunes, although Nada had teased him a bit a moment ago herself. "I wouldn't have put it quite like that, but let's see what we can do for the animal."

Whit agreed with a nod. His attention was drawn to the front of the barn, and he watched an old cowhand ambling in. The man was stooped and as bowlegged as a man could be. He had a shock of white hair hanging past the nape of his neck. The deep lines on his face told of years herding cattle in harsh weather and of a lifetime of hard work.

Mrs. Douglas motioned him forward. "Mort, this is Mr. Hawk. His horse needs attention. See what you can do for him."

The two men shook hands. "Glad to know ya, Mr. Hawk. What's ailing the animal?"

Nada raised the hoof so Mort could see it. "He has an infected hoof."

Mort nodded. "I'll see that he's doctored and settled in a stall."

Whit gazed around at the other stalls and saw that four of them were occupied. He would need a horse to get to Galveston, and he hoped they would sell him one. "I appreciate your help, Mort."

Nada walked toward the barn door. "When you're done down here, come on up to the house, Mr. Hawk. I have a pot roast warming on the stove. I wager you could use a good home-cooked meal."

Jackie was glancing out the window, and she watched Whit Hawk's progress across the yard. He moved with the assurance of a man who knew where he was going and how to get there.

When he knocked on the back door, Nada let him in with a smile of welcome. "You're just in time. I hope you like roast."

"Ma'am, if it's home cooking, I like about anything."

"Let's eat before it gets cold," Nada told him.

She was taken by surprise when Whit held her chair, then moved to Jackie and pulled out the chair for her.

"Your mama taught you right," Nada told him.

His gaze turned inward. "Actually, any manners I have come from a woman by the name of Mrs. Kingsley. She would rap my knuckles if I gave her any trouble. She always insisted we behave—" He broke off, realizing he'd said too much.

"This Mrs. Kingsley was your teacher?" Nada asked.

"Yes, in a way."

Nada caught Jackie studying their guest intently. Hawk was handsome enough to send any young woman's heart pounding. Jackie had never met anyone like Whit Hawk, and Nada didn't intend for her granddaughter to be swept away by a man who had too much charm and worldly knowledge. As pretty as Jackie was, she hadn't yet given her heart to any man. Of course, most of the young men in the county had gone off to war just when Jackie had been at an age for them to come courting and showering her with attention. There was Hutch Steiner, their neighbor, who had his eyes on Jackie, but she didn't show much interest in him. Jackie was always too busy to attend many of the functions for young people. From the way she kept watching Mr. Hawk, Nada realized Jackie was ripe and ready for some smooth-talking man to sweep into her life.

Nada also noticed that Mr. Hawk was doing some looking of his own, and there was a look in those golden eyes that troubled her. They were too intense. There was something important he had to do, and he wasn't about to let a woman get in his way.

Whit was about to reach for his water glass when Jackie and Mrs. Douglas lowered their heads to say grace. He quickly dipped his head, thinking about how long it had been since he'd been in a real home and enjoyed the niceties of everyday life.

After Nada had finished the prayer, she glanced at Whit. "So you were on your way to Galveston when your horse became lame."

Whit took the platter of meat Nada handed him. "Yes, ma'am, I was. Like I told your granddaughter earlier, my family once lived there."

"Hawk?" Nada tested the name. "I seem to recall a family by that name, years back. Were your folks in the shipping business?"

His gaze was guarded. "Yes, ma'am."

Nada nodded. "I never met any of your kin, but I recall my husband transported cattle on your family's ships a few times."

He reached into his pocket and handed her his ring. "Have you seen anyone wearing a ring like this one? My brother would be about my height, but other than that we don't look much alike. Or have you heard of anyone by the name of Drew Hawk living in Galveston?"

Nada examined the ring and shook her head. "No. I can't say that I have." She raised her gaze to his. "But we rarely go into Galveston since the place has been overrun with Yankees." She studied the ring carefully and handed it to Jackie so she could look at it, too. "That's a fancy ring."

"My father designed three just like it—one for me, Drew, and himself."

"If you don't mind my asking," the older woman inquired, "how did you lose your brother?"

Whit took the ring from Jackie and slid it back into his breast pocket. "It's a long story." He noticed Jackie was watching him with curiosity in her eyes. "I wouldn't want to bore either of you with the details," he said.

To Jackie's way of thinking, what he really meant was that he didn't want to talk about his personal life with strangers. She saw the flash of pain in his eyes, but again, it was quickly masked by a smile.

"I thank you both for your hospitality, and I'm afraid I'll have to impose further on your generosity." He directed his question to Jackie. "If you can spare one, I'd like to buy one of your horses. I need it get to Galveston as soon as possible."

Jackie reached across the table to remove a bowl, and felt the weight of his gaze as he waited for her to reply. "I'm sorry, Mr. Hawk. I can't sell you one of our horses." She stood to remove the plates from the table. "We don't have any to spare."

"I'd be willing to pay more than a fair price." His voice sounded deeper, troubled.

"I'm sorry. I can't help you . . ." She watched his slow, easy smile, and she forgot what she was about to say.

"Then can you tell me where I can buy a horse?"

Nada saw something happening between the two young people—she'd have to be blind not to recognize Hawk's fierce, hungry gaze when it fell on her granddaughter. Nada also saw that Jackie was confused and overwhelmed by the new feelings that swamped her.

Poor Jackie, she didn't want to admit to Mr. Hawk that most of their horses were attached to a mortgage, so Nada spoke up for her. "We don't have any extra horses here because we need ours to work the ranch. We could inquire at a neighboring ranch whether they have a horse to sell you."

Whit nodded gratefully "Thank you. I'd appreciate that."

Jackie was wiping the stove, and Whit watched her

hips move gracefully as she scrubbed back and forth, his heart slamming against his chest. He tore his gaze away from her, agitated because she kept drawing his attention. It was difficult to think about anyone else with her in the room.

That spunky little redhead was tugging at his heart, and he had to get away from her before he did something they'd both regret.

Whit turned to the grandmother. "Your grand-daughter told me how much land you have here. It's quite a spread."

"It would take more than a day to ride from one end of La Posada to the other."

Although Jackie had dropped her head and her silken red hair had curtained her face, Whit had caught a shimmer of tears in her eyes, and it felt like someone had delivered a blow to his heart. Something was wrong on this ranch, something serious enough to make her cry. He told himself he couldn't be bothered. It was none of his affair.

Jackie kept her back turned as she spoke. "I have decided that you can borrow my Arabian, Mr. Hawk."

Nada was taken aback by Jackie's offer. The girl loved the Arabian because it had been her brother's horse. She watched Whit's eyes widen with surprise, and she watched warmth pour into the golden depths.

"That's a very generous offer, but I'd insist on paying."

Patting his hand, Nada smiled. "Even though you're a stranger to us, Jackie must trust you, Mr. Hawk. She puts great store in that horse of hers, and she hardly ever lets anyone else ride him. If you borrow him, you'd better make sure you take good care of him and bring him back as soon as you can."

Whit stared at Jackie's rigid back. He hadn't wanted to feel anything for this family, or to become a part of their problems. But they were drawing him in with their kindness. He knew if he never saw Jackie again, he would always remember her sapphire blue eyes shimmering with tears. To him, she was like a rope thrown to a drowning man going down for the third time. "Why would you do that for me? Like you said, I'm a stranger."

It was Nada who spoke. "It comes down to trust, Whit Hawk. And don't ask me why, but my granddaughter has decided she can trust you. You go do your business in Galveston and then bring the Arabian back to her when you're finished. Our hospitality and the loan of the horse are freely given—there's no cost."

It had been so long since Whit had met with such kindness, it took him a moment to reply. "I'll take your offer, but I insist on making one of my own. I noticed that there are repairs that need attention about the place. I can put off going to Galveston long enough to lend a helping hand, if that's all right with you."

Jackie submerged a pan in the sudsy dishwater. "I thought you were in such a hurry to get to Galveston. You implied your trip couldn't wait."

He suddenly wished he had the right to pull her into his arms and comfort her, because she needed comforting badly. "What there is to do around here won't take that long—a couple of days."

Nada stood up and poured Whit a cup of coffee,

very aware that the tension had heightened between Jackie and Whit. "My granddaughter is too proud to take your help, but I'll accept it." She smiled. "It'll be good to have a young man about the place again. You'll have to sleep in the barn, though."

He took a sip of coffee and leaned back, studying the way Jackie's hair hung to her waist and swayed with each move she made. An unwelcome tightening hit him, and he tried to ignore it. "Thanks. I'll just get my gear and check on my horse." He drained his coffee and stood. "Thank you for all your help. And the meal was delicious, Mrs. Douglas."

Jackie watched Whit take his hat from the hat rack near the back door. "Breakfast is at five," she told him.

"I'll be here."

His smile sent Jackie's heart pounding, and it continued to pound after he'd gone. She found herself scrubbing hard on an already clean pot.

Her grandmother caught and held Jackie's hand. "You're going to rub a hole in that, child."

Jackie shook her head. "That man is the very reason I don't ever want to get married. He's so high-handed and demanding."

Nada hadn't lived to be as old as she was without gleaning some insight into human nature. For the first time in Jackie's life she was feeling the stirring of womanhood, and she was confused and disturbed by it. Nada would much rather Hutch had been the man Jackie wanted, but it wasn't to be. Hutch's father was not a man Nada respected, but the son had always been crazy about Jackie—he'd come running fast enough if Jackie gave him the least bit of encouragement.

She sighed. But human nature, being what it was, would not be shaped or dictated by anyone. This thing between Jackie and Hawk would soon play itself out, one way or another.

Chapter Five

Jackie stood on the porch, her back braced against a post, her thoughts in confusion. Her gaze kept straying to the barn. Although she tried not to think about Whit Hawk, he dominated her thoughts. She caught her lower lip between her teeth to keep it from trembling. Shards of light spilled from the barn, and she wondered what Whit was doing at that very moment. She was hit with such a deep longing, it made her press her hand against her stomach to still the fluttering there.

The screen door whooshed open behind Jackie, and her grandmother came out, fanning herself with her apron. "It surely is hot tonight. Not a breeze to cool a body down. There's dark clouds gathering, though, coming in off the gulf, so it might rain before morning. I hope not—that hay has to be harvested."

All Jackie could think about was Whit with his golden gaze and his obsidian-colored hair, and how much she wanted to feel his hands on her skin. "What do you suppose his story is, Gram?"

"Mr. Hawk? It's hard to know—he doesn't open up about himself. I could tell he was reluctant to tell us much about his past."

"Do you think he's running from the law?"

"Who can say?" Nada shrugged. "He has a cold streak in him, but I don't think he's mean. I do think he's dangerous. He's got trouble of some kind, and if I'm any judge of character, something is eating away at him."

Jackie lifted the weight of her hair off her neck and stared up at the clouds that were now boiling with energy. "I remember you once told me that when you met Grandpa, you knew right away he was the man you wanted to spend the rest of your life with."

Nada stopped fanning herself and dropped her apron. "That's right. And your grandpa knew it, too. Trouble was, he didn't want to be tied down to a woman. But in the end he came to me willingly enough. As his wife, I saw to it that he never had reason to regret the years we had together."

Jackie hesitated, leaning her elbows on the porch railing, realizing she would probably sound halfwitted when she put her thoughts into words. She had always considered herself a practical person. Well, there had been the incident today when she took her shoes off and danced barefoot—but most of the time she was hardworking and down-to-earth. "That's the way I feel about Whit Hawk. I don't know what happened to me, but I just know. What am I going to do?" Jackie blurted out, looking for guidance. "I have never felt this way about any man before. It has nothing to do with the way he looks, although I think he's the most beautiful man I've ever seen in my life."

"That's all well and good, but you don't really know anything about him. And he's older than you are by a few years. In some ways he's much older than you."

Jackie straightened, still staring toward the barn, wondering what had happened to her in the last few hours. Maybe all her troubles were just getting too big for her to handle; maybe she'd lost her mind. "I think I love him." Jackie turned a confused gaze on her grandmother. "Can I be wrong about that?"

Jackie's voice sounded so despondent. Nada gave her a quick look while she tried to digest that bit of information. Her granddaughter lived such a solitary life, and although Jackie had never said so, Nada knew she was often lonely. This was the first man who had ever touched Jackie's heart, and the last one Nada wanted to see her with. "Child, a moment ago you were wondering if Whit was running from the law. And I should warn you that there are other emotions a woman can feel for a man that shouldn't be mistaken for love."

Jackie slammed the palms of her hands against the porch railing, desperately trying to understand what was happening to her. "I know—I know. It doesn't make any sense to me. But I can't seem to help myself." She glanced into her grandmother's troubled eyes. "I will fight this, and I will win!" Her gaze was bewildered. "How do I do that, Gram?"

"I'm not sure I know. I wish I could tell you. This is something you'll have to work through on your own."

Jackie was clutching her hands together so tightly, her fingers whitened. "I sensed a loneliness in him, and it makes me sad. He needs someone to look after him."

"Maybe so. But not you."

"Did you know anything about Grandpa before you realized you loved him?"

"No," Nada admitted. "I didn't. I was just fortunate that he turned out to be a good man. I knew tonight that you were testing Whit Hawk in some way, and now I know why."

Jackie was not surprised her grandmother had seen through her—she always had. "You mean by loaning him my horse?"

"You want to see if he'll return the animal to you," Nada remarked sagely. "A lot of men would be tempted to keep such a valuable horse—you're betting Hawk will bring the gelding back."

Jackie was suddenly caught up in nameless fear. The thought of never seeing Whit again was almost more than she could bear. "My heart tells me he will return the horse to me."

None of the emotions Jackie was experiencing came as a surprise to Nada—she knew her granddaughter so well, and she had felt the longing in her when she had looked at Hawk tonight. "Use your head to judge this man—a heart can sometimes be deceived, but the mind rarely is. You have a lot of common sense. Use it in this situation."

Jackie nodded. "I'm trying. Anyway, he'll be gone in a few days when he finishes the work. If I never see him again, it might be for the best." She glanced up at the moon. "If I were smart, I'd accept Hutch's proposal. He's a good man, and if I married him I could save La Posada."

"But you don't love Hutch."

"No. I like him, but I will never love him." Guilt crushed down on Jackie. "Do you think it's selfish of me to turn Hutch down when I could save us from ruin by marrying him?"

Nada shook her head, feeling heavyhearted for the dear, sweet child who had to shoulder so much responsibility. "Marriage can be hard at times, even with a man you love. If you married Hutch, feeling the way you do about him, you'd both be cheated. And your life would get a lot harder."

"But Ortega and Mort would still have a home if I married Hutch."

Jackie had always thought she'd persevere through the hard times and save the ranch. But Nada realized the child was now on the verge of admitting defeat—a painful but necessary transition. "That's no reason to marry anyone, Jackie. You can't sacrifice yourself for the rest of us. I don't want it, and I know Mort and Ortega wouldn't either."

"I'm so confused. If I don't do something soon the ranch will be gone, and we will be moving to the house in Copper Springs."

They'd kept the house in town to use when they had to stay overnight in Copper Springs, and Nada was glad they had. "Whatever trouble comes, we'll face it together," Nada said, drawing her granddaughter into her arms.

Jackie leaned into her grandmother's comforting embrace, her gaze going back to the barn. "Yes. I suppose so. We won't have any choice, will we?"

Nada was suddenly struck by a plan to test the depth of her granddaughter's feelings—she was going to throw Jackie and Whit together and see what happened. Nada was depending on Jackie's good judgment to win over the confusion in her heart, and she hoped Jackie would realize that what she felt was just a physical reaction to a handsome and charming man.

"You need to take Mr. Hawk a pillow and quilt so he'll be more comfortable." She glanced up at the sky as thunder rumbled in the distance. "You'd better hurry before it starts to rain."

"Yes," Jackie said, turning away without hesitation, and entered the house, glad for any excuse to see Whit again.

Nada's heart hurt for Jackie because she was so confused. But then, she imagined Whit Hawk was somewhat confused himself. Jackie had to confront her feelings for Whit, for good or ill. Her granddaughter had to find out for herself if what she felt for that man was love or merely attraction. Some people would say a person couldn't love someone on first meeting, but Nada knew better. The love she'd felt for her husband had lasted for forty-two years, until his death. She smiled just thinking about him. Her spirit would always miss him, and her heart was his as surely as it had been that first day she'd seen him riding into town, so handsome and unsuspecting of how his life was about to be changed.

A slight breeze cooled her cheek. Anyway, La Posada was to be auctioned off in a little more than three weeks. They had lost so many people they loved. They had struggled with work that would overwhelm grown men. Jackie had worn herself out trying to hold the ranch together. And, in the end, none of it would matter.

She wished they'd had a horse to sell Whit Hawk so they could have sent him on his way. As soon as he'd finished the work that would satisfy any obligation he thought he owed them, he'd ride on. It might cost them a good horse to find out the cut of the man, but it would be worth it.

Whit opened the stall door and discovered his horse had been doctored, its hoof wrapped with wide bandages. He patted the animal and held a bucket of water for him to drink. Only after his horse settled down did he get his bedroll and spread it on the scattered hay near the back of the barn.

He lay down, resting his head on his folded arms as he listened to thunder crackle so near it shook the ground. He heard the first drops of rain hammer against the tin roof—a roof that leaked in several places, he observed. If he hadn't met Jackie today, he'd probably be sleeping out in the storm tonight. When he thought of her, his mind splintered in different directions, and his body hardened—he knew he wanted her.

Wanted, but could not have her.

His feelings for her scared the hell out of him. She made him feel too much. Want too much. All evening he'd been thinking about her soft lips, and that damned red hair that he couldn't get out of his mind.

That was crazy!

There was a black stain on his soul; he had a jaded past and an uncertain future—while Jackie was pure and sweet.

Innocent.

Directing his thoughts down a different path, he

glanced above him and noticed that most of the loft had rotted away. Earlier he'd noticed the barn door was warped and needed to be replaced. Even now it slammed open and shut with the force of the wind. The latch must be broken. There was a lot of work that needed doing around the place.

Whit would do as much as he could for the two women before going on to Galveston.

He closed his eyes, his thoughts turning once more to the beautiful redhead. She had been as affected by him as he was by her—he knew that. Everything had happened so quickly it disturbed him. Her sweetness beckoned to him, a call that he must not answer.

Whit frowned. His senses told him Jackie was lonely and knew little about life outside this ranch. He swore under his breath. He had to stop thinking about her. They were worlds apart, and he could never be anything in her life other than a stranger who passed through.

He stretched his long legs out on his bedroll. He was impatient to leave. He wanted to ride away from this ranch with no guilt and no attachments.

But he wanted her. Even now, just thinking about the soft swell of her breasts made him harden.

"Dammit," he ground out, trying to forget about the way his body was reacting to her.

But closing his eyes didn't help, because he could see visions of her dancing, her tangled hair swaying about her, her hips moving invitingly. The ache inside him grew deeper, the emptiness blacker. He wanted to be the man to take her hand and dance beside her, if only for a moment in time.

Whit's eyes snapped open. He couldn't allow anything to hinder his search for Drew. Guilt anchored him to the past, and determination dictated his future. His goal was a path he must follow to the end.

Whit had been so deep in thought he hadn't known someone entered the barn until a shadow came between him and the lantern. He rolled to his feet when he saw Jackie.

"Good evening, Miss Douglas."

Jackie noticed he'd removed his suit and was wearing dark trousers and a green work shirt—if anything he was even more handsome, with his ebony hair falling carelessly across his forehead.

Jackie brushed a damp curl from her cheek and gave him an uncertain smile. Holding the quilt and pillow out to him, she said, "Gram thought you might need these."

He took them from her, his fingers brushing against hers, causing her to quickly withdraw her hand.

"Thank you. You have both been most kind to a stranger."

The storm intensified, lightning crackled, and thunder rolled, matching the force that raged through Jackie's body. Whit's shirt was unbuttoned halfway down, and her gaze fastened on the curly black hair on his muscled chest. She wished she could touch him.

Whit saw where Jackie's gaze was directed and he quickly buttoned his shirt. "I'm sorry. I wasn't expecting anyone."

Jackie knew she shouldn't have come. Being alone with Whit only made her more confused than she already was. Tearing her gaze from his, she deliberately glanced upward at the rafters. "You'll want to sleep where the roof isn't leaking," she managed to say.

"Yes."

Jackie waited, as if she expected something from him. Surely he had experienced some of what she was feeling—she couldn't be wrong about that. He had probably met many women who reacted to him in the same way she did. She lowered her head, feeling humiliation. Her gaze fell on his hands—he had long, tapered fingers, beautifully shaped like the rest of him—and even now she was thinking about how it would feel to be stroked by those hands.

Before Jackie had met Whit Hawk, she had thought of herself as a sensible woman. Now she was behaving as if she hadn't a brain in her head or any morals.

How many different ways could she make a fool out of herself in one day?

Whit tossed the quilt and pillow onto his bedroll. She might not know it, but she was issuing him an invitation, loud and clear. It would take only one step to bring them together, but he wasn't about to take that step. The lantern glistened on the few raindrops that had dampened her hair, and he wanted to take fistfuls of curls and pull her to him, fitting her body against his; he ached to kiss her until her lips stopped trembling. In his imagination he was taking her onto the bedroll and covering her body with his.

His voice came out gruffly. "Mort took good care of my horse."

She glanced away from him. "He's always had a way with animals—they seem to gentle at the sound of his voice. Your horse couldn't be in better hands. Mort knows all about herbs and healing balms."

He didn't think she was aware that she'd stepped closer to him, but his body reacted to hers with raging hunger. He turned away and spread the quilt on his bedroll and plumped the pillow. "I should sleep soundly tonight with such comforts."

When he turned back to her, he read the hurt of rejection in her eyes, and it stabbed at his heart. "There is a lull in the rain." He moved around her to get the slicker that hung from a nail. "Take this to hold over your head—it'll keep you dry." He placed it in her hands and stepped back away from her, willing her to go before it was too late.

Jackie wanted to throw the slicker back in his face. It was obvious he just wanted her gone. She was startled when he took the slicker from her and placed it around her shoulders. "I'll see you to the door." He picked up the lantern and gripped her arm, pulling her forward.

Whit knew he had to get her out of there as soon as possible, because he wanted more from her than she could imagine. He wanted to lay her down on that quilt and bury himself inside her. He practically shoved her out into the rain and closed the barn door behind her, leaning against it, hoping his heart would settle down to a normal rate.

Jacqueline Douglas couldn't know what had nearly happened between them. She couldn't have known the tight rein he'd kept on his feelings. He had to make sure they were never alone again.

Whit was seated at the table while Nada piled his plate high with steak and eggs. She set a plate of mouthwatering biscuits in front of him, and a jar of her best homemade grape jam.

"If you feed me this well, I may never want to leave, Mrs. Douglas."

"If a man's going to do a day's work, he's got to be fed," she said, pouring him a second cup of coffee.

"I noticed while I was in the barn that the boards in the hayloft were warped and rotted, and you need a new barn door."

She sat down across from him, sliding the salt and pepper toward him. "It's funny you should mention that. Mort went into Copper Springs just last month to get the lumber to make that repair. Course, he can't go climbing around up there in the loft or he'd probably fall and break his neck. I'd be mighty beholden to you if you'd fix the hayloft for us."

He took a sip of coffee. "Where is your granddaughter this morning?"

"She left about an hour ago. It's too wet to gather the hay today, so she and Ortega are setting in new fence posts."

He took the last bite of his steak and another sip of coffee before he stood. "Thank you, Mrs. Douglas. You're an excellent cook."

She grinned. "Flattery such as that will get you something special for lunch." Her grin widened, because he was the kind of man any woman, no matter what her age, would want to please. "Maybe I'll make it hard for you to leave us."

His lashes swept over his eyes so she could not read his expression. "I have no choice, Mrs. Douglas. I have to get to Galveston."

"That's kind of what I thought you'd say." She stood. "Call me Nada. Everyone does."

He liked her informality. Again she reminded him of Mrs. Kingsley. "If you'll call me Whit."

"Get on out of here, you handsome rascal. You have work to do. Don't go trying to charm an old woman—I don't think my heart could take it."

He laughed on his way to the door. "Yes, ma'am. I'm on my way."

Using the heavy crowbar, Whit pried the rusty nails loose, splintering the rotten wood. It took him all morning to remove the old floor from the loft. He balanced his weight on a beam, shoving a new board into place. Mort was below, measuring and sawing planks while Whit nailed them in place. He was half finished when Jackie poked her head up the ladder.

"You're a fast worker."

He paused with a nail in his mouth to look at her. "So are you. Did you already set the new posts?"

"Yeah. It wasn't as bad as I thought—only three had to be replaced. It's too wet to bundle hay, so I came to see if I could help you."

It was on the tip of his tongue to tell her that a woman had no business doing such heavy work, but it wasn't his concern what she did, and she probably wouldn't want his advice anyway. "Fine. If you can hand me the boards as Mort saws them, it'll go much faster."

They had worked in companionable silence for over an hour when Jackie climbed up the ladder and handed him the last board, watching him shove it tightly into place. Her gaze followed the way his shoulder muscles rippled across his back each time he swung the hammer. His hair clung to the back of his neck, damp and oh, so black. His face glistened with sweat, and she ached to touch him. She bit her bottom lip until it hurt, trying to think of something besides how he looked.

Jackie had ridden away from the house earlier than usual that morning so she wouldn't have to sit across the breakfast table from Whit. But running away hadn't done any good—because Whit had been on her mind the entire time she and Ortega had been setting the posts.

What was the matter with her?

Whenever he turned his gaze on her, she could hardly breathe. She had to get her head together—there was work to do about the place.

"That's done, Mort." Whit drove in the last nail. "Now I'll get started on the barn door."

Mort slid the sawhorse to the side of the barn and hung the saw on a hook. "If you're through with me, I'll just go to my place to have a bite to eat," Mort told him. "You want to eat with me, Whit?"

Jackie wondered how the two men had gotten on such friendly terms. Mort was very particular about whom he befriended, and she couldn't remember a time he'd invited anyone to his house.

"He'll be eating with us, Mort," she said, stepping down one rung. "Gram has been fussing and cooking all morning. You're welcome to come, too, if you'd like."

"Thanks, but no. I got me a pot of beans simmering, and I think I'll just take me a little nap after I eat. Just for a short spell."

With a worried frown, Jackie watched Mort amble out of the barn. He spent more and more of his time in bed. She couldn't stand the thought of anything happening to him. He had been with the family long before she was born. She didn't want to lose another person in her life—especially not that dear man.

Whit wiped his face on his sleeve before he glanced at Jackie. She was standing halfway down the ladder, and he couldn't get down until she moved. "I need to see about that door," he reminded her.

"That can wait until after lunch. Gram is expecting you."

He sensed she was still troubled by him, and it was his bet that she didn't fully understand what was happening to her. He was a man, and he knew when a woman wanted him. He also knew his feelings for her could easily get out of control, but he mustn't let that happen. She was the kind of woman a man would never tire of—if he had her once, he'd want her again. But despite his good intentions, he couldn't help fantasizing about taking her down on the straw and—"I need to look in on my horse before I eat. Please tell your grandmother I won't be ten minutes behind you."

Jackie looked at his handsome face and the cynical twist to his lips, knowing he had just dismissed her. She reached for the canvas sack of nails, descended the ladder, and hung the sack on a hook.

As she walked toward the door, he made the mistake of watching. Her hips moved gracefully. Her hair swayed with each step she took, and it was driving him crazy.

Whit climbed down the steps and caught up with her before she reached the door. He saw the surprise in her eyes when he gripped her shoulders and turned her toward him. He had to get the hell off this ranch, and fast, but first he had to make her understand something. "There can never be anything between us, Jackie. You know that as well as I do," he said sardonically.

She raised her trembling chin to him and shoved him away. "You're mistaken if you think I want anything from you, Mr. Hawk. You're the most arrogant and self-centered man I've ever known."

It was easy to see by the bright sheen in her eyes that she was barely holding back tears. "You aren't the first woman who has said that to me," he told her, deliberately advising her that there had been many women in his life. "Forgive me if I was too bold. You have every right to ask me to leave."

Her temper roared into flame. "I do ask you to leave and never come back!"

"I'll have to come back to return your horse," he reminded her, his mouth easing into a smile. "Won't I?"

"You can hire someone to bring him back to me."

"No, I can't. If I borrow something, I see to it personally that it is safely returned to the owner. A woman named Mrs. Kingsley taught me that."

She stepped away from him, coming up against the door. "I wouldn't be surprised if you didn't bring my horse back at all."

He reached out and caught her face between his hands. "I will be back, and I think you know it in your heart."

"I never want to see you again."

"Yes, you do, sweet, sweet Jackie." His thumb feathered across her cheek. "I think you are going to break my heart."

She raised her chin to a higher angle. "Why would you say something like that to me?"

"You don't really know me, but understand this about me: I would never deceive you in any way or take advantage of your innocence." There was strain in his voice as he dipped his head, his lips only inches from hers. "Even now I want to kiss you. It would be so easy to—"

She whirled away from him, afraid now that he was so near. "You go too far!"

He took a deep breath and stepped back. "Again, I ask your pardon."

"Just don't touch me again," she said, turning and stalking out the door. She managed to get halfway to the house before her knees almost buckled.

Jackie had wanted him to kiss her, and he'd known it. She wanted him to do more than kiss her, and he knew that, too.

"Jackie Douglas, you're a fool," she muttered in distress. "A complete and utter fool!"

Chapter Six

The foreman of the Diamond S dismounted at the barn, observantly noticing that there had been some repairs done since the last time he'd been to La Posada. Hearing hammering inside the barn, Fletcher Langston figured he'd find Mort there, and he needed to talk to him about something. When Fletcher stepped into the cool interior, he found only a stranger nailing a board to the tack room door. The man didn't even look up from his task as Fletcher approached him.

"Hello," Fletcher said guardedly.

Whit turned to the newcomer and acknowledged him with a nod. "Mort's in the hayloft if you're looking for him." Whit turned back to his task, positioning a nail in just the right spot so it lined up with the others; hammering it into place, he tested it to make sure it was sturdy.

Mort had heard voices and was climbing down the loft ladder. He stared at the visitor, running his rheumatic fingers through his white hair. "How do,

Fletcher. We ain't seen you 'round here in quite a spell. How's your boss?"

Fletcher shrugged. "Mr. Steiner doesn't get out and about much anymore—his bum leg keeps him from riding or doing much of anything else."

George Steiner's leg had been crushed when a horse had fallen on him. The injury had been bad at the time, and Mort had heard his leg was getting worse. "I guess that puts most of the ranching on his son's shoulders."

"That's right. Hutch is down in Mexico on a cattle-buying trip right now. He should be back any day." As Fletcher spoke, he was sizing up the stranger, not liking what he saw. He supposed he was just another drifter, like so many others looking for work since the war had left them destitute. "Who's that?" he asked, nodding at Whit.

Mort wiped sweat from his face with a red bandanna and quickly introduced the two men. "This here's Whit Hawk. Whit, Fletcher Langston's the foreman at the Diamond S ranch."

Each man took the other's measure. They were about the same height, but while Whit's hair was black, Fletcher's was light brown and thinning, and his eyes were almost the exact same color as his hair. Whit judged the man to be in his late forties. His face was craggy, his nose wide, and it appeared to have been broken several times.

Fletcher held out his hand, and the two men exchanged handshakes, but there was nothing friendly about the glint in Fletcher's eyes.

"Glad to meet you, Mr. Hawk. Where are you from? Do you intend staying around here long?"

Whit immediately took a dislike to Fletcher, and he didn't appreciate his probing interrogation or his demanding tone. "I'm from here and there. And as to how long I'll be staying, I can't hazard a guess."

Fletcher's gaze hardened—he didn't like Hawk's attitude. "And if you do decide to leave, where would you be going?" he asked.

Whit shrugged. "Here and there."

Fletcher's eyes narrowed. He was foreman of one of the most successful ranches in the area, and this man was nothing but a hired hand. Fletcher demanded respect and usually got it. "You're a drifter," he insinuated insultingly.

Whit knew the man was looking for trouble, and he didn't want to tangle with him if he could help it. "Let's just say I travel around a lot."

"If you want permanent work, I'm always on the lookout for good hands."

Whit glanced back at the plank he'd just nailed into place and ran his hand over the wood. "I have a job."

Mort looked from one man to the other in bewilderment. Their words might be polite, but their attitudes certainly weren't friendly. Fletcher had a reputation for pushing people around, and a lot of men were scared of him. Suddenly Mort knew exactly why Fletcher was deliberately goading Whit—the foreman saw Whit as a suitor for Jackie's hand.

Mort grinned and said in a jocular tone, "Whit's helping out around here." He leaned an arthritic shoulder against the stall, watching with great interest as the drama unfolded before him. Mort didn't like Fletcher much, and he couldn't say he knew anyone who did. He hadn't known Whit for long, but he'd trust him with his best pair of boots, and that was saying a lot, 'cause he'd had them handmade and hand tooled down in San Antonio.

Fletcher's eyes hardened as he decided to goad Hawk into leaving. His boss wanted his son, Hutch, to marry Jackie so he could ally himself with the much-respected Douglas name. Steiner wouldn't take kindly to any man coming between him and what he wanted. "Miss Douglas can't afford to pay you as much as Mr. Steiner can."

Whit's eyes narrowed. "Is that right?"

Fletcher realized that Hawk wasn't just another saddle tramp, as he'd first thought. He was suspicious of a man with Hawk's obvious education and articulate way of speaking who hired on for menial labor. He took a threatening step forward. "Yeah, that's right."

Whit shook his head. "Thank you, but no. I'm happy where I am." He gathered the tools and stowed them on the top shelf in the tack room.

Mort was grinning from ear to ear. Fletcher was getting mighty upset 'cause he couldn't bring Whit 'round to his way of thinking. From the look of Whit's frown, he was getting plain aggravated by Fletcher's bullying.

Whit's dislike for the foreman grew, but he wouldn't allow the man to get under his skin. Fletcher was looking for a fight, and Whit didn't intend to oblige him if he could help it.

Mort thought it was time for him to step in before things got out of hand. "Fletcher, you wanted to see me 'bout something?"

The foreman blinked and turned his attention back

to the old man. "Yeah, I did. Mr. Steiner wanted me to warn you that a cougar is roaming the area. He took down one of our newborn calves, and Max Daniels lost three calves to the cat. If the size of his paw prints is any indication, the animal's huge. Me and some of the hands are going to track him tomorrow. Thought you and Ortega might want to come along." His gaze went to Whit. "You're welcome to come along, too, if you're of a mind to, Mr. Hawk."

"Thank you, but no. I have little interest in hunting at the moment."

Fletcher frowned. "You afraid, are you?" He shook his head in distaste. "You needn't worry; we'll protect you."

Whit's whole attitude changed. His shoulders straightened, and his eyes darkened. Mort saw the danger of goading a man like Whit, but it didn't seem that the foreman did. Fletcher was just asking for trouble, and Mort would bet Whit was about to give it to him. Mort almost laughed out loud when he realized Fletcher was trying to scare Whit into leaving. Fletcher was a fritter—and he was about to step off the deep end of trouble.

The foreman continued needling Whit. "Maybe you shouldn't go with us. Stay here and maybe the womenfolk can protect you if the cat comes near."

Whit let that pass. He'd seen men like Fletcher before, looking for a fight, trying to prove how tough they were. Whit had nothing to prove.

Fletcher rested his arm on a stall door, flexing a gloved hand. "Tracking a cougar is a job for a real man—one who isn't afraid of his own shadow."

Whit had just finished looping a rope and hanging

it on a hook. He slowly bent to pick up a second rope and began looping it. "Fletcher, you're looking at the wrong man if it's a fight you want. It'll take more than insults to my character from a man who doesn't even know me to make me mad enough to fight. If you're wise, you'll back down. Now."

"I'll give you a reason to fight—I say you're a coward!" Fletcher stood up straight and spread his legs wide apart while one hand went down to rest against the handle of his tooled gun.

Mort saw that things were turning mean real fast. He watched Whit's eyes, and if Fletcher had been wise, he'd have been watching them, too, because there was a deadly expression in those golden depths.

Whit casually made a wide loop in the rope as if he had all the time in the world. Before the foreman could react, the rope sailed through the air, the noose sliding over Fletcher's head and dropping to his waist. With a yank, Whit jerked the man forward. "I don't know you well enough to kill you, Fletcher. But just so you'll know this about me in the event we ever meet again, I don't like anyone implying I'm a coward."

Fletcher struggled and tried to work his arms free so he could get to his gun. Whit merely increased the tension on the rope, pinning the man's arms at his sides. The foreman wriggled and stretched his fingers toward his gun, but the rope was too tight.

"I still say you're a coward." But his accusation was delivered with less force this time.

Whit yanked on the rope and looped it a second time around the man. "If I were a coward, as you implied, I'd shoot you right now while you're helpless, wouldn't I?"

Fletcher saw something that scared him in the depths of Whit's eyes—and they certainly weren't the eyes of a coward. He nodded, licking lips that had suddenly gone dry. "I guess you aren't a coward."

Whit yanked the rope again, and Fletcher almost lost his footing. "You guess?"

"I know . . . I know you aren't a coward."

Whit dropped the rope and without glancing behind him, walked toward the barn door. "See that you remember it." He paused in front of Mort. "Help him, will you? And, Mort, I don't think we should mention this incident to anyone outside the three of us."

Mort would like nothing better than to tell every one what had just happened. A lot of people would be happy to know Whit had actually bested Fletcher without throwing a fist or pulling a gun. But Whit had asked him to keep it quiet, and that was what he'd do. Mort didn't think Whit would have any more trouble from the foreman of the Diamond S. Fletcher knew when he'd been beaten.

Chapter Seven

Jackie was troubled as she wrapped twine around a sheaf of hay with practiced skill and tossed it up to Ortega, who stacked it on the wagon. She was still stinging from the way she'd humiliated herself the day before. She grabbed the twine Ortega handed her and yanked it hard, trying to keep her anger under control. Jackie wasn't sure who she was angrier with—herself or Whit. Maybe both of them. That man certainly had a lofty opinion of himself, and she'd only added fuel to feed his arrogance. She imagined him gloating over another conquest and tossed the bundled hay so hard it hit Ortega in the stomach.

"Oof." He doubled over and burst into amused laughter. "Where is your mind today, señorita? Do you wish to knock me off this wagon?"

"Did I hurt you? I'm so sorry," she apologized.

"Of course you did not hurt me. You just knocked the wind out of me. You are very strong for a woman."

"I'm just in a hurry to get this job over with, and I was thinking of something else."

"Or some*one* else," he speculated with a smile.

The story of Ortega and Luisa, his wife, was wildly romantic. When Ortega had been a young man, Jackie's grandfather had sent him to Monterey, Mexico, to deliver a blooded mare to a Spanish don. While Ortega had been there, he'd met and fallen in love with the don's eldest daughter, Luisa. They had both known Luisa's father would never permit his daughter to marry a common cowhand from Texas. So one night, when everyone was asleep at the hacienda, Ortega spirited Luisa away, married her, and they crossed the border into Texas. By the time Luisa's father had finally tracked them down, Luisa was already carrying Ortega's baby. In a fury, the don had ridden away, swearing he'd never accept such a marriage and never again wanted to see his daughter.

For many years Luisa had not heard from any of her family. Finally she received a letter from her mother, informing her that her father had died. She invited her daughter to visit whenever she could, but wrote that her husband would not be welcome. Luisa had written her mother that if Ortega was not welcome, then she would not come home either.

If Luisa had regrets, she never spoke of them. The line cabin had been rebuilt years ago to accommodate Ortega's growing family. Luisa kept her house clean and took care of her family. It made Jackie sad to think that Luisa and Ortega would probably have to move if she lost the ranch.

Jackie was so deep in thought, she dropped the twine and it unrolled, bouncing away from her. With an exasperated sigh she picked it up and wound it around another sheaf of hay. She had risen an hour earlier than usual so she and Ortega could finish baling the hay before it got too hot, but it was taking longer than she'd hoped.

In another hour, the last of the hay was stacked on the wagon. Jackie removed her gloves and smiled at Ortega. He was a tall man, his once-black hair now streaked with gray. He had high cheekbones like many of his people, and the softest brown eyes she'd ever seen. He sometimes treated her like one of his daughters instead of his boss, and that was all right with her—he and Luisa were like family. She had grown up with their daughters as her playmates. Now their daughters were all married and had lives of their own. Jackie missed their companionship and was always happy when they brought the children home for a visit.

"That's the last of it," Jackie said, noticing for the first time that another storm was developing to the south. "You'd better hurry and take the wagon to the barn before the storm breaks. Mort and Whit can help you unload and stack the hay in the loft."

He looked at her suspiciously. "What is it you think you are going to do, *chiquita?*"

A while back, Jackie had bred one of her longhorns with a neighbor's Brahma bull in hopes of producing a hardier breed of stock. The bull was now a year old, and for a while he'd been her hope for the future, but not anymore. "The young bull broke out of the pen sometime yesterday, and he's missing," she answered cautiously, knowing Ortega wouldn't want her to go riding off on her own, since there was a cougar out there somewhere. "I'll ride along the river and see if I can pick up his tracks."

Ortega shook his head. "That young *bribón* has been nothing but trouble. He is forever breaking down fences and trampling your grandmother's garden. What are you going to do with him?"

She sighed. "I don't know. But I can't lose him. He was my dream for La Posada."

It hurt Ortega to speak so plainly to her, but there had always been truth between them. "That dream is all but over, little one."

"I know it is," she agreed in a resigned voice. "But I still need to take care of the yearling—I can't let anything happen to him."

"According to Mort, several ranchers lost stock to a cougar. You cannot go out there alone."

She stared at him stubbornly. "Oh, yes, I can."

Ortega studied her closely. When she was set on doing something, she was a very determined young woman. But Ortega feared for her with a storm brewing and a hungry cougar on the loose. "You should take the wagon back to the house and let me go in search of the bull," he suggested, jumping down from the wagon and approaching her horse, which was grazing nearby. "Mort and Señor Hawk can stow the hay in the loft for you. Night is coming on, and it will probably rain. You should not be out in such weather."

Ortega was being protective of her, and she knew it. He had to understand that she was trying to hold together the unraveling strands of her life. Lately she'd had very little control over anything, but this she *could* control. Her hands went to her hips in a show of authority. "If I were my brother, we wouldn't be having this conversation, and you know it, Ortega. I

101

am perfectly capable of tracking the bull. And I'm not afraid of the cougar."

His tone softened. "I know. But you work hard all the time. Let me do this for you."

Her chin rose a notch, and she shook her head while hopelessness and anger battled inside her. She was no longer a child, and he couldn't protect her anymore. There were some things she had to do for herself. "I'm boss here, and I'll say what you do and what I do."

Ortega digested what she was saying, not in the least offended by her attitude, but worried about her all the same. She always became defensive when she was troubled about something. Lately there had been nothing but trouble for her. "*Chiquita,* why do you think you have to do everything yourself? You cannot save the world. You know this."

Her shoulders suddenly slumped. "We will all be put off the ranch if I can't come up with the bank payment before the fifteenth of next month." She raised damp eyes to him. "What will you and Luisa do when that happens? What will happen to Mort? And what about Gram? She's lived on this ranch since she was a young bride. How will she survive in that small house in Copper Springs?"

Her sadness cut him like a knife. Ortega had known her all her life, had watched her take her first step, ride her first horse—she had cut her teeth on his heart. Now she was in trouble, and he could do nothing to help her. "I have found in hard times, *chiquita,* it is always best to put your troubles in God's hands."

She dipped her head, and her hair fell forward to

curtain her face, but not before Ortega saw her tears. "I know you're right about that; but I think God may be too busy to bother about my troubles. There are so many people who have bigger problems than I do and have suffered much more because of the war."

He remembered how devastated she had been that day the letter had arrived informing her of her brother's death. Losing La Posada would be almost as painful as the news that Matthew had died in battle. "Then I will say the prayers for you, *chiquita*. For I believe you are entitled to divine intervention as much as anyone else."

Jackie brushed straw from her leather skirt and walked purposefully toward her horse. "Tell Gram I'll be late. Tell her why."

Ortega watched her ride away, his heart heavy. He could not love her more if she had been one of his own daughters. She had had many troubles in her life, and no one to help her get through them—she had to do it all on her own. She was right to be concerned, though. What would happen to them all when the bank took the ranch, as surely it would?

Jackie halted her horse and dismounted beside the river. She had located the bull's hoofprints a mile back but lost them on a rocky ledge. She bent down so she could examine the muddy riverbank. He'd been there all right, and not long ago, maybe an hour or even less. As she glanced farther down the riverbank, her gaze hardened, and then her eyes widened with dread.

The cougar had also watered nearby!

Jackie walked downstream so she could get a better look at the cat's prints. Bending, she traced the outline with her finger and let out a worried sigh. Judging from the size of the paw prints, this cougar was huge. And unless she was mistaken, it was tracking her bull. She had to find the yearling before the cat did.

In a moment of fear, she considered riding to the house and bringing Ortega back with her—he could track anything, even in the dark. She shook her head and reconsidered. There was no time to ride back to the ranch. If she didn't find the bull quickly, he would probably end up being a meal for the cat tonight.

She ran to her horse and removed her rifle from the saddle holster. Mounting, she placed the rifle across her lap, riding along the river until she found the place where the bull had crossed to the other side. The cat was still trailing behind her bull. In a fight the yearling wouldn't have a chance, because his horns weren't yet fully developed—he would be no match for such a predator.

She jabbed her heels in her horse's flanks and rode across the river in pursuit. Except for the pounding of her horse's hooves, an eerie quiet settled over the land. Even the birds had fallen silent—it was as if they sensed something ominous was about to happen. She tasted fear and almost turned back toward the house, but her stubbornness would not allow her to abandon the bull. She urged her horse from a lope into a full run.

The sun was touching the western sky, and dark clouds gathered on the horizon as Nada stared in the direction of the river, frown lines creasing her brow. Jackie had her really worried this time. She couldn't

understand why her granddaughter insisted on looking for the stray by herself. It was too dangerous with
the cougar on the loose.

Whit removed his hat and stepped onto the porch.
"I finished patching the barn roof, and not a minute
too soon, by the looks of those clouds."

"Yes," Nada remarked, her gaze still skimming the
distance. "It's sure to storm before the night is over."

He frowned, sensing her unease. "Is something the
matter?"

"It's just that I'm worried about Jackie."

He followed her gaze. "She isn't in the house?"

"Ortega said she was tracking a yearling bull."
Nada turned to Whit. "There's a cougar out there—
it's getting dark, and she's out there alone. If I know
Jackie, she won't give up until she finds the bull."

Whit tensed when Nada met his gaze, and he saw
her deep concern. Jackie's grandmother wasn't the
kind of woman who would worry needlessly. "Did
Ortega say in which direction she went?"

"She told him she was going to follow the river."

Almost before Nada had finished speaking, Whit
was running for the barn. Only a short time later she
watched him ride toward the river, his rifle resting
across his thighs. She drew in a relieved breath—Whit
would find Jackie and bring her home.

Jackie glanced worriedly toward the dark clouds that
moved across the sun, casting the land in deep
shadow. She was often forced to dismount so she
could look for signs. Since she could find no evidence
of the cougar's tracks, she felt renewed hope. She

found a deep imprint of the bull's hoof and breathed a little easier. She hoped the cougar had found other game and moved on. But a prickle of fear touched the back of her neck when she found the cat's tracks in deep sand.

It was still following the bull.

Tears of frustration blinded Jackie. When the bull's mother had died, Jackie had fought hard to keep the animal alive. She certainly wasn't willing to give him to the predator who stalked him. If the bull died, she would never know if her crossbreeding had succeeded. To her, the yearling represented everything La Posada stood for.

Riding hard, she entered a deep canyon, her horse's hooves echoing against the limestone walls. Her gaze skimmed along the rim, then dipped to the ground as she searched in the near darkness for a broken twig, an overturned stone, anything that would help her locate the bull. Some way back she had lost the cougar's trail, but of course he had probably leaped up the face of the cliff to hide. By now the cat would know she was tracking the bull; perhaps the animal had abandoned the hunt.

The light was fading fast as dark, ominous clouds devoured the sunset. Streaks of lightning made a jagged path across the sky, and thunder rolled in the distance. Deep shadows crept across the canyon, and parts of it were already swallowed in darkness.

Jackie dismounted so she could get a closer look. A familiar sound—the bellow of the bull—sent a sigh of relief through her.

Her bull was safe, at least for the moment.

Until now Jackie's only concern had been for the yearling, but when she heard the unearthly scream of the cat above her on the cliff, a shiver of dread touched her spine and ran throughout her body. Her hand tightened on the rifle. This cougar was a cunning devil—it had doubled back on her, and it was hiding somewhere in the dark recesses of the cliff, watching her.

Her horse, catching the scent of danger, reared and recklessly backed away from the canyon wall. Jackie reached forward and ran her hands along the animal's neck, speaking soothingly. "Easy. Don't spook now."

A small rock slide just to the left of her sent her head jerking in that direction as her gaze tried to pierce the darkness. Although she could not see anything, another slide alerted her that the cat was on the move, and it was coming in her direction.

A chill hit her, and she swallowed a scream. The hunter was very near now.

Jackie's horse reared in fright, tearing the reins from her numb fingers and bolting toward the entrance of the canyon. A feeling of helplessness washed over Jackie, and fear made her heart race. She took a deep, steadying breath and gripped her rifle, quickly scanning the cliff face. It was too dark to see anything, and there were too many jagged overhangs and too much scrub brush where the cougar could hide. She held on to her courage by a thin thread. The thunder was closer now, and it rolled across the canyon, echoing loudly off the limestone walls. Her heart sank as the first drops of rain pelted her, stinging her face and blinding her.

Darkness had completely enveloped her.

With the realization that the cougar had lost interest in the bull and was now stalking her, Jackie cocked her rifle. Slowly she took a step away from the limestone wall, needing to put distance between herself and the cliff where the cougar could spring at her. She cradled the rifle on her arm, hoping she'd be able to see the cat when it charged. She tried to think of everything she'd been told about cougars: they struck with lightning speed; they could jump, climb, slither with power and ease; they were fast and had been known to bring down a full-grown cow.

Jackie caught a quick glimpse of red and stumbled back, wondering if her eyes had deceived her, or if what she'd seen was the reflection of the cougar's eyes in the darkness. She took several quick steps backward and gasped when her foot slid off a stone, twisting her ankle, tipping her off balance. Her feet skidded out from under her, and she went in one direction while her rifle flew in another.

Jackie landed hard, skinning her hands when she tried to break her fall, and felt gut-wrenching pain as her head struck a large boulder. For the first time in her life she knew what real fear felt like. She was in a situation where she had no control, and she had done everything wrong. The cat had maneuvered her, and she had reacted blindly. Ortega would never have made any of the mistakes she had, and she wished for him at that moment.

She was alone in the dark, it was raining, she was being stalked by an animal who wanted to kill her, and she had no gun!

Easing to her knees, she inched cautiously forward,

reaching out blindly with the urgent hope of locating her rifle. Even if she did find it, she would get only one shot, and even then it might not stop the animal before it hit her.

She gasped, her heart thudding inside her, when a sudden streak of lightning split the air, and she saw the cat poised on a ledge, ready to spring. She felt about frantically for her rifle and saw it no more than a few yards to her right.

But could she reach the gun before the cougar reached her?

Crackling lightning shimmered on the cat's tawny coat, and she watched in horror as it inched toward her on its belly. When the lightning played out, she was locked in the darkest night she had ever known. The cougar had the advantage over her because it could see in the dark, and she couldn't. With little hope of getting out of the situation alive, Jackie kept reaching toward the rifle.

The next streak of lightning shimmered and flashed across the sky. Jackie drew in her breath at the sight of the animal launching itself into the air, coming straight at her. She froze, unable to move.

The air was thick with her fear. When the lightning faded, she was once more swallowed in total darkness. She frantically jumped to her feet, scrambling backward. It felt like the heavens had opened up, dumping rain and drenching Jackie to the skin.

She waited for death.

Waited for the impact as she stumbled backward and fell.

Thunder cracked very near her. Still she waited; nothing happened. A scream formed in her mind, but it was locked behind the huge lump in her throat, and all she was able to do was whimper.

Where was the cougar?

Why hadn't it attacked?

Why had she not felt the impact of its body and its teeth tearing into her flesh?

Chapter Eight

Jackie's breath was trapped in her throat, and her body trembled with bone-chilling fear—she tasted death in her mouth like bitter bile that threatened to choke her. Her teeth chattered with terror, and coldness blanketed her.

A darkness blacker than any she'd ever known surrounded her. Fear had made her light-headed and faint. Because the cougar had the advantage, she thought it might be torturing her, playing with her, taking its time to move in for the kill.

Jackie found her voice, and a scream escaped her lips, only to be swallowed up by a peal of loud, ground-shaking thunder. Something solid brushed against her arm, and she jerked sideways, twisting her body toward the rifle, but she couldn't find it.

"It's all right, honey. It's only me." Whit bent down beside her, gathering her close. "You're in no danger now. The cougar is dead."

She could hardly speak above a whisper as she buried her face against him. "Are you sure?"

"Very sure."

She cried out in relief and threw her arms around Whit, comforted by his nearness. "I was so afraid."

He lifted her in his arms and held her against his chest. "I know you were." His grip tightened on her; his hands moved soothingly, stroking across her back as he attempted to stop her from trembling. He pushed her damp hair out of her face. "Don't be afraid anymore."

Jackie's head landed against his chest with a thud because she no longer had the strength to hold herself upright. She pressed her face against his neck, seeking protection from the onslaught of rain. "Are you really sure it's dead?"

Jackie was so small and defenseless—Whit wanted to spend the rest of his life keeping her safe. "Yes, sweetheart, it's really dead. I shot it at close range." Whit saw no reason to tell her he'd killed the animal the moment it launched its body at her. He crushed her to him, never wanting to let her go. "You must have heard the shot." He was spreading kisses across the top of her head as her body trembled with sobs. "Don't cry anymore, honey." Her tears were ripping him apart inside. "Don't cry."

The warmth in his voice, the endearing words he spoke, sheltered her from fear, but she couldn't seem to stop trembling. "I have never been that close to death before." She moved her face to his chest and buried it against his damp shirt. "It was so dark and cold." She clutched his arm to make sure he was really there. "I can't believe you came when you did."

He closed his eyes, trying to still his own racing heart. It hadn't slowed since he'd seen the cat leap at

Jackie. "Shh. Don't think about it anymore. It's over now. I have you."

When the next jagged flash of lightning speared across the sky, she turned her head, wanting to see for herself that the cougar was really dead. She sucked in her breath when she saw the crumpled body not four feet from where she had been huddled. She gulped in a breath of air and pressed her head back against Whit's chest. "I thought I heard thunder close by. It must have been when you fired your rifle." She shuddered, tightening her arms around his shoulders and moving her face back to his neck so she could feel his skin against her cheek. "I want to go home."

She wasn't trembling as much now, and Whit had time to relive the horrible moment when the cougar had leaped at her. He'd prayed that his aim would be true, and it had been. Emotions hit him strong and hard, and he gathered her closer. His mouth touched her cheek, and he closed his eyes. The world for him would be a drab place without Jackie in it. He wanted to keep her in his arms so he would always know where she was, and that she was safe. He raised his head and took a deep breath. That wish was not possible. "Let me be your strength, Jackie. Lean on me until I get you safely home."

She nestled closer to him, comforted by his words, even as the rain pounded down mercilessly on them both. Jackie gloried in the feel of his body against hers. "I should be dead now."

"I was not about to let that happen," Whit told Jackie in a deep tone, his hand moving up her arm, tightening his grip so he could absorb the quakes from her body.

His mouth skimmed across her ear, and she felt his warm breath stirring against her skin. Her voice trembled when she asked, "How did you know where to find me?"

"I followed the cat's tracks and then yours," he said simply. "When I heard the cougar scream and saw your riderless horse escape from the canyon, I knew you were in trouble."

She pulled back to look at him, but it was too dark to see his face. "You came just in time."

He pushed her damp hair away from her face and bunched it in his hand, wanting to raise the wet velvet curls to his lips. "I saw the cat when it sprang, and I thought . . ." He shook his head, unable to voice what he'd thought. "I'll take you home now."

Whit moved toward his horse and, without breaking his stride or dumping Jackie in the mud, scooped up his gun and hers. He shoved both rifles into his saddle holster and mounted his horse with her in his arms.

It was raining so hard they couldn't see a foot ahead of them. It was fortunate that Whit was riding Jackie's Arabian, because the horse would know the way home.

When they reached the mouth of the canyon, they heard the bellowing of the yearling as it ran past them, heading in the direction of the house. "I should have let the cougar have him," Jackie said in disgust. "He's nothing but trouble."

"You're the one who ended up being in trouble." Whit laughed as he settled her across his thighs, his chin resting on the top of her head. "If you had a hus-

band, you'd keep him in a fret every day of your life."
He nudged the mount forward. "Why did you do
such a dangerous thing?"

She closed her eyes, thinking what it would feel like
to be his wife, to have him love her and look after her
every day of her life. And at night he would take her
in his bed and—Jackie straightened away from him.
She had almost died, and here she was thinking about
Whit in the most intimate way.

He wrapped one arm around her. "Are you cold?"

"Not anymore." She didn't mind the rain or the
darkness, because it enabled her to press a kiss against
his chest, knowing he would never feel it through his
shirt. "If I hadn't gone after the bull, the cougar
would have killed him."

He distributed her weight and nudged the horse
into a lope. "But you didn't take into consideration
that the cat might turn on you, did you?" His reprimand was sharp. "What you did was beyond reason.
If I hadn't come after you, you'd be dead now,
Jackie."

She shivered. "I know."

He halted the horse for a moment and tilted her
face upward. "You're actually admitting you were
wrong?"

It was too dark for him to see her expression, but
she smiled. "I was wrong."

"Ortega and Mort are out there somewhere in the
rain looking for you. They'll have to be told you are
safe." His hand dropped away from her chin, and he
nudged the horse forward. "You are not shaking so
much now. Are you better?"

"I think so."

Heat radiated from his body, and nothing he said would make her mad at him tonight. Needing to feel his warmth, she unbuttoned the top button of his shirt and moved the material aside so she could touch her lips to his bare skin.

She heard him hiss, and he jerked her head up toward his. "Don't do that! Do you have any idea what you're doing to me? Do you know how hard it is to . . . Just don't do it again."

Jackie was glad for the darkness, because it hid the blush that crept up her cheeks. She wasn't promiscuous, or at least she hadn't been before he came into her life, but with Whit she committed reprehensible and bold acts. He'd always made it clear he didn't want her in that way.

For Jackie, the rest of the ride was silent and miserable, with the rain beating down on her. She couldn't wait to get away from Whit. She tried to put some distance between them, but he gathered her close. She could feel his every intake of breath, and she could hear the beating of his heart. His arms tightened around her, and although she tried to move away, he kept her pressed against him.

She could only imagine what Whit thought of her.

When they finally arrived at the ranch house, instead of taking Jackie to the house and depositing her on the porch as she expected him to, Whit rode the horse into the barn. Mort had left a lantern burning, and it sent faint light flickering against the rustic walls.

Whit dismounted with her in his arms and set her firmly on her feet. "We have to talk, Jackie."

"Gram will be worried about me," she said, backing away from him with every intention of scurrying to the house. She knew what he was going to say to her, and she didn't want a lecture from him about how she should behave. "Besides, there is nothing we have to say to each other." She paused. "No, that's not quite right, is it?" she amended. "I must thank you for saving my life."

"Jackie." He took her hand and pulled her closer to him. "I need to explain some things to you, and after the scare you've had, this is a hell of a time to do it." He breathed deeply before continuing. "You must be confused because I send out one message to you, and then retreat when we get too close."

"I'm soaking wet. I need to go in." Her heart quickened when she watched his expression change, becoming hard and ruthless. She would have thought him totally unfeeling if she hadn't seen the strain on his face.

"You can go in when I've finished what I have to say to you," Whit told her. "And as for your grandmother, she was watching out the window—she knows you're home." He tossed his hat aside and gripped her shoulders, turning her to face him. "I won't keep you long, because you need to change into something dry."

His gaze skimmed along her delicate throat and then settled on her mouth. She stood there looking so fragile, so worried about what he was going to say to her. He wanted to grind his mouth against those tempting, trembling lips. "First of all, I want to know if you were hurt in any way."

She could have told him she had a broken heart, and that hurt more than any physical pain she could suffer, but he wouldn't be interested in hearing that. "I'm not hurt, except my head . . . and"—she held her palms out for him to inspect—"I skinned my hands when I fell."

She looked so helpless and endearing that he paced away from her and poked his hands in his back pockets to keep from grabbing her. Her blouse was soaked and almost transparent, her breasts clearly visible to his hungry gaze. He jerked a drying cloth off a hook and came back to her, noticing that her long hair was a deeper red when it was wet. He stroked the strands back from her face lovingly while gazing into the blue eyes that had kept him awake at night.

She stood there so grave and silent, he could not imagine her thoughts. "Show me where you hit your head."

She pointed to a spot near her crown and winced when he touched it.

"It's a bit swollen, but the skin isn't broken. Does it hurt?"

She nodded.

"Have Nada look at it when you go into the house. I should think ointment would help your skinned palms."

"I'm going in."

He held on to her. "Why did you do it, Jackie? Why didn't you come back when you knew the cougar was after you?"

"Because I was doing my job," she said, raising her head and glaring at him. "If I hadn't lost my rifle, I would have shot the cougar myself."

"But you did lose your rifle." He shook his head. "You were no match for the cougar."

"I'm a good shot. My grandmother can tell you that."

"Under different circumstances you probably could have shot the animal, or at least shot near enough to scare it away."

"This a big ranch, and everything on it is my responsibility. If I didn't do what was expected of me, I'd be letting down my dead father and my brother."

Whit knew only too well how someone could feel an obligation to dead relatives, and he knew about the guilt involved. "You have men on this ranch who can do the dangerous chores for you. La Posada is a good spread. You can hire more men to help you. Your grandmother told me the ranch once supported fifty cowhands. There are men coming home from the war every day. Many of them need jobs—hire some of them. You don't even have a foreman to help you. You need to hire one. It shouldn't be too hard to find good wranglers." He was frustrated, and more than a little frightened because she could have died tonight. "Stop trying to do everything yourself."

She shook her head, unwilling to tell him there was no money to hire more men. It would be humiliating if he knew they were going to lose the ranch. "When I ask for your advice, then you can give it. Until that time, I'll just muddle through in my own way, the same as I did before you came along."

She stalked toward the door, but he caught up with her, turning her to him. "I'm not finished talking to you."

"You're finished, all right." She shoved against his chest, but he didn't budge, holding her arm firmly in his grasp. Her heart was beating wildly inside her. She wanted to rest her head against him and pour out all her troubles. "Let go of my arm," she demanded.

"Dammit," he said, his hand gliding about her slender waist. With the slightest pressure, he drew her tighter against him. "I need to tell you I'm leaving."

She went still and quiet.

"I can't stay here to make sure you don't get into more trouble." His heart rate speeded up a notch as he touched a bruise on her smooth cheek. Her skin felt like silk, and he gripped her chin, wanting to feel all of her. She was the world he wanted and couldn't have. He ached to take her right there in the middle of the barn. "If I were free to do as I choose, I would stay and help you, but I'm not."

Her eyes slid shut, and she swallowed hard before she could meet his amber gaze. "It's another woman, isn't it? You're married, aren't you?"

A reluctant smile tugged at his lips. "No, Jackie. If there were a woman in my life, it would be you."

She stared at him for a long moment, not sure she believed him. "Then you're leaving because I've made it impossible for you to stay, haven't I?"

He looked into her eyes, feeling as if he could drown in them. "I could easily lose myself in you, Jackie." His hand dropped away from her. "But I can't allow that to happen."

"Why?" There was a world of feeling in her plea. "What would be the matter with that?"

He felt her tremble when he gathered her closer,

running his hand through her damp hair that had spiraled into tighter curls because it was wet. He could hardly say the words because his feelings were so raw. He wanted to take her, and damn the consequences. He wanted to be with her, to take what life had thrown in his path, to have her for his own. "I'll be leaving in the morning."

She pressed her cheek against his damp shirtfront, then pulled back to gaze into those incredible eyes that held such softness. Jackie felt as though she would die if she couldn't kiss that sensuous mouth. "I'll never see you again, will I?"

His mouth touched the lobe of her ear, featherlight. "Yes, you will. I'll have your horse, and you'll have mine. I have to come back."

Jackie's senses were more acute than they had ever been before—she heard the roughness of his voice, felt the gentleness in his hands, the heat from his body. She was also aware that the lantern flickered, running low on oil, and she heard rain lightly peppering the tin roof—and she knew she would have no future with Whit. Tomorrow, and for the rest of her life, she would be lonely for him.

"Keep the Arabian as a gift from me to you for saving my life."

"No. I will bring him back to you." His mouth moved to her temple, then brushed softly against her cheek in pursuit of those tempting lips that quivered, begging to be kissed. He paused, then moved to her mouth. "Just one kiss to take away with me so I will always remember."

A cry escaped from deep within her throat when his mouth settled on hers, soft, nurturing, unhurried, as if he had all the time in the world. She grabbed his shirt to keep her knees from buckling. His lips conveyed tenderness, but she felt him holding back his deeper needs. She went on tiptoe to press her mouth tighter against his, and his hands came down to her waist, bringing her closer to his body.

Whit knew that if he deepened the kiss, a floodgate of emotions would open, swamping them both.

Jackie clung to him, wanting him as a man, as a lover. He would never know about the love she felt for him—a love that would not die or grow old, not even when she did.

Whit pressed her slight body against his, needing more from her than just a kiss. His hand swept up her rib cage, and he felt her delicate bones. He'd never given love much thought until he met Jackie. She was so small, a little package with spirit and kindness, a treasure wrapped in fiery hair that rivaled the sun. Whoever she married—and she would marry one day—would need to have a strong hand to guide her. His chest rose and fell. He would not be that man, so the honorable act would be to leave with only this kiss between them.

But her lips were like velvet, and he refused to relinquish them.

Not just yet.

He wanted to touch the firm breasts that were pressed against his chest, but he didn't dare—as it was, he was barely holding on to what control he had. This family had been kind to him, and he couldn't take advantage of Jackie's innocence and then just ride away.

Jackie buried her fingers in his dark hair, her body

softening against his. She could feel the swell of him, and she trembled and ached, needing what his body promised hers. She pressed tighter against him.

Whit struggled against the need to take his actions beyond a kiss, but she wasn't making it easy for him. Her soft curves beckoned to him, and he wanted more than anything to take her all the way.

Whit tore his mouth from Jackie's and looked into eyes that were glazed with desire. "In my dreams I have kissed you like this a hundred times."

His whispered words melted her heart and brought her hope. She reached out and laid her hand on his cheek. "I know you are having some kind of trouble that has to do with your search for your brother. Let me help you."

Whit closed his eyes to her tender touch and her offer of help. His heart was torn and bleeding; she couldn't help him—no one could. He moved her hand from his face and held it in his for a moment, reluctant to let her go.

"You are mistaken. I don't need anyone's help." The words were spoken harshly, because he felt so much and was reluctant to let it show. "I should never have allowed it to go this far between us."

In confusion, she backed away from him. "You have nothing to blame yourself for." Her voice trembled with hurt. "Let's just forget this ever happened."

Her innocence was pulling at him, while her eyes offered him everything he'd ever wanted. He took a deep breath to steady his heartbeat. She had become important to him too fast. Whit watched a wounded expression darken her eyes. If he stayed another day, he might give in to the temptation to take all she had to give. "None of this was your doing. I ask your pardon."

Whit took another steadying breath to stop the trembling in his voice. "You'd better go in the house now, Jackie." If she only knew that he was undressing her in his mind, wanting to touch every inch of her soft skin, she'd run away as fast as she could.

"Is what you have to do dangerous?"

"No. I don't think so."

"I'll never see you again. I know I won't."

His heart skipped a beat. "Yes, you will." He managed a strained smile. "I'll be back to watch you dance. Only next time I'll be your partner. Remember, you owe me a dance." He followed her to the door, trying to ignore the blush on her cheeks. He had awakened a need in her that she didn't understand, and tomorrow he would be leaving her confused and alone.

"Go on into the house now or your grandmother will be worried." He sounded impatient. "Before I bed down, I'll ride out and make sure the bull made it safely back to the herd. I'll see if I can find Ortega and Mort to tell them you're safely home."

Jackie turned away before the tight grip she'd kept on her emotions crumbled. She hurried toward the house, welcoming the rain on her face so her grandmother wouldn't know she'd been crying. She was breaking apart inside, and she might never be whole again.

What would she do when Whit left?

How would she survive if she never saw him again?

*   *   *

The minute Jackie entered the house, she was drawn into Nada's embrace.

"Child, child, what am I going to do with you?"

"I don't know, Gram."

Jackie tried to hide her tears, but she couldn't fool her grandmother.

"Tell me everything that happened."

"I was attacked by the mountain lion. If Whit hadn't come along when he did, I would be dead."

Nada's face paled. "Land of mercy, what happened?"

"That cat was tracking the bull, and I tracked the cat, but it turned on me."

Nada let out a tense breath. "Get yourself into dry clothing and then come into the kitchen. I saved your supper, and I'll make you a cup of hot tea and doctor your scrapes."

Jackie took her grandmother's hand for courage. "He's leaving tomorrow." Fresh tears moistened her eyes. "Did you know that?"

Nada's heart was breaking for her granddaughter, but there was nothing she could do about the situation. In the few days she had known Whit Hawk, Nada had gained a great deal of respect for him. But he was a man with something eating away at him. "I knew he would be leaving soon, but I had no notion it would be tomorrow."

There was anguish in Jackie's voice when she asked, "You remember when I told you I loved him?"

"I remember."

Jackie wiped tears on the pads of her hands. "I love him so much more now, Gram."

Nada caught Jackie in her arms. "Cry it out. That's all you can do, honey."

Jackie took a deep breath and raised her head, not wanting to further upset her grandmother. "He says he'll be back to get his horse and bring me mine."

Nada guided Jackie toward her bedroom so she could change into something dry. "If he said so, then I think he will."

Jackie wasn't so sure. She had probably driven him away by throwing herself at him. What man wouldn't run when he felt trapped by a woman's attentions? She lowered her head, totally despondent. She had lost him. But then, he'd never really belonged to her, and he never would.

It was nearly dawn when Whit slid his arms into his black suit jacket and retied his tie for the third time. He led Jackie's Arabian out of the barn and glanced toward the house with a sense of regret and loss. Going to Galveston would help him to get his head on straight, and get that little redhead out of his mind— once and for all.

Jackie watched Whit shove his boot into the stirrup and mount. She willed herself not to cry as he rode away and disappeared over a hill.

"God bless you and keep you safe, Whit." The prayer was wrung from her very soul. She felt the tears drying on her face, and she was completely engulfed in sorrow.

After a moment she went to the ewer, poured water into a bowl, and washed her face. It wouldn't do for her grandmother to discover she'd been crying. Glancing at the mirror that hung above her dressing table, she noticed the circles beneath her eyes.

"You would have been better off if you'd never met Whit Hawk," she told her reflection.

With a deep sigh, she squared her shoulders and dressed. There was work to do. She didn't have time to weep over a man who didn't even want her.

Chapter Nine

It was a hot day with only a few scattered clouds hanging over the gulf. A brisk wind was blowing from the north, and Whit thought it unlikely the clouds would make landfall. Even if they did, he doubted it would rain.

Sweat trickled between Whit's shoulder blades, and he wiped his forehead with his shirtsleeve. He had forgotten how thick the humidity could be in Galveston. He'd been so young when he'd lived there that things like the heat hadn't bothered him. Now it pressed in on him like a heavy weight.

He breathed in the heady salt air and smiled as waves of memories swamped him. After all the years of wandering, he had come home at last.

He guided the Arabian down Broadway, recalling the lazy Sunday afternoons when the whole family had taken open carriage rides down the wide boulevard. Flashes of bright-colored flowers, salt-tinged air, events that had happened in childhood, darted through his mind, making him smile now.

Not all memories were good ones. He remembered vividly the day the housekeeper had been in tears, covering all the furniture with large dust drapes; later that same day their house had been boarded up by his father. Whit recalled how his young sisters believed their father when he told them they were setting out on some great adventure.

He dragged his thoughts out of the past so he could concentrate on the scenes around him. Evidently the Union blockade had taken its toll on the city because there was evidence of destruction all about him. He felt a dull ache in his heart. Nothing in his life was as it should be—he'd once had a family; now he had no one, and the town that held such happy memories for him had been ravaged by war and neglect.

Whit gazed at a once statuesque palm, the leaves splintered and ragged, the trunk showing evidence of bullet holes. It was probably dying. One enormous oak lay on the grassy bed it had once shaded, its roots withered and dying. He recognized many of the old stately homes. He'd visited some of them with his family. He saw crumbling bricks, warped boards, and splintered verandas.

But there was also evidence of repairs and rebuilding. Apparently prosperity was slowly returning to the area. He guided his mount over to the side of the road to allow a heavy freight wagon loaded with lumber and bricks to pass by.

His lips met in a firm line—something new had been added. Union soldiers were very much in evidence as they mingled with the populace. In the past Whit had not had strong feelings about the confrontation between the North and South. He hadn't felt inspired to join his fellow Texans in fighting a senseless war that never should have involved Texas at all. The war hadn't seemed real to him until now. He felt anger well up inside him because the Yankees were occupying Galveston, and martial law had been declared.

Nada had warned him he would find Galveston overrun with Union soldiers, but seeing the occupation for himself was another matter. Yankees mingled with local citizens, and from all appearances it seemed the Union kept a light hold on the people, not harsh and punishing, as he'd seen in some parts of Texas.

He tensed, halting the horse, undecided whether to go any farther. Just beyond a huge oleander hedge stood the house his family had once owned. From where he was he should be able to see the six huge white columns of the Greek Revival structure, but they weren't there. With a heavy heart he dismounted and hitched his horse to the rusted lion-head post where his father had always tied his mount. He stepped around the oleander bush and froze; all that was left of the house was the back part and the veranda that had circled the front. Apparently the house had taken several direct hits from Yankee cannons.

The sight of his boyhood home in ruins tore at his heart; it was another loss, another disappointment. He stood there for a long time before mounting and riding away. When would he give up and accept the fact that he'd lost everything? His sisters were dead, and he was never going to find Drew.

Whit shook his head. He couldn't give up—not until he had proof of what had happened to Drew. He patted the neck of the Arabian and nudged it forward.

He rode directly to the Strand, the streets that had always held quaint little shops that had fascinated him as a child. The store where he and Drew had spent their pocket money on rock candy was still standing and still had the same sign swaying in the wind. There were late afternoon shoppers dashing in and out of stores, just like before. Life was coming back to the town, and businesses seemed to be thriving.

He stopped at the Wainwright Hotel and checked at the front desk, asking the desk clerk to stable his horse and to have someone give the animal a good rubdown. He wanted Jackie's horse to have the same careful attention it had received under Mort's care. Having Jackie's horse with him had brought him a strange sense of calm, as if a part of her accompanied him in this troubled time. He brushed that thought aside—on the ride to Galveston she had taken up too much of his thoughts. She still did.

Tossing his saddlebag over his shoulder, Whit climbed the stairs. Too weary to think, he let the leather bag slide to the floor while he went directly to the bed and lay down without even removing his boots. Weary in mind and body, he fell into a deep sleep.

It was early the next morning when Whit dismounted before the warehouse that had once belonged to his family. The desk clerk at the hotel had told him that the business was now owned by a man named Simon Gault. To Whit's way of thinking, if Drew had come back to Galveston, this would have been the first place he'd have gone, looking for information.

The front of the two-story warehouse and office building spread out along the dock. The steeple roof was just the way Whit remembered it, tall and imposing—of course, it had looked taller when he'd been a child than it did now. He was surprised by how much he remembered of what his father had told him. He knew that the beautiful stone used to construct the building had come from a quarry in England and had been shipped to Galveston, brick by brick. The building sat high off the ground so it could withstand the worst flooding. The steps that led to the front door were steep—he remembered his father's office and where it had been located.

As he touched the brass railings, memories flooded his mind: he and Drew sliding down those railings, and their mother scolding them because she'd been afraid they'd be hurt.

He closed his mind to those memories—he was getting good at that. He needed to talk to the new owner and find out if he had heard anything from Drew. He was afraid to hope; he had met with disappointment too many times.

Whit entered the cool interior, his boots silent as he crossed the black-and-white mosaic floor. That hadn't changed.

It was painful to see something so familiar after so many years. The last time he had walked this hallway he'd been a boy, with no inkling of the trouble that lurked in his future.

He opened the door to an outer office. There were changes here. The polished wooden floors had been covered with a thick green-and-yellow patterned rug that he found offensive, gaudy. He stepped up to the desk, wondering why anyone would cover the beautiful floors when his father had told him the wood had been brought to Galveston at great expense. He forgot where the wood had been shipped from, but his father had been proud of it.

The man at the desk glanced up at him. "How can I help you?"

"I would like to see Mr. Gault."

The slight, gray-haired man studied him above his wire-rimmed glasses. "You don't have an appointment."

"No. I don't," Whit answered, stating the obvious. "If Mr. Gault can't see me today, I'd like to make an appointment and see him tomorrow, or perhaps later today."

The man poised his pen above the ledger he'd been working on. "And your name would be?"

"Whit. Whit Hawk."

The clerk's head jerked up. "Hawk?" He stared at Whit as if he'd seen a ghost. "Are you a member of the family who once owned Hawk Shipping Company?"

Whit looked at the man, assessing his features. If he'd ever known him, he didn't remember him. "My father once owned the business here, yes."

Bruce Carlton realized he'd been staring at Whit and managed a smile that deepened the crags on either side of his mouth. "Everyone wondered what had happened to your family."

Whit took an instant dislike to the man. "Is that so?"

"Your family had friends here who didn't know what had happened to you."

"I was young when we left. I don't remember many people."

"So, you've come back."

"As you see."

Bruce took out his handkerchief and polished his glasses, his tone tinged with irritation. "How about the rest of your family? Where are they?"

Whit wasn't willing to discuss his family with a man he didn't know. "May I make an appointment?"

The clerk's whole demeanor changed, and his eyes became watchful. "At one time I worked in your father's warehouse. When Mr. Gault came to Galveston, I started working for him. When he bought the place, he made me his assistant."

"I'm sorry," Whit said, searching his memory. "I don't remember you."

"There would be no reason why you should. I was just a dockworker, and you wouldn't have remembered me out of the many who worked for your father." He stood up and extended his hand. "I'm Bruce Carlton. I often saw you kids when you came to visit your father."

Whit shook his hand, but something in the man's eyes bothered him, although he could not have said what it was—something fleeting, like a smirk, and then it was gone. "When can I see Mr. Gault?"

"He isn't in today. He had to go to Houston, but he should be back by the end of the week. I'll tell him you were here. I'm sure he'll want to talk to you. Where can I find you?"

"I'll come back here on Monday if I'm still in town. I don't expect to remain in Galveston for very long."

"That's a pity. So many of our finer families have left town."

Again Whit thought he saw a smirk. "That happens in war, I suppose."

"Yeah. New people come in every day, and I don't know many of those that stayed. I'm sure you're finding the Galveston you knew no longer exists."

"Yes. I've noticed that."

"Is there anything I can help you with while you're here?"

Whit thought for a moment. "You could tell me where to find the best place in town to play poker."

"That's easy. Madame Chantalle's is the best in town. Her games are honest, because she doesn't put up with any nonsense. I play there myself on occasion. Her girls are pretty, too—if your tastes run in that direction." Bruce smiled. "It's a bordello, but a fancy one."

Whit moved to the door, wanting to get away from the place that held so many memories for him. "Good day, Mr. Carlton. Thank you for your help."

Chapter Ten

Jackie lifted the hoof of Whit's horse and examined it closely. "Gram, it looks like it has healed. Do you think Mort could shoe him tomorrow so I can ride him?"

Nada bent down beside her granddaughter and nodded. "It's healed, all right. As soon as he's shod, I see no reason why you can't ride him."

Jackie stood, her eyes troubled. "You haven't asked me what the bank had to say."

Nada stood slowly, her gaze on her granddaughter, who had just returned from Copper Springs. She could tell by Jackie's defeated expression that she hadn't gotten the loan extended. "I knew if it was good news you'd have told me right away."

"They won't give me any more time." Jackie's shoulders slumped, and she shook her head. "I knew it was a waste of time to ask for an extension, but I had to try. I don't know what else to do." She glanced at her grandmother with a guarded look. "Bart Everett—you know, the teller at the bank—told me about this woman in Galveston; he said she charges very high interest but she sometimes loans money to people the bank turns down."

"What's the name of the woman he spoke of?"

Jackie tried to avoid her grandmother's all-seeing, all-knowing eyes. "She's a businesswoman. Her name is Miss Beauchamp."

"I've never heard of anyone by that name, and I know a lot of people in Galveston."

Jackie didn't want to tell her grandmother that she would have no reason to know this person. Chantalle Beauchamp was a madam who owned a house of pleasure—or whatever the place was called. Jackie would never consider approaching such a woman if she weren't desperate. There was nowhere else to turn, no one to ask for help. "I thought I'd go to Galveston the first part of next week and find out if she'll see me."

Nada nodded, absently running her hand over the sleek neck of Whit's horse. Jackie wasn't going to give up until she had explored every possibility and knocked on every door. "You'll need to take Mort with you. I don't want you going to Galveston alone. I hear the streets are crowded with Yankees."

Jackie was relieved her grandmother hadn't insisted on going with her—it saved her the complication of explaining about Miss Beauchamp's profession. As it was, she felt guilty about deceiving Gram by omission.

Nada watched Jackie as she said, "You probably won't run into Whit while you're there."

Tears lurked just behind Jackie's eyes. "I don't care if I never see him again. I'm over that childish infatuation. As soon as he left I put him out of my mind, and I won't ever have to think of him again."

"That's not quite true, honey. I know what you feel for him." Nada walked toward the house. Nothing had gone right for Jackie in a long time. Before she died, Nada wanted to see her granddaughter married to a good man. Now there wasn't much chance of that, since the girl had her heart set on Whit Hawk. No matter what Jackie said, she still had deep feelings for Whit, and no other man would do.

Whit noticed Madame Chantalle's establishment was a two-story redbrick mansion set back from the road some fifty feet, no doubt to provide privacy for her clientele. Live oaks arched over the walkway, and the breeze stirred the gray moss that clung to the branches. Brilliant pink oleander hedges gave a manicured look to the yard. The place seemed to have escaped the devastation of war and hadn't been damaged like many other stately buildings.

Whit had been told that Madame Chantalle allowed Union soldiers to mix with her local customers, and only an occasional fracas broke out between them. He had also been told that she was strict about the way her girls behaved. He noticed there was no front porch, and he assumed the madam wanted it that way to discourage her girls from lounging out front scantily clad.

He dismounted and an elderly servant ambled forward, took his horse, and led it toward the back of the house—he assumed the stables would be in that direction.

Whit hadn't come to the bordello to fraternize with

the women. He wanted to ask some questions, and earlier in the week he'd been told by Bruce Carlton that Chantalle Beauchamp's house was the best place to gamble. The waiter at the hotel had told him Miss Beauchamp's honest games drew high-stakes gamblers from all over the state. If Drew was alive, someone had to have seen him here in Galveston, and Miss Beauchamp might know something about him.

On entering the establishment, Whit examined the interior carefully. The anteroom was expensively decorated, although the colors were as bright as one would expect to find in a bordello. Large, ornate gilded mirrors hung against red-velvet flocked wallpaper. Heavy red velvet draperies drawn back with tasseled golden cords hung at the windows. The sun hit a huge stained-glass image of Aphrodite in a blue toga and splashed brilliant colors across parquet floors. There was a wide oak staircase that led to the second floor and veered off in two different directions. The parlor had numerous scarlet-and-white striped couches scattered about, but what drew Whit's interest was the huge oak bar with heavy brass trim.

He was early and there didn't seem to be anyone about, so he inspected the brands of wine displayed behind the bar. Some of them were very expensive imports. A first-class establishment, he thought with a twist of his lip.

A sudden sound on the stairs caught his attention, and he watched a woman descend, fanning herself with a red feathered fan that matched her low-cut red gown. He decided it was the madam herself: apparently she had carried her love of red to her own clothing. Her hair was the brightest red he'd ever seen—certainly not a natural color. She was very well-endowed, with a waist cinched tight and wide hips. Whit judged her to be somewhere in her late forties, but she was still a handsome woman, if he overlooked the heavy makeup she wore for effect.

"Good morning. I'm Chantalle Beauchamp." She forced a smile, her practiced gaze sweeping over the handsome, dark-haired man dressed in a tasteful black suit. There was an intensity in his amber eyes that set off warning bells in her brain. She knew a lot about men, and this one looked like trouble to her. "You are a bit early if you want to see one of my girls. We don't usually open to the public until mid-afternoon."

He flashed her a smile as she moved off the last step and approached him, not in the least immune to his mesmerizing appeal. She summed him up, knowing he would probably use his charm on every woman he met, even one of her age. Handsome devil—he'd probably broken many hearts.

"I'm not here to see one of your girls, ma'am. I have heard that you run a clean game of cards."

"Ah, that's right." She moved behind the bar and set a glass before him. "Allow me to buy you a drink; then you can come back later when we are open."

He turned his head slowly and looked at her. "I'm not an early drinker, ma'am. But if you have a glass of water, I'd like one—this heat has parched my throat."

"A gambler, but not a drinker," she mused. "A rare combination these days." Her gaze swept over his handsome face and then locked with his golden eyes. "You are new in town."

He saw the alertness in her eyes—she gave the impression she had seen and heard it all and knew just how to deal with whatever life handed her. "Yes and no. I once lived here. But that was a long time ago."

"That seems to be the way of it with many people these days—they fled during the blockade, and now that it's over they're returning home."

"That's not the case with me. I'm looking for a man."

She shook her head, pouring him a glass of water from a crystal pitcher. "I make it a practice never to discuss any of my clients with anyone. So," she said, shrugging, "I can't help you there." She handed him the glass. "Tell me, do you want to find this man to kill him?"

He took his ring out of his breast pocket and laid it on the bar. "The man I'm looking for is my brother. If you saw him, he'd have a ring just like this one." He was weary of asking about Drew—he'd been in almost every shop and business in Galveston, but the answer was always the same: no one had seen Drew, and he really didn't expect this woman to know anything about him either. Still he asked, "Have you seen him? His name is Drew Hawk."

She glanced up from the ring and slowly shook her head. "If a man had come in here wearing a ring like that one, I would have remembered him."

He took in a deep breath and let it out slowly. Raising the glass to his lips, he drank deeply.

"Thank you for your trouble. I'll be leaving now."

"Wait!" she called out. "Tell me what your brother looks like so I'll recognize him if he should come here."

"I haven't seen him since he was seventeen, so he

will have changed somewhat. He has dark hair like mine, and his eyes are blue."

"Does he look like you?" She winked. "I don't know if my heart could take it if there were two like you running around out there."

She made him smile with her quick humor. There was sharp intelligence in her eyes as they rested on his face. "I was told when we were younger that we didn't look anything alike." His hand was on the doorknob. "If he comes here, you will know him by the ring. Should you see him, I'd appreciate it if you'd let him know I'm looking for him."

She smiled slightly. Her heavy makeup had been artfully applied, but it couldn't hide the deep wrinkles around her mouth and beside her eyes. "Did you lose him in the war, Mr. Hawk? Surely you have some other family that would have kept up with him?"

He returned to the bar. "My name is Whit Hawk, ma'am. Forgive me for not introducing myself in the beginning." The familiar ache stirred inside him. "I had two sisters, but they died in a fire in El Paso some years back." He hooked the heel of one boot on the brass railing and stared at her, surprised that he had told this woman even that much. He had never discussed the deaths of Laura Anne or Jena Leigh with anyone.

She turned and poured herself a shot of whiskey and quickly downed it. When she turned back to him, her smile was melancholy. "Everyone has a sad tale to relate, and I hear many of them here in my place."

"I'm sure you do."

"Why don't you come back this evening, and I'll serve you the best meal you've had in a long time. If playing cards is your game, you won't be disappointed."

He nodded and walked to the door. "I may just do that."

Unlike the anteroom, the card room was decorated with subtle colors: the walls were covered with a deep green; the ceiling and baseboards were a stark contrast in white. English hunting scenes hung on the walls, and six round card tables were complemented by cushioned leather chairs. There was also a small bar in the corner of the room. Whit was glad he didn't have to listen to tinny music, like in most saloons. One of the girls sat at the piano in the main room, playing music, soft and pleasant.

Whit played cards with four men, one a merchant from New Orleans, the others locals, one of whom was Bruce Carlton, the man Whit had met earlier at Simon Gault's business. Three of the men were the kind of players Whit liked to sit down with, professional, not talking too much, and not asking questions. But Bruce, as he insisted everyone call him, kept talking *and* asking questions, irritating everyone else at the table.

"Just how long are you planning on being in town, Hawk?" Carlton asked, folding his losing hand and tossing it on the table.

"I haven't quite decided," Whit answered, fanning a full house out on the table.

"You didn't say where the rest of your family is," Bruce pressed.

Whit's heavy gaze landed on the man. "No. I didn't."

"Where are they?"

"Do you usually talk this much when you're playing cards?" Whit asked pointedly.

The clerk's light blue gaze snapped with anger, but his voice came out smooth and calm. "I was just interested, since I once knew them."

Whit raked the chips toward himself. "Are you in or out on this next hand?" His tone was brusque, showing his irritation. He would prefer that Bruce either leave or stop talking so much.

Bruce met Whit's gaze. "I'll stay in for one more hand."

One of the other men scooted his chair away from Bruce. "Don't stay on my account. You can't seem to take the hint that Hawk does not want to tell you anything about his family. So just shut up and ante up!"

Bruce's hands tightened on the cards he'd been dealt. "I thought this was just a friendly game," he said sulkily.

At that moment Chantalle appeared in the room and went around the table filling drinks. Hawk was not drinking, so she skipped him. "Gentlemen, if you would like to take a break after this hand, dinner will be served in the dining room. Goldie will show you in."

She indicated one of her girls, who sauntered into the room, her sultry gaze going directly to the handsome dark-headed man. Chantalle watched as Goldie slid behind Whit, rubbing her body along his back and brushing a hand against his shoulder. Goldie was just what her name might imply. Her hair was corn yellow, and her eyes big and blue. She wore a low-cut blue gown that revealed an ample amount of her

144

breasts; the skirt fell only as far as her knees, showing a pair of shapely legs.

"Maybe you want me to stay with you and bring you luck," Goldie crooned, leaning close to Whit's ear.

Whit smiled up at her, then glanced back at his three aces. "Lady Luck has already been smiling on me tonight." He pressed a silver piece in her hand. "Maybe you need to offer your *luck* to one of the others at the table."

The man from New Orleans laughed and grabbed Goldie's hand, pulling her toward him. "Come sit on my lap, honey. I need all the help I can get."

Chantalle had watched the exchange between Whit and Goldie and then faded into the other room, where several new customers had just arrived. It appeared that Whit Hawk was a man with a single mission, and that was to find his brother. It didn't appear that anyone, not even Goldie, could derail him from that mission.

The hour was late, and most of the men had either gone home or disappeared upstairs with one of the women. Whit stretched and flexed his shoulders as he left the card room.

Chantalle smiled at him. "Looks like you had a run of luck." She already had a drink ready for him and handed it to him, patting the bottom step where she was sitting. "Won't you join me?"

He took the whiskey and sat down beside her. "I am considerably heavier in the pockets than I was when I came." He tilted the glass up and swallowed, the whiskey burning a trail down his throat.

"I notice you never drink while you are playing cards."

"You're very observant. I've always found that a clear head gives me a slight advantage."

"Apparently that was so tonight."

He swirled the whiskey in the glass. "I'm going to call it a night."

"None of my girls interests you?"

"It isn't that. It's . . ." He fell silent. He didn't want to tell anyone about Jackie and his feelings for her. He didn't want any other woman; he wanted Jackie. The miles he'd put between them hadn't dulled his need for her.

She chuckled. "It's another woman, isn't it?"

He glanced at her hair. "Like you, she's a redhead, and she has the devil's own temper."

"Is she your wife?"

"No." He laughed. "I see how it is—you can ask questions, but I'm not allowed to."

She shrugged. "When a handsome fellow like you comes into my place and doesn't like any of my girls, I have to ask why."

He took another sip of whiskey. "If I stay here much longer, I'll be telling you all my secrets." He got a faraway look in his eyes. "I've made a lot of mistakes in my life, Chantalle, but marriage wasn't one of them. I have no room in my life for a wife and family."

"And this redheaded woman would want marriage?"

"Yes. I can't expect her to understand all the mistakes I've made in my life."

She clinked her glass to his. "Here's a toast to all the mistakes I've made in *my* life. I'll stack mine up

146

against yours anytime." She downed the remainder of her whiskey.

Whit finished his whiskey and then handed her his glass. "Thanks for the dinner and the card game." He smiled at her. It didn't matter to him what Chantalle's profession was—there was something about her that he liked and even respected.

"Good night, Madame Chantalle."

"Good night, Whit Hawk. Will we see you tomorrow night?"

"If you can promise a dinner like the one we had tonight, you very well may."

Again he flashed her that wonderful smile of his, and she watched him leave.

Chantalle stood and leaned her elbows on the bar, staring out the window until she heard the sound of Whit's horse fade in the distance.

She sighed, walking around the room extinguishing the lamps, and finally moved wearily upstairs to her office. It had been a long day.

Chapter Eleven

Whit's boots sank into the soft sand as he stood on the beach watching the sunset turn the ebbing tide a deep crimson color. The horizon was awash with dark purples and reds, reminding him of a time when he had watched his father's ships sail out of port riding the restless waves on their way to distant lands. The ebbing and flowing of the tide was an eternal phenomenon, always predictable unless a storm crashed the waves past the beach and across the road. Whit could remember that happening before.

He took a deep breath and stared into the distance, unaware of the passing of time. When he finally realized it was getting late, a quarter moon had muted the colors of the landscape, washing them in shadows. In that moment Whit felt very insignificant in comparison to the wide sky that flowed endlessly across the gulf. He opened his mind, allowing happy memories to flood his thoughts. He had been fighting so long and hard to bury his boyhood memories, but now, in this place, they were all coming back to him.

This part of the beach was familiar to him. His gaze moved past the salt marshes and skimmed along the spiky cordgrass. Wildlife abounded on this side of the island. He turned to watch a seabird fly low, its call reverberating across the swaying cattails.

Cattails.

He had to smile as he remembered how much Laura Anne had loved cattails. Just two years old, she had been afraid of the shadows and the darkness, so when they came to the beach at night, they would all make a ritual of planting cattails in the sand and pouring a dab of kerosene over the top—then their father would ignite each one, sending shimmering light across the sand, making it look like sifting gold. Whit could almost see Laura Ann clapping her hands and jumping with glee at the sight.

He also remembered those times when her eyes would cloud with fear, and he would go down on his knees, holding her close to him while telling her that fear was the enemy, and she couldn't let it win. Those words had always seemed to calm her, although Whit was sure she'd been too young to understand their real meaning.

Another smile tugged at his lips as he thought of fearless little Jena Leigh, who had just learned to walk. Her adventuresome spirit had meant that one family member had to watch her every minute, or she would have toddled right into the sea.

Funny how he had forgotten about that until now.

He shook his head to clear his memories. It was still painful to think about his sisters. Maybe it always would be.

*　　*　　*

Sunrise was still an hour away when Simon Gault made his way up the back steps of Madame Chantalle's establishment. He always used the back entrance because he was considered a respectable businessman, and it wouldn't do for any of the women of the town to see him entering a bordello. Simon was no longer the oafish man he'd been when he first arrived in Galveston. He'd watched how the respectable folks acted and patterned himself after them. He read books, learned everything he could about the behavior of a gentleman. He took particular care with his appearance, and concentrated on his manner of speaking. He was wealthy now, and he was crafty, knowing just what he should do to impress others. He was honest with himself—his greatest weakness his desire for rough sex. He thought about it a lot and was addicted to it. Even now, he was burning to have a willing woman under him.

Simon maintained his own room at Chantalle's place. She never allowed loose talk about any of her clients, so he didn't worry that anyone would find out.

Today anger motivated his heavy tread as he moved down the hallway to Chantalle's office. Sliding into the shadows, he took a quick glance downstairs to make sure no one saw him. The door to her office was open a crack, and light spilled into the hallway. Chantalle must still be up working on her books.

He shoved the door all the way open, banging it against the wall. "Tell me what you know about Whit Hawk!" he demanded. "Where is he staying and how long has he been here? Bruce said he was here last night. I want to know everything he said and did. I understand he's looking for me—do you know why that is?"

Chantalle's green dressing gown gaped open, and she pulled it together when his gaze settled on the curve of her breasts. Simon Gault always made her uneasy with his lustful gaze. He had a mean streak in him, and more than one of her girls had complained about how rough he was with them. Now when he came to her place, she would allow only Angie to be with him. Angie didn't mind a man getting rough with her—in fact, she liked it that way.

"Good morning, Simon." She looked into black eyes that were so cold, they sent a shiver down her spine. There was nothing behind those eyes, no warmth, no feelings other than anger churning in the dark depths. "You're up and about early."

"Spare me the pleasantries, Chantalle. I asked you a question, and I demand an answer."

"Actually, you asked me several questions."

"And I want answers."

"Sit down, Simon—you're giving me a headache."

"A woman's stock response when she doesn't want to do something."

She waited for him to ease onto the chair near the window and noticed that his face was a mask of fury. "Now, first of all, don't come in here making demands on me. This is my place, and I decide what I say and what I don't say. Second, I am not your sycophant like Bruce Carlton. I don't take orders from you or anyone."

He slammed his hand against the arm of the chair. "You're the only woman in this town who ever dares defy me. I have the power to bring this place down around your head if I decide you are no longer useful to me."

Her laughter held a hint of mockery. "You don't scare me, Simon. You see, I know your dirty little secrets, the ones you wouldn't want the rest of the town to find out about." Her eyes narrowed with disgust. "Don't ever threaten me again."

He moved forward, his eyes hard and glaring. "It sounds to me like you just threatened me."

"Not at all. I'm just telling you to leave me alone. Don't come in here trying to throw your weight around." She managed to smile. "Besides, if you could drive me out of business, where would you go for your pleasure, and who then would keep your dirty little secrets? There are people in this town who would give a lot to find out what I know about you."

He leaned back, a satisfied smile on his face. "It seems every argument we've ever had ends in a stalemate."

She closed her ledger. "So it would appear." She shoved a loose curl to the top of her head and pinned it into place. Courtesy dictated that she should offer Simon a cup of coffee from the pot she kept on her desk, but she didn't feel generous where Simon was concerned. "Now, what was it you wanted to ask me?"

He gazed out the window, troubled. "I want to know everything you can tell me about Whit Hawk."

She sat back in her swivel chair and studied him for a moment. If she didn't know him so well, she might have been inclined to think he was a handsome man. He had broad shoulders and looked younger than his fifty odd years. He was always well-groomed, and his suits were of the best cut. But she knew he was capable of destroying lives without pity if someone got in his way. She'd rather turn her back on a rattlesnake than trust him.

"I know very little about Mr. Hawk. He came in here last night, played cards, had dinner, played cards again, and left around midnight."

"Did he say or do anything that seemed . . . that caught your attention?"

"I can't think of a thing."

"Bruce said he didn't drink while he played cards."

She shrugged. "Which allowed him to be clear minded and come out the big winner last night."

"How about the girls—did he go upstairs with any of them?"

She looked into dark, cunning eyes. "No. He didn't. What I'm wondering is why you're taking such an interest in him."

Simon stood up, jammed his hands in his pockets, and stared out the window to watch the first streaks of light touch the eastern horizon. "I thought he was dead."

"Apparently not."

He cast a dark glance at her and moved to the door. "I'll be watching him. And if he makes one move I don't like, he'll be a dead man. If he comes here again, send me word."

"No. I don't think I'll do that."

He glared at her with pure hatred. Simon despised anyone who didn't do what he demanded of them. "Don't push me too far, Chantalle."

"Don't think you have any say over what I do, Simon. I think it's best for you to leave now."

"I want to see Angie."

"She's asleep."

"Wake her up. I need her."

"Good lord, Simon, it's barely sunup. You need to curb some of your passions."

"I didn't come here for a lecture from you. Your business is furnishing me with a whore. I want one now."

She shook her head. "No."

He literally stomped out of the room and slammed the door, and Chantalle heard his footsteps fade down the hallway. But his threats still hung in the air. She poured herself another cup of coffee and sat silently thinking.

When had Whit's path crossed Simon's?

Why would Simon be so afraid of Whit?

Why would he want him dead?

It was just after sundown when Whit arrived at Chantalle's place. She had been watching for him, hoping he'd come. He nodded in her direction and flashed her that smile that would melt the heart of any sane woman. She watched him disappear into the card room with Goldie hot on his trail.

A short time later Goldie returned, shaking her head, a pout on her lips. "All that man wants to do is play cards. I could show him such a good time if he'd let me."

"Maybe you aren't his type, Goldie," Chantalle advised, smiling. "It seems none of my girls are. Even Marian has approached him and got only a silver piece for her trouble."

Goldie soon forgot the sting of rejection when one

of her regulars arrived, and she sauntered forward to meet him.

Chantalle allowed Whit to play cards for an hour before she approached him. She bent near his ear and whispered to him that she'd like to see him on the back veranda. He nodded, throwing in his hand and following her.

As Whit stepped onto the veranda he breathed in the flowery scent that he'd always associated with Galveston. The smell came from a honeysuckle vine that twined through the wooden latticework. "I never knew how much I missed this place."

"Galveston?"

He nodded. "I guess it'll always be home to me, although I'll be leaving before long."

"I would never want to leave here."

"I love this time of day," he said, leaning on the porch railing and staring across the yard. "It brings back so many memories."

Chantalle stood on the first step leading to the garden. "Are they pleasant memories?"

He took another breath, and let it out slowly. "Some of them are." He watched her closely, wondering what kind of life she had. "Have you ever married, Chantalle?"

She arched a delicate brow at him. "Now who's getting personal?"

"I know it's none of my business."

Her gaze became wistful, as if she were looking back in time; then she smiled and turned to him. "As it happens, there is someone I am quite fond of. If you hang around long enough, you'll meet Joshua."

"Is he away?"

"He's Captain Joshua Knowles." A bright smile transformed her face, and she was beautiful in that moment. "With him at sea a great deal of the time, we are always glad to see each other."

"An ideal arrangement, some would say."

"Walk with me," she said, nodding toward the path.

He flashed her a smile. "It would be a pleasure to walk in the garden with you, Chantalle."

She laid her hand lightly on his arm. "My girls will be jealous. They quite fancy you as the most handsome man to hit Galveston in a long time."

He paused, looking into her eyes questioningly. "You didn't ask me out here to make your girls jealous. You have something on your mind. What is it?"

Chantalle laughed, amusement dancing in her eyes. "I like a man who cuts right through the preliminaries and goes straight to the heart of the matter." She watched his face as she asked, "What have you done to anger Simon Gault?"

His brow furrowed in puzzlement. "Simon Gault? I don't even know the man. I did go to his office and talked to his clerk, Bruce, but Mr. Gault was out at the time. I told Bruce I'd like to talk to Gault. That's all."

"Why ever would you want to talk to that man?"

He still looked baffled. "I wanted to ask him the same questions I asked you about my brother." He paused near the honeysuckle vine and breathed deeply. "I don't know Mr. Gault's temperament, but maybe he objects to me because I relieved his clerk of three hundred dollars in the game last night."

"It's none of my business, but Simon is a dangerous man when he has it in for someone. He's a relentless enemy. For some reason he's taken an interest in you, and it isn't friendly."

"That's very curious, because the only connection I could possibly have with the man is that he now owns the business that once belonged to my family."

"That doesn't seem like a good enough reason for him to be angry with you. There has to be some other problem."

Whit's jaw tightened, and he stared into the darkness. "Then I will make certain that Mr. Gault finds me so I can learn what his intentions are."

She nodded. "Or you could just leave town."

Whit glanced down at Chantalle, aware that she was serious. "Now why would you want me to do such a thing? Give me one good reason."

"I can give you one good reason—Simon Gault."

"I appreciate your taking an interest in my health, but I think I can handle that man by myself."

"I hope so, Whit."

"Now, why would you care what happens to me, one way or another—we don't really know each other all that well."

"Maybe it's because I'm partial to handsome young men. Maybe it's that I have a weakness for gamblers."

He laughed as he reached out and plucked a bloom from a honeysuckle vine and handed it to her. "Thank you for the warning. I'll keep my eye out for Mr. Gault."

Chapter Twelve

Jackie liked riding Whit's horse. The gelding instantly responded to the touch of her heels in his flanks. He was a superb animal, like his owner.

She dismounted and walked toward Ortega. He had skinned and tanned the cougar and had stretched the hide on the barbed-wire fence.

"Look at the size of this animal, *chiquita*. He is the biggest cougar I have seen in my lifetime."

Jackie stared at the paws of the cat that had terrorized and almost killed her. She couldn't bring herself to look at the head, because a quick glance showed the cat's sharp yellow teeth. "I wish Whit were here so he could see the size of this thing."

"It is tanned now. Do you want to keep it or save it for him when he returns?" Ortega asked.

She shivered, glancing down the mile or so of fence that disappeared past a slope and then ran several more miles. "No. I'm surprised I can even look at it after all I went through that night. Do with it whatever you want, Ortega."

Before he could tell her that several people had wanted to buy the skin, they heard a rider approaching, and Hutch Steiner came into sight. Jackie smiled warmly at him when he drew even up to them and swung from his saddle.

Whistling through his lips, Hutch laid his hand on the dead cougar's paw. "He's as big as I've seen. He must have migrated up from Mexico."

Hutch was tall, blond, and tan from the sun. His gray eyes sometimes looked green if the light caught them just right. He was a handsome man, and Jackie wondered why he hadn't married before now. He hadn't appeared to be dejected by her refusal to accept his proposal. Half the single females in the county imagined themselves in love with Hutch. He had a great personality, and it was easy to like him.

"Hello, Jackie." He touched the brim of his hat. "You and this cougar have everyone talking."

"The cat comes up in our conversations pretty often, too," Jackie informed him. "Seeing it now, I'm surprised Whit killed it with one shot."

Ortega pressed his finger in the hole where the cougar's chest had been. "Whit shot him right in the heart—that is what stopped him dead."

"A good clean shot," Hutch agreed. "I would like to meet the man. My foreman had a run-in with him, from what I understand."

"I didn't know Whit and Fletcher had met," Jackie stated. "Anyway, Whit's not here anymore."

"Too bad. I'd like to shake the hand of the man who brought down a cougar with one shot."

Jackie could feel the sun's heat beating down on her, and looked longingly at the shade tree just a few feet away. "Unfortunately, I don't know when or if he'll return."

Hutch smiled, and his cheeks dimpled. "You know you should never have gone after that cat on your own, don't you?"

A swift breeze touched Jackie's face, and she tightened the leather straps on her hat to keep it from blowing away. "Not you too, Hutch. I've heard the same thing from everyone I meet."

Ortega was walking toward his horse, but he couldn't resist sharing his thoughts with Jackie. "Then you should listen."

Jackie sighed. "It was a mistake. I admit it. And I won't do it again."

Hutch clamped his hand on Jackie's arm and guided her toward the oak tree. "Let's get you out of this heat."

"How are you doing?" she asked, removing her hat once they were under the shade and allowing the wind to blow through her hair.

"I can't complain. In fact, the ranch is doing better than ever." He watched Ortega ride over the rise and turned back to her. "I just got back from Mexico, where I purchased five Brahman bulls. In a year or two, I'll have a herd that I can be proud of."

"I'm glad for you, Hutch." And she was. His family had been good neighbors through the years.

Hutch stared into her eyes. "That's kind of why I'm here."

"You want to buy my bull?"

He reached out and touched her hair, allowing his hand to slide down to her shoulder. "No, dammit—I don't care about your bull. How can you not know how I feel about you?"

She removed his hand from her shoulder and held it in hers so he would leave her hair alone. "Hutch, we have been friends for a long time. You were Matthew's friend. You're like a brother to me."

His hand clamped painfully around hers. "I don't want to be your brother—I want to be your husband, your lover. I want to be everything to you."

She blinked and stepped back, wresting her hand from his. He'd never talked this way to her before. "I've already told you I won't marry you. I haven't changed my mind."

"Why not?" His tone was deep with feeling. "You only have three weeks to come up with the money to save La Posada. I can help you with that. Together, La Posada and the Diamond S would be the biggest ranch in Texas."

"Hutch, if you want my ranch, all you have to do is show up at the auction and bid on it." She frowned. "Although I do have one more person to see about a loan."

"I could loan you the money to pay off the bank. I had a talk with my papa, and he agrees."

She shook her head. "I could never take that kind of help from you. But I thank you and your father all the same."

Jackie was taken by surprise when Hutch grabbed her and yanked her forward. Before she could protest, he pressed his lips against hers, stunning her into silence. His hands ran up and down her body, and she felt him yank at her blouse, popping several buttons.

She could not believe the man she had always known and trusted would treat her in such a way. She struggled to get away from him, but he only tightened his hold—he was strong, and she couldn't get free of him. Her heart was beating with fear—she had never seen him like this. She twisted and pushed against him, but his mouth plundered hers. She felt her stomach lurch when he jabbed his tongue down her throat, and she thought she was going to be sick. His hand was rough as he shoved it inside her blouse and squeezed her breast.

He was breathing hard when he raised his head. "I want you. I've always wanted you. Why do you think I have never married anyone else?"

She shoved his hand away. "If you ever try to kiss me or touch me like that again, I'll shoot you."

He pulled her back to him. "Why can't you see what we could have together? I can't go back to my papa and tell him you refused my offer."

She tried to step away from him, but he grabbed the front of her blouse and ripped it, popping the rest of the buttons. "If I can't have you one way, I'll have you the other."

"Please don't." She struggled to grab his hands, but he was too strong for her.

When he clamped her breast, she saw an expression in his eyes she'd never seen before. "Don't do this, Hutch."

He pulled her against him. "I'm going to have you, and you might be mad at me for a while, but you'll come around to my way of thinking when you realize it's the only way you can save your ranch."

She worked one hand free and managed to wedge her elbow between them and move him backward.

In that moment they both heard a rifle cock.

"Step away from Jackie," a deadly voice ordered. "Do it now, or I will shoot you down like the dog you are!"

Hutch turned toward Ortega, and Jackie grabbed her blouse, holding it together and blushing with shame. "You'd better listen to him, Hutch," she managed to say through trembling lips. "Ortega always means what he says."

Hutch spoke as if he hadn't heard Jackie's warning. "This is between me and Jackie. I'm asking her to marry me."

The rifle centered on Hutch's chest. "I do not like the way you ask." He nodded toward Jackie. "And neither does she. Get on your horse and ride away."

Hutch glared at Jackie, his tone menacing when he warned, "This isn't over between us, and you know it."

She trembled while he stalked to his horse, mounted, and rode away. With tears in her eyes, she turned to the tree trunk, braced one arm on the rough bark, and lowered her head, sobbing so hard her body shook. That wasn't the Hutch she had known all her life. She couldn't imagine what had made him act in such a way.

Ortega put his leather vest around Jackie's shoulders, and he waited for her to pull it across her bare midriff. With a sob, she turned into his comforting arms. "You are safe now, *chiquita*. He is gone."

She rested her head against Ortega's shoulder. "Why did he do that to me?"

"I do not know. I have thought for some time now that he watches you too closely. I had a feeling I should return, because something just did not feel right to me."

She clutched his arm. "Thank you. I don't know what I would have done if you hadn't come when you did."

There was sorrow in his voice. "Let us get you home."

She paused, pulling his vest together. "No. Take me to your house first so I can borrow one of Luisa's blouses. I can't go home like this. Gram—she can't know what Hutch did."

"Very well," he said soothingly, guiding Jackie to her horse.

She was still shaking when she swung onto the saddle. "We can't ever tell Gram about this. I don't know what she would do."

Ortega nodded. He was sure he and Hutch were going to have a very serious conversation. He was angry, and he was sad. Jackie's world was falling apart around her, and it hurt him to see this thing that had happened between her and Hutch. The young man was weak, a shadow doing what his overbearing father told him to do. Old man Steiner wanted La Posada, but Hutch wanted Jackie. It had been hard to resist the urge to put a bullet in Hutch. If the man ever came near Jackie again, Ortega would do it.

Hutch was angry. He hadn't intended to let things get out of hand with Jackie; it had just happened. His father had always wanted to join the Diamond S with La Posada. After Jackie's father and brother died and the ranch became hers, his father saw a way to gain the land through marriage.

Hutch's eyes narrowed. He had very different reasons for wanting Jackie as his wife—he'd wanted her for a long time. He'd tried to be patient, thinking that if he gave her time she'd come around to his way of thinking. But when he got the news that the bank was about to foreclose on La Posada, he knew he had run out of time, and he needed to do something fast. It didn't help that his father was always telling him to "go get that gal no matter what you have to do."

Now that his passion had cooled a bit, he felt ashamed of himself. Jackie would never want to see him again after today. And he didn't blame her. What had he been thinking?

He dismounted and slowly climbed the steps to his house. The wooden structure was nothing fancy, not like the house at La Posada. But the rooms were large, and his mother had made it a comfortable place to live. Hutch's heart sank—his father was waiting for him at the front door.

George Steiner had been a tall man, but since his accident he was stooped and walked with a limp, leaning heavily on a cane. His hair was white and thick, his gray eyes fraught with cunning. As a young man he'd taken five hundred acres and turned it into two sections. His ambitions didn't stop at the border of his land—he wanted to add La Posada to his holdings.

"Well," George Steiner demanded, his gaze searching his son's face, "how did it go? Did she agree to marry you if we paid off the bank note?"

Hutch hooked his hat on the hat rack. "It didn't go well. Jackie is a stubborn woman."

His father glared at him long and hard. "What in the hell does that mean—give it to me in plain English."

"She said no."

George shrugged. "Women always say no when they mean yes."

"Not Jackie."

His father's voice took on a deadly tone. "I want that ranch. You get it one way or another."

"I'm not going to push her any further. You don't know what I did today. I did not . . . behave in a proper manner toward her."

"Oh, well, in the heat of passion, young men do things they regret. Go back and apologize. Make it up to her somehow."

"It'll take her a long time to forgive me for what I did—and I can't say I blame her."

Rage drove through Steiner. "My only son is afraid of a woman. When I saw your mama and wanted her for my wife, she turned me down. But I didn't take that as her final answer. When I was finished with her, she had no choice but to marry me to save her reputation."

Hutch felt sick inside. His mother was sweet and kind, and everyone liked her. But she very rarely smiled, and at times Hutch thought she might be afraid of his father. "I don't want to be like you. I couldn't live with myself if I treated a woman like you treat Mama."

Instead of taking offense, George roared with laughter. "Whether you want to admit it or not, you are like me. It would seem you proved that today."

Hutch turned and went back out the door, wanting to get away from the man he despised. His father's laughter followed him outside, and his own guilt took Hutch to his horse. He mounted and rode away, wishing he could just keep riding.

Chapter Thirteen

Simon was out of breath when he reached the top step, so he paused, gasping, sweat pouring off him. He and Bruce had been scouring the town looking for Whit Hawk—they'd found the hotel where he was staying, but Hawk wasn't in, and the desk clerk said he rarely saw him.

Simon was tired and not in a good frame of mind.

Lately he'd begun to despise himself for the weakness that tempted him to frequent a place like Chantalle's. That hunger in him grew stronger with each passing day, and it had to be sated more often now. Recently he'd been spending more and more time with Angie in his rented room.

He thought about the argument he'd had with Chantalle the week before. She wasn't a woman he could bend to his will, and he hadn't won that round with her—but he wasn't worried that she would betray him. She was a stubborn woman and held tightly to her belief that her clients' visits were to be kept strictly confidential.

There had actually been times when Simon had found Chantalle herself desirable—but she made it clear to everyone that she didn't fraternize with her clients—not in bed anyway. And Simon was too smart to push her, knowing that if he laid a hand on her, he'd find himself evicted from his room. He'd never seen Chantalle with anyone but Captain Knowles, and he supposed they had an understanding between them.

Simon gave Chantalle grudging respect because she knew how to turn a penny into a dollar. She was an extremely successful businesswoman.

The door creaked as he opened it, and he waited to see if anyone would come to investigate. But the hallway was deserted, so he quietly made his way to his room. He tossed his hat on a chair as excitement stirred inside him—just thinking about the plans he'd made for tonight made him pace the room. For a long time now he'd had an itch for pretty little Marian. He'd actually been with her once, but his lovemaking had gotten out of hand, and he'd scared her. Since that night Chantalle had kept Marian away from him, sending Angie, instead, to look after his needs.

Angie was all right—she knew what Simon liked, and she didn't mind if he got rough at times. But he was losing interest in her—there was no mystery with her anymore, and he needed someone new. He hadn't been able to get Marian out of his mind.

Weariness drained out of him when he thought of sweet Marian. In frustration he jerked the curtains together, shutting out the moonlight. He then lowered the wick on the lamp, casting the room in shadow, and smiled cunningly. He'd struck a bargain with

Angie, paid her well, and she'd promised that he'd have Marian tonight.

He grunted. Angie was a bitch; she'd do anything for money. Anything.

All the women here were whores, just like his mother. It angered him that Marian thought she was too good for him. She was small and pretty and had a gentleness that got under Simon's skin. No woman was worth much, and Marian had no reason to hold herself so high and mighty.

When he heard the hall clock strike nine o'clock, Simon felt the first stirring of annoyance. If Angie had taken his money and played him for a fool, she'd live to regret it. He considered the fact that Marian might be with another man, and that irked him. He paced the room, his annoyance growing into anger, and then into fury. He didn't like to be kept waiting by anyone.

Especially not some little whore.

He felt a surge of excitement when he heard someone rattle the door handle, and the door opened a crack.

"Angie, are you in here?" Marian asked, a nervous tremor in her voice.

He was hidden in the shadows, watching the slight figure in the doorway. She wore something white and filmy, and with the light behind her he could see the outline of her sweet, lush body. Simon had deliberately stationed himself behind the door so she wouldn't see him. He almost stopped breathing as she advanced farther into the room.

Marian's gaze swept the seemingly empty room. "Angie, you said you wanted to show me something. Are you here?"

When she advanced past the bed, Simon slammed the door and turned the key in the lock. "Angie's not here. But I've been waiting for you."

Marian cringed at the sound of Simon's voice. She was deathly afraid of him because he'd hurt her real bad once before. She backed away from him, coming up against the bed. "You can't want to see me, Mr. Gault. I'll just go get Angie for you." But Marian already knew Angie had betrayed her, had tricked her into coming to Mr. Gault's room. She tried to swallow, but her throat was too tight.

If she screamed, would anyone hear her?

Angie had been very clever. Marian heard someone playing a lively piece, and Angie, who never sang because she couldn't carry a tune, was singing at the top of her voice. Marian shuddered as she saw the lust in Simon's eyes. There was no escape for her.

"I don't want Angie," Simon said, stepping toward her. "I want you."

She pushed down the scream that rose inside her. "No! Please, no."

"I've had a hankering for you for a long time, Marian."

His voice repulsed her, and as he gripped her shoulders she wanted to shove him away. But she took a steadying breath and tried another tactic, although she doubted it would help. "You wouldn't like me. I'm not anything like Angie. She likes you a lot, Mr. Gault, and she'll probably get mad if she finds out I'm in here with you."

He gripped her arms and jerked her forward, eagerness growing inside him. "Don't play the innocent with me. You have already guessed that Angie did exactly what I told her to do." With a swift tug he ripped her gown all the way across the midriff. He felt her tremble in fear, and it excited him, reminding him of a time when he'd held a baby bird in his hand—it had trembled in his palm until he'd crushed it, just the way he was going to crush Marian.

Chantalle was in the card room, and she heard Angie singing. Gritting her teeth, she hurried to the anteroom. She'd stuff a gag in Angie's throat if need be to shut her up. Goldie rolled her eyes and groaned, and one of the men had actually put his hands over his ears.

"That will be quite enough, Angie," Chantalle said, scooting onto the piano bench and forcing Angie to slide off. "It's all right, folks, I'll take over from here," Chantalle promised.

After Chantalle finished playing her first piece, a haunting melody, she started to feel uneasy. Something wasn't right. Angie knew she couldn't sing, and always refused to join in when the others sang. As Chantalle's fingers ran over the ivory keys, she stopped abruptly.

Marian should have been playing the piano.

Chantalle's heart skipped a beat. She hadn't seen Marian since dinner, when she'd been conversing with Whit Hawk.

She'd heard Simon enter sometime earlier. Could it be that he . . . ? Chantalle moved off the piano bench, her footsteps hurried as she went upstairs. Even before she reached Simon's room, she knew that Marian was in there with him.

Marian had come to Chantalle at age seventeen,

more child than woman, her spirit crushed, her mind in fragments. She had worked at a saloon down on the border, and she had been badly used by the man who had owned the place. There were scars on her body and in her heart. Chantalle had taken her in and nursed her back to health. When she discovered that Marian was talented at music, Chantalle had given her the job of playing the piano and told her she didn't have to entertain any of the men if she didn't want to. Sometimes Marian would serve drinks to the men, and on a few occasions she had gone upstairs with clients.

She thought back to the night Simon had taken Marian to his room. It was still fresh in her mind, for she could never forget what Simon had done to the girl. He'd been rough, slapping her around and even breaking Marian's wrist. After that night, Chantalle promised Marian she'd never again have to go any-where near Simon.

Chantalle rushed down the hallway, and when she reached Simon's room she heard a soft keening noise coming from inside. It was Marian crying out in fear and pain.

"Simon, send Marian out right now. I mean it!"

She heard a deep sob, and then a slap that reverber-ated all the way to Chantalle's heart. She frantically rattled the doorknob. "Simon, you open this door right now," she demanded.

His voice was muted, and he was breathing hard. "Go to hell!"

Fear for Marian tore at Chantalle's mind. She shoved her shoulder against the door, but it didn't give an inch. The locks were designed to keep people out, and she could not budge it. "Simon, if you don't open this door immediately, you'll regret the day you were born!"

Chantalle heard Marian's muffled cry. She had to help her! Not knowing what else to do, she ran to the stairs, gripped the railing, and almost collided with Whit, who had heard the commotion and was rushing upstairs.

"Help me," Chantalle cried, tugging on his arm and leading him down the hallway. "Marian is in there with Simon Gault, and he's hurting her."

Without pausing to ask pointless questions, Whit tried the doorknob. When it didn't open he slammed his shoulder into it, but it still held fast. He drew his gun and fired at the lock. The wood splintered when he kicked it open.

Whit saw Marian sobbing as a man pressed her into the mattress. Whit didn't take time to think before he moved forward, yanked the man off the bed, and shoved him to the floor. "Be wise and stay where you are," Whit warned Simon in a deadly calm voice.

Whit grabbed the quilt off the bed and quickly wrapped it around a naked and terrified Marian. All the while his cold gaze was on Simon, daring him to move.

Not wanting anyone else to get involved or to know what had happened, Chantalle ran to the railing and yelled down the stairs, "Nothing's wrong. A gun went off accidently. Go on with what you're doing." She then rushed back into the room and gathered Marian into her arms. She drew the quilt tighter against the girl and led her toward the door.

"I'm sorry, Marian. I promised to keep you safe,

and I failed you." Chantalle's gaze went to Simon. "You will be sorry for this," she said bluntly. "Someday, some way, you'll pay for this piece of work."

Simon glared at Chantalle; then his gaze shot back to Whit. "I don't think so."

Marian leaned into Chantalle, her body trembling, her teeth chattering. She held her hand over her mouth, feeling as if she were going to be sick.

Whit's gaze was riveted on the man he'd just thrown to the floor. He stood over him, hoping he'd try to get up so Whit could smash his fist into the man's face. And it didn't take long for Simon to oblige him—he shook his head to clear it and rose to his feet.

Simon looked into the angry, appraising eyes of the man who'd busted the door open. "Who the hell do you think you are?" Simon demanded.

Cold fury hardened Whit's voice. "I know who you are, and I know what you are: You're a poor excuse for a man, treating a woman the way you did Marian."

Simon's fists were doubled, and he was almost blinded by the red rage that flared before his eyes. "I don't know you, and you have no reason to come in here butting into my business."

Whit's voice was controlled, cold, and merciless. "What you did to Marian made it my business, Mr. Gault."

Simon's eyes darkened, and hot fury pumped through his body. "Who do you think you are, talking to me that way?"

"I'm about to become your worst nightmare," Whit said mockingly. "I don't approve of craven men who hurt women."

"You can't call me a coward and get away with it," Simon spit, with sarcasm dripping from each word. Caught up in a fury he lunged forward, but Whit was too fast for him and sidestepped the charge. Whit was several inches taller than Simon, younger and stronger—and at the moment he was just as angry as Simon was. Whit caught Simon by the collar of his shirt, swung him around, and slammed him into the wall.

Simon sank to his knees, wiping blood from his mouth. Seeing his own blood only fired his anger more. He raised his head to glare at the man who had interfered with his plans. "Tell me your name."

"I'm Whit Hawk, Mr. Gault. Have you ever heard of me—or a man named Drew Hawk?"

Simon felt the weight of Whit's gaze cut through him like shards of glass, so he lowered his head while hatred ate away at him. "If I had I wouldn't tell you. Go to hell."

"I heard you've been looking for me. Now that you've found me, I want you to remember my name—I'll certainly remember yours."

Whit watched the man grip the back of a chair to lever himself to his feet and lunge at him, his fist clipping Whit's jaw and jerking his head back. Whit shook his head and was ready for the next rush. When Simon swung at him, Whit grabbed his arm and twisted it behind him, applying enough pressure to send the man to his knees.

Simon screamed in pain, cradling his arm. "You broke it, you bastard. You broke my arm." He slid to the floor, moaning in pain.

Whit stood over him unmoved, assessing Simon's

injury. "If I had intended to break your arm, I would have," he informed him. "It isn't broken, but it'll pain you for some time. If I ever hear of you hurting that girl again, I will come back and finish what I started here tonight."

By now Chantalle had rejoined them. "Simon, you have gone too far this time. I want you out of here!"

"He broke a bone."

Chantalle bent down beside Simon and examined the arm. "It isn't broken," she said, glancing up at Whit. "It's probably sprained."

Grudgingly she tried to help Simon to his feet, but they both teetered, so she moved away from him. "You are a bastard, Simon. I won't forget what you did to Marian tonight."

Simon's eyes were cold and dark. "She got what she deserved."

"I've told you to leave Marian alone, but you wouldn't listen."

"That little whore sashays around making a man want her. And she's no better than any of your other women. They're here to do what I tell them to do."

Chantalle felt bile rise in her throat, but she managed to push it down. "Marian is here to do what *I* tell her to do," she corrected. "And *I've* told her to stay away from you, and *I'm* telling you, you'd better leave her alone."

Simon was about to say something when Will, the man who tended Chantalle's stable, appeared in the doorway. "Goldie told me there was trouble up here," he said, stepping into the room and staring openmouthed at Simon.

"Will, hook up the buggy and take Mr. Gault

home." Chantalle looked at Simon. "Did you ride your horse here tonight?"

"Of course I did," Simon said, glowering and trying to pull himself to his feet by gripping the bedpost. He fell back to the floor in frustration. "I don't care what you say, I think my arm's broken."

Chantalle gave Will instructions. "Tie Mr. Gault's horse to the buggy and take him down the back stairs. After you see him home, go by Doc Wesley's and ask him to look in on Mr. Gault."

Will was a huge man with broad shoulders and a thick neck. He pulled Simon up as if he weighed nothing.

Simon shoved at him, cradling his injured arm. His hate-filled eyes settled on Whit. "This isn't over between us."

Whit stared into cold, unfeeling eyes and saw stark evil. "No. I don't suppose it is. I won't be hard to find when you want to finish what you started tonight."

Simon was still curious to know why Hawk had come by his office. He doubted Hawk had connected the death of his father with him in any way. Still, there was always a danger that Hawk knew something, and he couldn't allow him to dig too deeply into the past. "I'll find you, all right, and you'll pay for daring to interfere in my business."

Whit merely looked at him. "Save your threats, Mr. Gault. I have little fear of any man who would hit a woman."

Chantalle guided Whit out of the room and down the hallway to her office. "Simon doesn't make threats unless he means to act on them, Whit," she warned, her expression dire.

"I'm not worried about him. How is the girl doing?"

"I got her settled in her room, but she's still shaking. She has cuts and bruises mostly. It would have been much worse if you hadn't helped us." She placed her hand on his arm. "Thank you for what you did tonight."

They entered Chantalle's office, and she closed the door. "We can talk freely here."

Whit was still angry at Simon. "He got off too easy for what he did. I should have broken his neck."

She handed Whit a shot of whiskey.

"That man is deranged. If I were you, I wouldn't allow him around any of your girls."

Nothing would have given Chantalle greater pleasure than to forbid Simon to ever again enter her place. But now that she had involved Whit in the situation, she knew Simon would go after him with a vengeance. She would allow Simon to return so she could keep an eye on him. If he was up to something, she might find out in time to warn Whit.

"I've told you before, he's dangerous. He's a man with no conscience, no scruples. He wants his way in everything, and when he doesn't get it, he retaliates." She took a sip of whiskey. "Take my warning to heart and watch out for him."

Whit rubbed his forehead. Simon had given him a fairly good punch—it was beginning to ache. "I won't be staying in Galveston for much longer," he said blandly. "I've been told that the adjutant general's office keeps records on Confederate prisoners who are still in custody. I need to find out if my brother is one of them. Do you know anything about that office?"

Chantalle would be sorry to see Whit leave, but he was a man with a mission, and no one could hold him back from it. "I understand they have an office just off the Strand. I believe Major Clay Madison is the attending officer. I was told they are holding twenty-odd prisoners at that location."

"I went there today, but they are closed until Monday. If my brother isn't among the prisoners, I'll be leaving." Whit drew in a weary breath. "What can you tell me about Major Madison?"

"Not much. He has never been to my place. I've heard he's a fair man, but I can't swear to it." She smiled up at Whit. "Would you leave Galveston without telling me good-bye?"

His devastating smile slid into place, and she wondered why some woman hadn't already claimed him. There was the redhead he'd spoken about; maybe she was the one he was returning to.

"Now how could I leave town without saying good-bye to my best girl?"

She chuckled. "What about the redhead?"

Whit gave her a guarded look.

"I know, I know; you don't want to talk about her."

He drained the whiskey and walked to the door. "Good night, Chantalle."

"Whit. Good luck finding your brother."

It was two hours until sunrise, and the place was quiet. Everyone had gone home. Chantalle sat at her desk, reliving the incident between Marian and Simon. She suspected that Angie had purposely sent Marian to Simon's room. But Angie had denied it when she had questioned her, and Marian would say nothing against the other woman.

She intended to keep her eye on Angie. Her jealousy of the other girls was beginning to become a real problem.

Chantalle rubbed her throbbing head and stood up, gazing out the window. After tonight Simon was off the leash, and she knew from past experience that he could be vindictive. He would go after Whit; she knew he would. She still couldn't understand why Simon had it in for Whit. In the future she'd watch Simon more closely. Maybe she could prevent him from harming Whit.

Chapter Fourteen

Bruce grumbled under his breath and then cursed aloud as he stared at the huge brass lion-head doorknocker. He was not in a good mood, because Simon's stable boy had come pounding on his door in the middle of the night with a message that Simon wanted to see him immediately.

Simon had no thought for anyone but himself. He had no compunction about waking anyone at any hour if it suited his purpose.

Bruce swallowed his anger as he entered the opulent showplace Simon called home. The place was a bit too overembellished for Bruce's taste, but Simon liked to flaunt his wealth and held the belief that if something was expensive, it was worthy of being displayed in his home.

The green marble floor was so shiny Bruce could see his reflection in it. Heavy green velvet draperies hung on the floor-to-ceiling windows, and heavy mahogany furnishings were placed about the room.

A smirk touched Bruce's lips as he wondered how

anyone could feel comfortable living in such a place. Of course, he knew everything in this house was for show. Simon held lavish parties here, and invitations were sent to only the best families in Galveston and across Texas.

He made his way to Simon's office and rapped lightly on the door, wondering what his boss wanted at this time of night. A fixed smile slid into place. His duties as Simon's sycophant had required Bruce to do many things he didn't like, and he was sure he'd do many more. This wasn't the first time he'd been roused out of bed in the middle of the night.

"Bruce, that had better be you," Simon called out in a disgruntled voice. When Bruce entered, Simon gave him a dark look.

The study was where Simon spent most of his time. Bookshelves were filled with leather-bound books, and some were lying open on Simon's desk with dog-eared pages. Simon was an avid reader—in fact, it was an obsession with him, because he was always trying to improve himself, to rise above his humble beginnings. Bruce knew some of Simon's background, but most of the details his boss kept to himself.

Bruce shrugged. "Who else would it be at this time of night?"

Simon was seated in a wing-back chair, a book open on his lap, his arm in a sling. He glared at Bruce, and the bottom of Bruce's stomach dropped. When Simon was in this mood, it meant that someone's head was about to roll—he just hoped it wouldn't be his.

"It's about time you got here," Simon ground out between clenched teeth. "I sent for you over an hour ago."

Bruce was hoping Simon would at least offer him a drink from the crystal decanter on the sideboard, since he'd had to leave his warm bed. But Simon remained in the chair, his eyes cold and deadly.

"I got here as soon as I could." Bruce nodded at the sling. "What happened to you?"

"Sit down so I don't have to keep looking up at you, and I'll tell you." He nodded to the green leather chair across from him.

Bruce wondered what could have happened that had made Simon so angry. In any case, it was going to be a long night for him. Simon's attitude warned Bruce that there would be trouble for someone. "Did you fall and hurt your arm?"

"No, dammit, I didn't. Whit Hawk did this to me." He raised his arm, wincing in pain. "But as far as everyone else is concerned, I was in the warehouse and a crate fell and hit my arm." Simon's dark eyes were piercing and cunning. "Is that understood?"

"That's the way everybody will hear it from me." Bruce rested his elbows on the arms of the chair. "How *did* it happen?"

"If I wanted you to know, I'd already have told you."

Bruce shrugged, glancing absently at the fireplace and the flickering flames that licked at a log there. "I was told you wanted me for something important. The boy said it couldn't wait until morning."

Simon stared into space, reliving the scene between himself and Whit Hawk. "I want you to watch every move Hawk makes. Shadow him, become his friend, his confidant. I don't care how you do it—just do it!"

"I don't think he likes me very well." Bruce smothered a yawn, trying to stay alert so he wouldn't further annoy Simon. "I just don't see me and Hawk becoming friends."

"Then play cards with him, find out what he's thinking, what he's doing. Lose money to him."

Bruce adjusted his glasses on his nose. "I've already lost money to him, and he still didn't like me afterward. I can't afford to play cards with him again—he's too good at it."

Simon let out an impatient breath. "I'll give you the money to play. Nothing loosens a man's tongue more than winning at cards," Simon declared stiffly.

"I tried talking to him when we played the last time. He doesn't like to talk when he's playing poker."

Simon turned his cold gaze on his clerk. "Do I have to map everything out for you? Get Angie to help you. She likes pretty baubles, and she'll do anything for money. Have her watch him and question him, find out what he's doing here, and report back to you."

Bruce studied Simon for a long moment. He'd known his employer for years, and yet he still didn't understand him. Simon had an obsession with being accepted by the upper crust of the community. He gave heavily to charities and headed several committees, but as far as Bruce could tell, the only person Simon really cared about was himself.

His boss had a dark hole inside him where his heart should have been. Bruce didn't really mind how warped Simon was in his thinking as long as he didn't turn his cunning on him. Simon paid him very well for what he did—and he'd bought Bruce's soul years ago.

Bruce had often been the instrument Simon used to strike out at those he wanted to destroy. The good people of Galveston didn't know Simon had played both ends against the middle during the war. Simon had felt no compunction about dealing with the Yankees when it suited his purpose.

Bruce had done many unspeakable things for Simon. He had arranged little accidents for many of Simon's enemies. The two of them were tied together by such dark deeds it would earn them both the hangman's noose if anyone ever found out the truth.

Theirs was an unholy alliance at best, but Simon had bought only Bruce's soul, not necessarily his loyalty. He'd stay with Simon as long as it was in his own best interests. "I'll watch Hawk so closely he'll think I'm his shadow."

Simon waved his uninjured arm in dismissal. "See that you do. Report everything to me: I want to know where he goes, whom he sees, and what he does. I want you to learn about his habits, and even his intentions. Find out which one of the girls at Chantalle's he's sleeping with." He stared for a long moment at the clerk. "If anything goes wrong, I'll hold you entirely responsible."

Bruce stood, knowing Simon didn't make idle threats. "You know you can depend on me."

Simon's tone was cold and deadly, his eyes expressionless. "The day I can't depend on you is the day I'll no longer need you. Think about that, and remember what happens to people I no longer need."

Bruce knew only too well what would happen if Simon found him more of a hindrance than a help. The man was deranged, his mind full of evil. The ocean did not give up its secrets—if a body was properly weighted down, it would never be found. Bruce knew that because he'd dumped a number of bodies in the gulf. He also knew that if he made one wrong move, he could easily be food for the sharks himself.

His stomach suddenly tightened into knots, and fear crept into his mind. Simon didn't trust anyone. Bruce wouldn't put it past him to have someone watching him right now.

Working for his boss was something like walking a tightrope—one wrong move and he'd plunge to his death. Simon reminded him of a tiger he'd once seen in a tent show in Houston—the animal had turned on its trainer and mauled him to death.

He stepped out into the crisp air, wondering why Simon and Hawk had engaged in a fight.

Whit Hawk might not know it, but he had just been marked for death.

Chapter Fifteen

It was late afternoon as Bruce Carlton entered Chantalle's establishment with a pocketful of gambling money, thanks to Simon. On Simon's orders, Bruce was there with the express purpose of playing cards with Whit Hawk and losing to him. Losing to the man wouldn't be a problem—Bruce had proved to be good at that.

Chantalle was leaning her elbows on the bar, listening to Marian play a plaintive tune. Hawk must have entered moments before Bruce, because he was heading for the card room.

"Chantalle, I need to speak to you," Bruce said with a slight nod in Marian's direction.

"You'll have to wait a minute. I'm serving Tom, here," Chantalle told him, placing a drink in front of a smiling gentleman who'd already had too much to drink.

Bruce looked irritated. "I need to speak to you now!"

"Sure." Her bare shoulders rolled in a shrug. "What's on your mind?"

"In private."

Chantalle watched the drunk weave his way up the stairs with Goldie's aid. Then she turned her attention back to Simon's weasel. "This is as private as it gets between you and me. What have you to say?"

Bruce glared at her, thinking she always acted so superior. She probably resented him, he speculated, because he rarely frequented her place. He couldn't afford her prices and usually went to a bordello on Post Office Street. "I want to hear everything you know about Whit Hawk."

"Do you, now?"

He nodded his head toward the card room. "It's my understanding that you know Hawk quite well."

Chantalle drew in an intolerant breath and shook her head. "You were misinformed. He's a mystery to me. If you find out anything about him, I wish you'd let me know."

He gave her a disgusted look and said scornfully, "You know much more than you're telling. Simon says you always keep things to yourself."

She gave him a smile, and if he'd known her better, it would have given him cause to worry. "If you know that about me, I'm surprised you would waste your time asking me questions. To talk about those who come to my place would be a bit indelicate, don't you think? Surely you aren't asking me to spy on one of my clients?" She looked pointedly at him. "Are you?"

Bruce crammed his fists in his pockets and stalked off to the card room, mumbling under his breath. He pulled out a chair at Hawk's table and tried to bury his anger. "I hope you don't mind if I try to get back some of the money I lost to you last week."

Whit nodded. He didn't like the man, but he didn't have to like a man to take his money. "Sure. Why not."

An hour later, one of the men at the table pushed his chair back and left; the other one was Ed Morrison, a rancher from the panhandle who had plenty of money to throw around. Bruce's gaze moved to Whit Hawk. It was uncanny how Hawk won most of the hands. He looked into Whit's eyes—they were totally devoid of warmth. He shifted uncomfortably in his chair. Bruce's pride was on the line here, but he'd have to swallow it tonight. He'd been given two hundred dollars to lose to Hawk, and he didn't dare refuse to follow Simon's orders.

Bruce fanned out his cards one by one and stared in disbelief; he had three queens! Excitement thrummed through him until he remembered he was supposed to lose. "I call," he said, matching Whit's bet.

The rancher had dropped out, but Whit laid his cards faceup. Bruce threw his cards into the pile in the middle of the table. "Your three jacks beat my pair of treys," he ground out grudgingly. He could have won that pot.

Whit didn't trust Bruce. Maybe because he worked for Simon, or maybe because there was something secretive about his demeanor, something forced about his smile. Most of the time the man bet wildly on nothing more than an ace high. Whit had read Bruce's face during the last play, and knew the man had thrown in a winning hand. What he hadn't figured out was Bruce's motives for doing such a thing. Again,

Bruce had asked several personal questions about Whit's family, which he'd managed to sidestep. But Bruce kept pushing, irritating the hell out of Whit.

"You don't ever lose on the big pots," Bruce lamented, the crags on either side of his mouth deepening, his gaze boring into Whit.

Although Bruce had attempted not to accuse Whit of cheating, his words were harsh, and there was a thread of anger in his tone.

"Maybe you should take up another pastime, Bruce," Whit suggested in a terse tone. "One more suited to your talents."

Ed Morrison sneered at Bruce. "You play too reckless. It's no wonder you lose all the time. My granddaughter could beat you."

Bruce whipped his head around in Morrison's direction, his eyes cold with malice. "I don't need you to tell me how to play poker. I haven't seen you win many hands tonight."

"Suit yourself. If you like throwing away money, you've sat down at the right table."

Bruce remembered how the Hawks had once been accepted as one of the most elite families in town. But when the mother ran off with another man, shocking all of Galveston society, the family seemed to crumble. The father lost his business and everything else he owned—it was rumored that he'd gambled it all away. It gave Bruce a great deal of satisfaction to know that Whit had been reduced to gambling in a brothel. But he had to keep his thoughts to himself.

How the mighty have fallen!

According to what Angie had told Bruce, Hawk hadn't gone upstairs with any of the women. Bruce was determined to change that. He had already approached Angie about enticing Hawk upstairs. He hoped that in a moment of passion, Angie might ask Hawk the right questions and get some answers.

As if on cue, Angie suddenly appeared in the doorway, waiting for instructions from Bruce. When he nodded, she moved into the room, sidling up to Whit's back. She placed her hand on his shoulder and then allowed her fingers to slide up his neck and through his thick black hair. He was a handsome man, and since he showed no interest in any of the women there, it made him even more desirable to Angie. She wanted to be the one he took upstairs so she could throw her conquest in the other girls' faces. And her body quivered as she thought of those strong hands gliding over her naked body.

"You've been playing poker for four hours straight," Angie said, leaning close to Whit and blowing in his ear. "Why don't you come upstairs with me?" she suggested breathlessly. "I could show you a real good time."

He grabbed her hand and moved it away from him. Chantalle had told Whit she suspected Angie of luring Marian to Simon's room that night. "*I* choose the women I want to be with," he told her. "Why don't you run along and play nice with one of the other men."

She jerked her hand out of his grasp, humiliated by the sneer on Ed Morrison's face. "Maybe later?" she asked, trying to smile and knowing Bruce would expect her to keep trying. He had promised to pay her if she could come up with some information on Hawk. So far, all her attempts had failed.

"Hell. I'll go with you, little lady," Morrison said, throwing in his hand. "I'm not having any luck at cards today."

Bruce removed his glasses and cleaned them with a handkerchief, a nervous habit Whit had observed in the clerk whenever he was upset about something. His gaze went from Angie to Bruce, and Whit put two and two together. He knew exactly what the two of them had attempted to do.

Bruce shoved his glasses back on the bridge of his nose. "I'm done for today. But if you're here tomorrow, I'll be around."

Whit stacked the cards on the table. "I'm not sure. I may be leaving town tomorrow."

Bruce stared at Whit for a long moment. "Where did you say you were going when you left here?"

Whit stood, towering over Bruce. "I didn't."

"So, you've concluded all the business you had in Galveston?"

Whit smiled at Bruce's bungling attempt to extract information from him. "Why would you want to know that? You take entirely too much interest in my personal business."

Bruce glared. "I take an interest in all my friends."

"I'm not your friend."

Bruce swallowed his anger. Simon wasn't going to be happy when he heard Hawk was leaving town without his ever learning why he'd come to Galveston. If Simon wanted Hawk dead, it would probably have to be done soon. "Excuse me," Bruce said, taking his hat off the hat rack and moving toward the door. "I've got business to attend to."

*   *   *

Jackie had worn her best gown, a green cotton day dress with a matching bonnet. It had been over two years since she'd worn a hoop beneath her gown, and she'd almost forgotten how to walk to keep it from swaying with each step she took. As she gazed down the long avenue of trees that led up to Madame Chantalle's establishment, she momentarily considered fleeing back to the buggy, where Mort waited for her. Jackie swayed, feeling dizzy. She should have eaten breakfast or lunch. The heat was so oppressive it crushed in on her like a weight. The layers of clothing she wore made it even hotter.

She pressed her handkerchief to her forehead and drew in a deep breath. She was desperate, and Miss Beauchamp was her last hope. If the woman refused to loan her money, Jackie had nowhere else to look for help.

Mort didn't seem to know what kind of establishment Jackie was going to, or if he did, he didn't mention it to her. When he'd handed her out of the buggy, he'd remarked that he'd stay with the horses until she concluded her business.

Jackie was grateful for the shade when she reached the trees. The establishment looked nothing like she'd imagined it would. It looked like the residence of someone who had money.

When she reached the door she paused, unsure whether she should simply knock or just enter on her own. She chose to knock. She waited, and when no one came, she knocked again.

Finally the door was whisked open, and Jackie had to swallow several times and still couldn't find her voice. The woman was dressed in a pink gown that plunged in front, showing entirely too much of her bosom, and the skirt was so short it didn't cover her legs. She wore heavy makeup, and her lips were bright red.

Goldie looked the young woman over. "What's the matter, honey, did you get lost on your way to a camp meeting?"

Jackie shook her head. "I . . . wish to see Miss Beauchamp on a business matter."

"Sure. Come on in, honey. She's serving drinks at the bar."

Jackie gathered her courage and stepped inside the house. She was startled by the flamboyant colors of the decor. She didn't belong there, and considered leaving. She called on all her strength to cross the room. The redheaded older woman behind the bar caught Jackie's attention—she'd never seen hair that color red before. The woman was laughing at something one of the two men said to her, and her large breasts looked like they were about to spill over the top of her low-cut gown.

Jackie questioned her sanity in coming to such a place. The woman had been pouring liquor for one of the men, and she paused, staring at Jackie as if she'd just sprouted a second head. The two men turned their attention to Jackie as well. Everyone had stopped what they were doing to stare at her.

"Well, hello, you pretty little thing," one of the men remarked, his gaze sweeping Jackie from head to toe. "Let me buy you a drink."

"No, thank you, sir." Her hands were trembling, so she clasped them in front of her. "I am here to see Miss Beauchamp."

Chantalle nodded at her and came around the bar. She had hired several well-dressed, innocent-looking women to work for her over the years, but this one was beautiful—and as nervous as they came. Instinct told Chantalle that the little beauty wasn't there for a job—she had something else on her mind.

"I'm Miss Beauchamp. Follow me upstairs, where we can talk in private."

One of the men reached out and caught Jackie's hand. "Come on, honey, have a drink with me. Tell me your name."

"Let go of her, Walter," Chantalle told him. She reached for Jackie's hand and drew her away from the slightly drunk cowboy. "Don't you know a lady when you see one?"

The cowboy laughed and shook his head regretfully. "I sure do, and I've never been that lucky, Chantalle."

"Follow me," Chantalle said, leading the way upstairs. "You'll have to overlook Walter—he's harmless."

Jackie heard the sweep of the woman's expensive silk gown on the stairs. She could tell by the plush furnishings in the house that the woman had money. But Jackie wasn't so sure she could convince Miss Beauchamp to give her a loan.

When they reached the office, it was unlike the rooms Jackie had seen downstairs. Here the walls were sunshine yellow, with lace curtains at the windows. The desk and chairs had the fine, delicate lines of expensive French furniture.

Chantalle glanced at Jackie's hand and saw no wedding ring. "Won't you be seated, Mrs. . . ."

"It's 'Miss.' Miss Jacqueline Douglas. I own the La Posada ranch on this side of Copper Springs."

Chantalle went behind her desk and motioned for Jackie to be seated in a nearby chair. "I have heard of your ranch. But I don't know you or any of your family, do I?"

Jackie gripped her hands so tightly her fingers whitened. "We hardly ever come into Galveston, so we wouldn't have had a chance to meet. We get most of our supplies in Copper Springs."

Chantalle could tell the young woman was uncomfortable and nervous. She was an absolute beauty, with bright blue eyes and smooth skin. Her copper hair had been swept up on top of her head, and a pert bonnet that matched her gown was perched there. She could already guess why Miss Douglas had come to see her, if her outdated gown was any indication of her mission. "What can I do for you, Miss Douglas?"

Jackie met the woman's gaze, deciding to tell her everything. "My parents and my brother are dead. I run the ranch with my grandmother and two hired hands. With the war, and cattle prices dropping, I had to mortgage everything to get by. Now cattle prices are high again, but I can't sell mine because they are attached to a note at the bank."

There was desperation in the blue eyes that searched Chantalle's face so hopefully. Chantalle laced her fingers together on the top of the desk. "I see. Then you have come to me for a loan? How much?"

Jackie bit her trembling lip before answering. "I have three hundred head of cattle that I could sell if the bank note were paid off. You would be getting your money back within a year, maybe less."

"How much?" she repeated.

Jackie was so weary she could hardly hold her head up. She hadn't slept well in the hotel the night before, and she was so upset she hadn't eaten all day. She felt sick to her stomach. "Five thousand dollars. If I don't have the money within three days, it'll be too late. The letter from the bank informed me they were going to auction off La Posada."

Chantalle didn't blink at the amount of money. "I'm sorry to have to say this to you, but you aren't what I would consider a good risk, Miss Douglas. I'd like to help you—truly I would. But I'm sure you understand it wouldn't be good business judgment on my part to loan you money under your circumstances." There was compassion in her voice. "I've heard so many sad stories like yours. The whole South is bankrupt, and it's dragged Texas down with it. I only give loans to people I can trust to repay them."

Jackie moved forward in her chair in desperation. Drawing in a deep breath to fortify herself, she said, "I will work hard. If you loan me the money, I won't stop until I pay back every penny."

Chantalle felt her heart ache for the young woman who was in such a desperate situation. There were dark circles under those beautiful eyes—the woman must already be working herself into exhaustion. "Surely, as pretty as you are, there is some man who will take care of you."

Jackie stood, her pride coming to her aid. "Thank you for your time. And good day."

Chantalle nodded. "Good day, and good luck to

GET UP TO 4 FREE BOOKS!

You can have the best romance delivered to your door for less than what you'd pay in a bookstore or online. Sign up for one of our book clubs today, and we'll send you **FREE* BOOKS** just for trying it out...**with no obligation to buy, ever!**

HISTORICAL ROMANCE BOOK CLUB

Travel from the Scottish Highlands to the American West, the decadent ballrooms of Regency England to Viking ships. Your shipments will include authors such as CONNIE MASON, SANDRA HILL, CASSIE EDWARDS, JENNIFER ASHLEY, LEIGH GREENWOOD, and many, many more.

LOVE SPELL BOOK CLUB

Bring a little magic into your life with the romances of Love Spell—fun contemporaries, paranormals, time-travels, futuristics, and more. Your shipments will include authors such as LYNSAY SANDS, CJ BARRY, COLLEEN THOMPSON, NINA BANGS, MARJORIE LIU and more.

As a book club member you also receive the following special benefits:

- **30% OFF all orders through our website & telecenter!**
- **Exclusive access to special discounts!**
- **Convenient home delivery and 10 day examination period to return any books you don't want to keep.**

There is no minimum number of books to buy, and you may cancel membership at any time. See back to sign up!

*Please include $2.00 for shipping and handling.

YES! ☐

Sign me up for the **Historical Romance Book Club** and send my TWO FREE BOOKS! If I choose to stay in the club, I will pay only $8.50* each month, a savings of $5.48!

YES! ☐

Sign me up for the **Love Spell Book Club** and send my TWO FREE BOOKS! If I choose to stay in the club, I will pay only $8.50* each month, a savings of $5.48!

NAME: _____

ADDRESS: _____

_____

TELEPHONE: _____

E-MAIL: _____

☐ **I WANT TO PAY BY CREDIT CARD.**

☐ VISA   ☐ MasterCard   ☐ DISCOVER

ACCOUNT #: _____

EXPIRATION DATE: _____

SIGNATURE: _____

Send this card along with $2.00 shipping & handling for each club you wish to join, to:

**Romance Book Clubs
20 Academy Street
Norwalk, CT 06850-4032**

Or fax (must include credit card information!) to: 610.995.9274. You can also sign up online at www.dorchesterpub.com.

*Plus $2.00 for shipping. Offer open to residents of the U.S. and Canada only. Canadian residents please call 1.800.481.9191 for pricing information.

If under 18, a parent or guardian must sign. Terms, prices and conditions subject to change. Subscription subject to acceptance. Dorchester Publishing reserves the right to reject any order or cancel any subscription.

you, Miss Douglas. I hope you find a way out of your trouble."

Jackie held back her tears. She had known before she came to Galveston that there wasn't much hope of Miss Beauchamp helping her. But she'd had to try. As she descended the stairs, she noticed the two men she'd seen earlier were still at the bar. She hoped they wouldn't bother her. Tears gathered behind her eyes. Everything was so hopeless.

Before she reached the bottom step, she stopped dead still, her heart pounding inside her. Whit was seated beside one of the brothel women, and she was looking at him adoringly. Jackie felt her heart shatter into a thousand pieces. No wonder Whit hadn't wanted anything to do with her. Apparently he was attracted to women with painted faces and plunging necklines.

She wished the floor would open up and swallow her so she would not have to face him. But to get to the door, she had to walk right past him.

Whit smiled at Marian. "I'm glad you are feeling better. The bruises are fading. And," he said, trying to cheer her, "I miss your piano playing. I hope you will play for us tonight."

"If you want me to, I will." Marian took his hand, almost coyly, and covered it with her other hand. "Whit, how can I say thank-you for helping me? I don't know what would have happened to me if you hadn't stopped Simon when you did."

"There is no need to—" Whit shot to his feet, dislodging Marian's hand from his. "Jackie, what are you doing here?"

Shock at seeing Whit so cozy with that painted

woman sent Jackie reeling backward, and she gripped the stair railing. With iron will she stared at the front door, thinking she had to get out of this place.

"Why are you here? Were you looking for me?"

Jackie raised her gaze to Whit's, and she could see he was angry. "No. I wasn't looking for you." Hurt stabbed at her like a knife. "If I had been, this kind of establishment would have been the last place I'd search for you." Anger compelled her next words, "Why would you think I am looking for you?"

"Something has happened. You are almost crying. Why?"

Chantalle was coming down the stairs, and she watched the drama play out at the front door. She saw the anger in Whit, but she saw something else—this woman was the redhead he'd spoken of. Whit cared a great deal for Miss Douglas. He was in love with her.

Whit gripped Jackie's arm and led her outside. "I asked you a question, and I want an answer," he said when he'd closed the door behind them.

"My business here has nothing to do with you." Her eyes were brimming because she'd just been dealt two heavy blows to her heart—the loan she'd hoped for had been denied, and she'd seen Whit with another woman. She was hurt and disappointed in him—she'd thought better of him. "Let go of my arm."

"No," he told her bluntly. Then, when she glared at him, he released her reluctantly. She was pale; her skin looked almost translucent. The delicate curve of her cheek caught his attention, and he wanted to touch her. "Did you come to Galveston to get your horse or to see me?" he asked.

"Neither." Her chin went up, and she had to struggle to speak past the tightening in her throat. "You flatter yourself if you believe I ever want to see you again. The reason I came here is between myself and Miss Beauchamp, and it has nothing to do with you. I didn't even know you were here. You'd better go back inside—your friend will be wondering what happened to you."

"Jackie, will you let me talk so I can explain?"

She shrugged her delicate shoulders and turned her back. "You don't owe me an explanation—I have eyes." She was humiliated, mortified, and hurt.

"It's not what you think."

"I suppose you were looking for your brother—in that woman's eyes? I have to go now. Move out of my way."

Not knowing what to say, he took her arm, although she tried to struggle free of his grasp. "Let me escort you to your buggy."

"No." He watched her struggle with her composure, but it didn't slip, and she regained control of her emotions. "Thank you anyway. I am capable of finding my own way."

Whit knew that from Jackie's point of view, the situation she'd observed between him and Marian must have looked bad. He didn't know how to make her understand what had really happened. "Jackie, just spare me a minute of your time and listen to what I have to say."

"Whit, stand aside." She looked past him as she added, "Get out of my way."

His eyes became cold, his body rigid. When he didn't move Jackie twisted away and stepped around him, hurrying down the pathway. She was careful to hold her head high, her shoulders straight. But inside she was crumbling—the whole world was falling apart around her.

Whit watched as Mort helped Jackie into the buggy. He watched until they drove out of sight.

What reason could Jackie have for coming to Chantalle's?

She had been shocked to see him there, so that disproved the notion that she'd come to find him. There was another reason, and he'd find out what it was.

With determined steps he went directly to Chantalle, who was standing halfway down the stairs as if she were waiting for him. Confusion and anger raged inside him. "I want to talk to you."

Chantalle smiled, arching an eyebrow. "Do you now?" She laughed and winked. "I kind of figured you might. That's why I was waiting for you. Let's go into my office so we can talk undisturbed."

Chapter Sixteen

Whit paced restlessly around the room, then stepped to the window and braced his hands on the window casing. "What did Miss Douglas want to see you about, Chantalle?" He moved the lace curtain aside and peered into the twilight. "What did she want?"

"Whit, when someone comes to this office to do business with me, I feel obligated to keep all transactions between us secret. I can't break Miss Douglas's trust. Surely you can understand and appreciate that."

"But something was wrong. I could tell when I spoke to her. I need to know if she's in trouble."

"I saw you walk outside with her, and if she didn't tell you why she came here, then neither can I."

He swung around to face her, his eyes smoldering with anger. "The very thing I admire about you the most is what's making me frustrated with you at the moment, Chantalle. I do appreciate how you can keep a secret, and people trust you. But you don't understand—I need to know if Jackie is in trouble."

Neither of them heard Angie creep quietly up the stairs and stop to listen just outside the door. They were unaware that she could hear every word that was being said.

"Sit down, Whit, and let's play the guessing game."

He looked confused. "I'm not playing games at a time like this."

"Yes, you are." She nodded at the chair. "I can't tell you why Miss Douglas was here, but if you guess right, I won't deny it."

He grudgingly dropped onto the chair. "I don't like games where Jackie's concerned. You can imagine what she thinks of me right now. She believes something was going on between me and Marian."

"You could tell her the truth. Explain to her that you saved Marian from a rowdy customer, and she was expressing her thanks to you."

"You don't understand: I didn't . . . I never—"

"Touched your little redhead. Yes, I believe that about you. I would be surprised if you had, Whit."

"Jackie wouldn't agree with you."

"She's the redhead you spoke about, isn't she?"

"Now who's guessing?"

"It doesn't take much guessing to see you're in a regular tear because you think she's in some kind of trouble. She means a great deal to you." Chantalle shrugged. "Had I known she was the one . . ." She leaned into her desk. "How I do rattle on."

His amber gaze swept her face. "Is she in trouble?"

"I won't deny it."

"I think we can assume she didn't come to you looking for a job?"

Chantalle smiled. "You assume correctly."

"Then she came here . . . because there is trouble at her ranch, La Posada?"

"I won't deny it."

He rubbed the back of his neck in frustration. "Can't you tell me?"

"I can tell you this much," Chantalle answered, her heart going out to him. "The bank in Copper Springs is going to auction off a ranch on the fifteenth. I'm not saying it's her ranch, just someone's ranch."

That bit of news hit him hard. "Why didn't she tell me? I never knew. All the time I stayed at the ranch she never let me know about her trouble."

"I suspect Miss Douglas suffers from a great deal of pride. I can only imagine the courage it took for her to come here today."

"The fifteenth," Whit said, trying to think what to do. "That doesn't give me a lot of time. How much money does the bank need to halt the auction?"

"How much have you got?"

He shook his head. "I don't know—eight, maybe nine hundred dollars."

"The bank wants five thousand dollars."

"Damn. I couldn't raise half that amount in so short a time."

"You are in love with her, aren't you?" She already knew the answer, but she would bet Whit had never admitted it to himself.

"Yes." He was in torment. "Hell, that first day I met her I knew she was going to complicate my life. That's why I left La Posada before I did something I'd be sorry for." He gripped the arms of the chair. "I have to help her."

Chantalle laughed. "If I read her reaction correctly,

you'll have a lot of explaining to do about Marian the next time the two of you meet."

"And this is the one time I'm innocent." He closed his eyes. "But she'll never believe me."

Chantalle saw Whit's anguish and ached for him. "I think you should forget about the bank loan and go to the auction. Bid on the ranch. You never know what could happen."

"I *will* be there. Although I don't know what I can do to help her." He stood up and started pacing again. "Can you put out the word that there is to be a high-dollar poker game here this evening?"

Chantalle nodded. "You could lose, you know."

"I have no choice but to try to win as much money as I can." He moved to the door. "I have some business in town. I should be back by sundown."

Chantalle sat there in silence long after he'd left. "Here's a pretty wrinkle in the fabric," she said aloud.

When Whit reached the stairs, he saw Angie hurrying down in front of him. She waited at the bottom for him.

"I hear there was quite a fracas between you and some lady that came here a while ago."

"You hear too many things, Angie," he said coldly.

She watched him leave with a frown on her face. She had no way of knowing if what she had overheard would be important to Bruce. But she would tell him and see what he made of it.

Marian appeared beside Angie with a slight smile on her face. "If you're thinking you can catch Whit's interest, you'd better think twice. He wants a woman, all right, but it ain't you, and it ain't me. He likes that pretty little redhead that just left here." Marian's smile widened—she found satisfaction in knowing Angie couldn't have every man she wanted. "I've seen that look in men's eyes before—no one but the red-head will do for Whit. He's in love with her—I could tell."

Angie turned on Marian. "What do you know about love? You're just a shadow of a woman. You should have taken up shopkeeping, for all the good you do around here."

Marian knew that Angie had lured her to Simon's room that night Whit had saved her. "At least I don't sneak around and betray friends like you do. My word can be trusted; you wouldn't know the truth if it hit you in the face."

Angie gripped Marian's wrist and yanked her forward, hissing a warning. "If you ever tell anyone about what happened that night, your face won't be so pretty when I get through with you."

Marian's eyes widened with fear. The more she tried to struggle, the tighter Angie clamped her arm. "I haven't told anyone," Marian swore.

Angie flung her arm away. "And you'd better not!" she commanded.

Simon looked disgruntled when Bruce entered his office. "You can just go on home and leave me alone." Simon's voice sounded belligerent, as it did most of the time when he was irritated—and he was always irritated. "I'll be working late tonight."

Bruce didn't seem in the least deterred as he flopped down in a chair, grinning. "I think I know something you might like to hear."

"I doubt it."

Bruce smiled knowingly. "It's about Hawk." That got Simon's entire attention. "You were right about Angie—she's a good one to have on our side."

Simon stared at Bruce. "What did she find out?"

"It seems Hawk has a soft spot," Bruce announced triumphantly, his eyes gleaming. "A lady."

Simon shook his head. "Don't come telling me this. I know he doesn't go to bed with any of Chantalle's girls."

"I said a *lady*," Bruce stipulated blandly.

Simon looked doubtful. "Who is she, and why would I care?"

"Have you ever heard of the La Posada ranch?"

"Of course," Simon bit out in irritation. "Everyone has. It used to be the grande dame of all ranches. But I understand the family who owns it has fallen on hard times." He searched his mind. "It's owned by the Douglas family, if I recall correctly." He tapped his fingers on the top of his desk, trying to remember what he knew about that family. "Mr. and Mrs. Douglas are both dead. I believe their only son was killed in a battle somewhere. I don't know where. That's all I know, and even that is only hearsay."

"Well, it seems the Douglas family had a daughter. From what Angie said, she's a real beauty. And you know how critical Angie can be about another woman's looks."

"What else did Angie tell you?"

"She overheard Chantalle and Hawk talking. It seems the ranch is in foreclosure and is about to be auctioned off. Angie told me that Hawk was pretty upset about the whole thing. He's going to try to bid on the ranch himself."

HAWK'S PLEDGE

Simon leaned back in his chair and smiled. "Is that right?" He stroked his chin. He would do all he could to thwart Hawk's plans. "I've been thinking about owning a ranch lately. I think you'll drive me down to that auction. Find out from Chantalle when the auction is being held and ask around town for directions to the place." His smile broadened. "Yes, indeed—I think I'll buy me a ranch." His eyes hardened when he glanced at Bruce. "Of course, if you get a chance to kill him first, it'll save me some money."

In the hotel dining room, Mort sat across the table from Jackie. Her eyes were red and swollen from crying. She was trying to be brave for his sake, but he knew she was hurting. "I'd like to tell you that something will come along to help you, but we both know better."

Jackie speared a carrot with her fork, but instead of eating it, she dropped it back on the plate. "I know nothing can be done. I have exhausted every avenue. I don't know how I'm going to tell Gram that we have to start packing right away and be ready to move into town. Although Gram already knows this day must come."

"Yeah," he said morosely. "We all did."

Jackie gripped Mort's misshapen hand. "I'll speak to the new owners about you and Ortega. No one knows the ranch as well as the two of you, and I'm sure whoever buys it will want you both to stay on there."

"Don't you go fretting 'bout us. Me and Ortega will be all right, and so will you."

She shook her head, tears burning in her throat.

209

The sight of Whit with that woman had shredded her heart. Jackie would never have the one man she loved—she'd never have Whit's children. Any children she had in the future would not grow up on La Posada as she had. She ached with wounds so deep they would never heal. "It's my fault that we're losing La Posada. If Matthew had lived, he would have found a way to save us all."

"Jackie, no one coulda done better. You worked yourself to death trying to save us."

Her eyes filled with fresh tears, and she knew she had to tell him what had happened at Miss Beauchamp's. "I saw Whit today."

"Did you?" His eyes widened. "Where at?"

"He was at Miss Beauchamp's." She raised her gaze to Mort's. "I let you and Gram think I was visiting a businesswoman, and I suppose she is in a way, but she's . . . That place is . . ."

He lowered his head and awkwardly patted her hand, unable to watch the tears run down her cheeks. "I knowed all the time what kind of place it was. Don't go fretting 'bout that."

"Whit . . . He was with a woman."

Mort wanted to go back to that place and knock some sense into Whit Hawk. He understood better than Jackie that a man sometimes had to scratch an itch, but he couldn't tell her that. Mort was surprised, though, that Whit would let a woman like Jackie get away from him and go for some floozy in a whorehouse.

"I saw you talking to some man outside that place, but my eyesight ain't what it once was, and I couldn't make out who it was. Was that Whit I saw you with?"

"Yes."

"Well, I do declare. Do you want to talk 'bout it?"

"No. I don't think I do."

Mort didn't feel qualified to comfort her or advise her on matters of the heart. "All right then, we'll just eat in silence."

Jackie placed her napkin on the table and stood. "I'm going to my room. I'd like to leave Galveston at first light."

Mort nodded. "I'll have everything ready."

Chapter Seventeen

The wind had kicked up, and a few drops of rain splattered on the walk. Whit passed between several soldiers in blue uniforms who were lounging in front of the Galveston branch of the adjutant general's office. Whit had one purpose in mind, and that was to find out if Drew was among the Confederate prisoners being detained there.

One of the soldiers spit tobacco juice on the walkway, barely missing Whit. Whit's eyes filled with contempt, but he wasn't there to stir up trouble; he wanted some answers.

Whit removed his hat and stepped inside the building. The reception room was small, with five desks crowded closely together. There were three doors leading to other offices, where Whit suspected the higher-ranking officers resided. He remembered from his childhood that this building had once been a leather shop. His lip curled in disgust—it seemed the Yankees were occupying every available building they could find.

At the moment there was only one soldier in the room, a burly sergeant who glanced up from his paperwork inquiringly. "How can I help you?"

"My name is Whit Hawk. I heard you're keeping several Confederate prisoners here. I would like permission to see if my brother is among them."

"You'd have to see Major Madison about that. That's his department, and he makes all those decisions."

"Is he in?"

"Yes. But he may be busy." He gained his feet, moving his heavy bulk across the room. "I'll find out if he'll see you." He disappeared inside an office and moments later reappeared, motioning to Whit. "Major Madison will see you, Mr. Hawk."

The man who stood up when Whit entered was about Whit's height, with dark hair, and in the dim light his eyes looked silver-blue.

"I understand you are looking for your brother." He offered Whit his hand and they shook hands, a gesture that took Whit by surprise. He hadn't expected such courtesy from a Yankee officer.

The major sat back in his chair and motioned for Whit to take a seat in the folding chair in front of his desk. "Sergeant Walker told me your last name is Hawk."

"That's right. Whit Hawk. I've been looking for my brother, Drew, for several years. I'm told that you are holding Confederate prisoners here, and I wondered if he might be among them."

"We have a few here. Most of them have already been released. You need to understand that the prisoners detained by this office are under investigation

213

for crimes against the Union—if found guilty, they will be brought up on charges."

"I thought as much. Do you have anyone here by the name of Drew Hawk?"

Major Madison shuffled through a stack of papers and removed a file, opening it in front of him. "Can you tell me which regiment your brother was with?" he queried. "That might help speed things up."

Whit moved back in his chair, hoping he could make the major understand his dilemma. "That's the tricky part. I'm not altogether sure Drew even joined the Confederacy. But it would be in his nature to have joined as soon as the war broke out."

"I see." The major read down the list of names, turned a page, and scanned it as well. After a few moments, while Whit waited anxiously for his answer, the major shook his head. "Your brother isn't on my list."

Whit swallowed another disappointment. "I didn't think he'd be here, but I've run out of options."

Silver-blue eyes filled with sympathy as the officer looked at Whit. "I know exactly how you must be feeling. My brother fought for the Confederacy, and I have been unable to find out whether he survived the war. It's hell not knowing."

Whit was astounded. "You and your brother fought on opposite sides in the conflict?"

"It happened a lot. In my case it's rather complicated. My mother was from Texas, and we grew up listening to her wonderful tales about her girlhood. When my brother was old enough to be on his own, he came to Texas and started a business in Houston. When the war broke out, he joined the Eleventh Texas Cavalry. Like you, I would like to know if he's alive."

Whit stood, and the two men exchanged handshakes. "Thank you for your help. I hope you find your brother, Major Madison."

"May God help us both in our endeavors," the major said, then turned to the stack of paperwork on his desk.

Whit entered his hotel room. It was his last night in Galveston. He would be riding out for La Posada first thing in the morning.

He had to help Jackie if he could. And he needed to explain to her what he'd been doing at Chantalle's place. He knew that would take some doing. She'd never believe that he hadn't been with any of the women there.

Whit was haunted by the stricken look on Jackie's face when she'd seen him with Marian. He hated the idea that she'd been disillusioned by him. He didn't owe her an explanation. He'd been honest with her from the very beginning. She knew he had no room in his life for any woman. He'd tried to make it clear to her there could never be anything between the two of them.

But that had all changed now. She needed him.

Whit frowned. How could he have been such a fool? He'd noticed that first day that La Posada was run-down, and there had been only the two older cowhands to help run the place. He should have realized then that Jackie was in trouble—if he hadn't been so immersed in his own problems, he would have guessed something was wrong.

Jackie had so damn much pride. She would rather lose the ranch than ask him for help. As Chantalle had intimated, Jackie must have swallowed a great deal of that pride to go to the madam for help.

Whit removed his boots and unbuttoned his shirt, draping it across a chair. He was too weary to finish undressing. He sank onto the bed, closing his eyes. He was disheartened because he hadn't found Drew in Galveston. Even though every road he'd taken had led nowhere, he couldn't yet face the fact that his brother might be dead.

Whit closed his eyes, thinking of Jackie. Even now his body ached for her. But she probably wouldn't ever speak to him again.

With Jackie still in his thoughts, Whit drifted off to sleep. His breathing was even, and his limp hand fell off the side of the bed. His dreams took him on a fanciful journey, back to the day he'd first seen Jackie. Her sweet voice called to him while she danced through his mind. His heart was beating wildly, because in his dreams he took her hand and danced her around the meadow.

His dream swept him where he wanted to go. He felt her hand in his, the silkiness of her hair, the sweet scent of her body enticing him. He knew how it would feel to be with her, exciting, heart-stopping—once he had her beneath him and tasted her sweet kisses, he would want her again and again. When he bent his head to touch his mouth to hers, he jerked awake.

He sat up, waiting for his heartbeat to return to normal. That woman was driving him crazy. He had to either get her out of his system or take her in his arms and—

Whit suddenly stilled. Someone was standing just outside his room, attempting to open the door. Shards of moonlight fell across the room, illuminating the door handle. He watched it turn slowly. With catlike quickness, Whit slid off the bed and moved so he'd be behind the door when it opened.

The door creaked open a crack, and a hand holding a gun came into view. Whit threw his body against the door and slammed it on the man's hand. He heard a muffled curse and the gun fell to the floor.

Whit could hear footsteps retreating down the hallway, but by the time he'd struggled into his boots and scooped up the gun, the man had already escaped. Whit hurried downstairs, only to find the lobby empty. There wasn't even a desk clerk on duty. It would have been easy for the intruder to take the spare key to his room.

His eyes narrowed to slits, and anger swept through him. He'd made only one enemy that he knew of while he'd been in Galveston, and that was Simon Gault. He had no proof, and yet he was almost certain that the culprit had been Simon's right-hand man, Bruce Carlton. He had no time to chase shadows; Jackie needed him. But the time would come when he'd have to confront Simon Gault. It wasn't over between him and Simon—he knew that for sure. They would meet again.

Whit returned to his room, realizing he wasn't going to get any more sleep, so he finished dressing and gathered his belongings, heading for the stable.

It was still dark when he rode away from Galveston, and he didn't even give the town a backward glance. He had gone there to find Drew, and he had failed. He'd dredged old memories, found an enemy in Simon, and made a friend in Chantalle.

He still had problems to face: Chantalle had come through for him in the poker game. She'd sent word out to high-stakes gamblers, and five of them had shown up to play. Whit had a little over five thousand dollars in his pocket. It was too late to go to the bank in Copper Springs to pay off the mortgage on La Posada, but as Chantalle had suggested, he'd be at the auction that would take place in two days' time.

The most he could hope for was to come away from the auction as the high bidder. But he wasn't sure of that. There had to be many people interested in La Posada, people with enough money to buy it outright.

Whit didn't know where life would take him if he couldn't save the ranch for Jackie. He wanted peace in his life; he wanted a lifetime of commitment from Jackie. But that would come with a price. Responsibility. No more roaming from one place to another.

His heart was open. He was ready to accept anything Jackie would give him. For the first time in his life he knew what it felt like to love a woman so much that he ached inside, day and night.

The sun was coming up by the time he'd reached open country. Galveston no longer held any interest for Whit. His home would always be wherever Jackie was.

He dug his booted heels into the Arabian's flanks. "Come on, boy. Let's go home."

Chapter Eighteen

Jackie carefully folded a quilt and placed it in a crate, her mind on all the work entailed in packing up three generations of memories. Today was the most difficult of all because she had to go through Matthew's belongings.

Jackie and her grandmother had left Matthew's room the way it had been the day he rode away to join the Confederate forces. She'd known her grandmother kept it clean, but Jackie had rarely gone into the room.

Tears brightened her eyes, and she ran her hand over Matthew's favorite tan leather jacket. "Matthew," she said, holding the jacket to her face, wanting to feel closer to him. "You would be so disappointed in me—I failed you and the whole family. I lost our home."

With a sigh, she carefully put the jacket into the wooden crate. There was no time for self-recrimination or for feeling sorry for herself. Matthew had met life head-on, and that was what he'd expect her to do.

Trying to feel detached, she methodically packed up

his belongings, knowing Reverend Witherspoon would find some worthy person who would make use of Matthew's clothing. She should have given the clothes to him long ago, but she just hadn't been able to part with them until now.

The bank was giving them three weeks after the auction to move out of the house, but Jackie had decided it would be best to get it over with as soon as possible. Already the house in town was stacked with crates and furniture that Mort and Ortega had taken there.

The auction was tomorrow—how would they get through it? Jackie considered allowing Ortega to oversee the showing of the house, but that would be the coward's way out. It was up to her to represent the family when curious people tramped through their lives.

She picked up Matthew's spurs, thinking they needed oiling and knowing she couldn't bear to part with them—their father had given them to Matthew on his twelfth birthday. How proud Matthew had been that day, strutting around the house just so he could hear the spurs tinkle.

It took Jackie a moment to realize her grandmother had been speaking to her from the doorway. "I'm sorry, Gram—I didn't hear what you said. I guess my mind was somewhere else."

Nada walked over to Jackie and took Matthew's spurs out of her hand. "We'll keep these. I know you want them."

"Yes. I can't seem to part with them."

"Mr. Booth has arrived. He's ready to take the bull. He's waiting for you in the barn."

Another heartbreak. Jackie hadn't wanted to sell the yearling, but she'd had no choice in the matter. They needed the money, and besides, there was nowhere to keep him in town.

"I'll be back to help you as soon as I finish with Mr. Booth, Gram. I don't want you to do any heavy lifting while I'm gone."

Nada watched Jackie leave and wiped tears on her apron. She never cried, but seeing the torment Jackie was going through was too much for her. Her shoulders sagged, and she felt old, helpless to aid her granddaughter.

She heard the back screen door slam and sighed heavily. Nada didn't know what was going to happen to her granddaughter. Even though Jackie didn't love Hutch, maybe she should have married him so she could keep the ranch.

Nada heard the tread of boots in the front room and assumed it was Ortega. "I'm back here in Matthew's bedroom," she called out.

Whit turned left out of the living room and moved down the hallway, following the sound of a box being dragged across the floor. When he entered the bedroom, he rushed forward to help Nada lift the heavy crate. "Here, let me do that for you."

Nada stared up at him, her gaze wide with amazement. "I wasn't sure I'd see you again."

"I had to return a horse." He frowned at her with concern. "It looks like you're moving."

Nada settled on the edge of the bed, tiredly brushing a strand of hair back from her face. "That's exactly what we're doing."

He walked to the window and slid his hands into

his pockets, speaking to Nada with his back to her. "I know something of what is going on, but I'd like for you to tell me everything."

"It's no secret—it's common knowledge. La Posada will be auctioned off tomorrow."

"Why didn't someone tell me about this while I was here before?" Whit turned back to her. "Why didn't you tell me?"

"Why should I? We don't go around telling anyone our troubles. Besides, it has nothing to do with you. We Douglases take care of our own problems and don't ask for help from anyone."

"Your granddaughter has your same pride, Nada. I'm going to try to help her whether she wants me to or not."

She folded a shirt and placed it lovingly in the crate. "There's nothing you can do to help her, and we wouldn't want you to even if you could. In case you don't know it, she's mad at you. She wouldn't stoop to pick you up off the ground if you were a greenback dollar."

"I know that, but it doesn't matter." He swept his hand toward the half-packed crate. "How did this happen? And don't say it's none of my business, because I'm making it my business."

Nada lowered her head as if it were too heavy to hold upright. "Our troubles started with the death of Jackie's mother and father and escalated with the coming of the war. Everything crumbled when Jackie got word that her brother had died in the war. Everyone was having a hard time, but Jackie fought hard to keep the ranch going. She had to mortgage the ranch, and later on the stock. The reason she couldn't sell you one of our horses was because her Arabian is the only horse she still owns."

Whit took that piece of news hard. She'd loaned him the only horse that belonged to her. It had been a supremely unselfish act, and she hadn't even known anything about him as a person.

Nada stared down at her blue-veined hands as if she didn't recognize them as her own. "I know you are offering to help us, out of some feeling of obligation, but Jackie won't take it that way. She told me what happened while she was in Galveston."

Whit stood silently for a moment, then turned back to the window, looking toward the barn, where a stranger was leading Jackie's prize yearling toward his horse. "I know what happened looked pretty bad," he remarked without turning his gaze. "But it wasn't the way it seemed."

"Are we talking about the same thing—you holding hands with a . . . a whore at a whorehouse? It's not our concern how you spend your time. I'm sorry Jackie had to see you there, but she'll have to get over it, won't she?"

Whit had never heard Nada speak in anger. He turned his head upward, as if he were communicating with the ceiling. "Nada, you may not believe this, but I never once went up those stairs with one of those women for the reason Jackie thinks. I'm a gambler, and that's what I was doing there. That's *all* I was doing there."

Nada sighed. "You are a good-looking bachelor, and how you spend your time is up to you. But it would be better for Jackie if you could leave before she sees you."

"I can't. I won't."

"And why is that?"

"I want you to stop packing right now. I'm going to be at that auction tomorrow—if I am high bidder, none of you will have to leave."

Nada studied him closely. "Why would you do that?"

"I think you know." He moved away from the window and began pacing. "I have never had time in my life to love a woman—I never wanted the responsibility."

"But?"

"I can't put a name to what I feel for Jackie, because I don't know myself. I only know that when she's hurt, I have thorns in my heart."

"And what are you going to do about it?"

"Help her keep this ranch if I can."

She nodded. "Even if you do get the ranch, you won't get Jackie. I don't think you know how deeply she was hurt."

"I'm beginning to understand. I've never known a more courageous woman than Jackie—she's headstrong, impossible, and, for me, unforgettable. I want to help her. I need to help her."

"So you can walk away again?"

"No," he protested.

Nada used the bedpost to pull herself to her feet. "You'll have to leave—Jackie won't have you, Whit. You see, the way she looks at it, you didn't want her. You wanted some cheap, tawdry woman you could buy for a few hours and then walk away from, uncommitted."

"I didn't do it, Nada. If I had, I'd admit it to you. I hope you believe me."

Nada was quiet for a moment while she looked into his eyes. Whit might be many things, but she didn't think he'd tell an outright lie. "I do believe you—but Jackie won't."

Whit wearily flexed his shoulders and massaged his neck. He hadn't slept much since he'd found out about Jackie's troubles. "Nevertheless, I am going to be here tomorrow. And if I should be fortunate enough to be the high bidder, you'll have to help me convince Jackie that the ranch is hers with no strings attached."

"Whit," she said, studying him carefully. "You say you are a gambler. Is that all you are? Could you just walk away from gambling?"

"Without ever looking back," he replied forcefully. He decided he needed to tell Nada something about himself, but no more than he had to. "I gambled because I was good at it. I didn't have to be tied to one place and could move around so I could search for my brother."

"I was just wondering. To some men it's a way of life and eventually leads to their ruin."

"You just described my father." He stared at her, his gaze hard. "I'm not like him."

She nodded and said for the second time, "I believe you."

"But as you said, your granddaughter won't."

"Not without some convincing," she agreed.

"I've never known a woman like your Jackie. She makes me crazy. She's . . . unpredictable, unforgettable."

"I know; she's all that and more."

"Well," he admitted, staring into space, "she sure has managed to complicate my life."

Jackie came around to the front of the house so she could watch Mr. Booth lead the yearling away. She had no more tears left, and she had too much to do to dabble in self-pity. Glancing at the ground as she walked toward the house, she went over everything that needed her attention. When she glanced up, she came to a dead halt.

Her Arabian was tied to the hitching post. The last person in the world she wanted to see at this time was Whit.

Jackie approached her horse and ran her hands over his flanks. "So you came home?"

With a clinking of bridle hardware, the gelding turned his head and nudged Jackie's hand, as if he was glad to see her. Jackie looked him over carefully. It was obvious her horse had been well taken care of and had been combed and curried, although he was covered with dust from the road.

With a heavy heart and a deep sigh, she moved up the steps to the front door. Jackie hadn't been sure if she'd ever see Whit again, and she wasn't certain she wanted to, but he was here now, and she had to face him.

The screen door slammed shut behind her, and she heard her grandmother call from the kitchen, "We're in here."

She removed her hat and tossed it on a chair, then ran her fingers through her hair, trying to assemble it into some kind of order. When Jackie entered the kitchen, Whit and her grandmother were seated at the table, having a cup of coffee.

Whit glanced at Jackie and nodded. "Hello."

She gave him a brief nod in return and cleared her throat, but still her voice came out in a whisper. "Whit." She went to the cupboard, took down a glass, and poured water from a pitcher. She hoped Whit hadn't noticed her hands were trembling. "It won't take you long to change your saddle from my horse to yours," she said, leaning her hip against the stove.

Whit met Jackie's steady gaze, noticing that her eyes were brightened by her anger. "It wouldn't if I were going anywhere. I'm not."

He was staring at her so intently, Jackie could hardly catch her breath. She took a sip of water, hoping she could swallow it past the painful lump in her throat. "As you can see for yourself, we are somewhat busy around here today. Work just piles up."

Whit was not going to allow her to order him off the place. She needed him whether she knew it or not. "I noticed."

Her grandmother nodded at a chair. "Why don't you sit down, Jackie? You need to take a rest—you've been going at it hard since before sunup."

Jackie gestured toward Whit. "I'm going take his saddle off my horse, so he can leave as soon as possible." She slammed the glass down on the table and stalked out of the kitchen without a backward glance.

"She's still mad at me," Whit observed, his eyes narrowing.

Nada agreed with a nod of her head. "Check back

in about a hundred years from now, and she'll be more amenable toward you."

Whit took a quick sip of coffee, his mood darkening. He grabbed his hat and moved toward the door. "I need to talk to her." His gaze captured Nada's. "I need to make her understand what happened in Galveston."

Nada watched Whit rush out of the room. If she were a betting woman, she'd wager that Whit cared more for her granddaughter than he'd even admitted to himself. He'd have his hands full winning Jackie over. She could be stubborn when she believed strongly about something—and she believed strongly that Whit had betrayed her.

Chapter Nineteen

Jackie was unfastening Whit's saddle when he came outside, and she slid it off the horse before he could reach her. Whit took the saddle from her and hoisted it and his rifle onto his shoulder.

"I'll just put this in the barn," he told her, walking around the horse before she could protest.

She led the animal toward the barn, catching up with him, still unnerved by his sudden appearance. "Put your saddle on your own horse and ride away," she said, choosing anger rather than confusion. She glanced at him, but his expression didn't betray what he was feeling.

His expression was grim. "No."

She paused, but he kept walking. "No? You're telling me no?"

"Yes," he said determinedly, his stride strong and purposeful. His jaw was set in a stubborn line.

Jackie pulled her horse forward, almost running to keep up with Whit's long strides. "Whit Hawk, until nine o'clock tomorrow morning, I am still owner of

La Posada." She gave him a frigid glare. "Until then, *I* say who stays on my ranch and who goes."

They had reached the interior of the barn, and he hoisted the saddle over a stall door. "Force me to leave if you can." A smile lurked near his lips. "That's the only way you'll get me to go."

"You aren't staying here," she reiterated in angry frustration.

A smile touched the corner of his mouth as he turned to her, centering his attention on her glorious hair. "Jackie, I'm staying right here in the barn tonight, just like I did before. I will be here when the auctioneer begins the bidding in the morning, and I will be bidding on La Posada."

Hurt hit her like a tight fist—surely she had heard wrong. "You want to own my ranch?"

At the moment he wanted nothing more than to kiss the look of betrayal off her face, but she wouldn't welcome such a move from him. He started to speak and then paused. "I hope you will understand what I'm about to tell you, Jackie."

She folded her arms across her chest and tapped her boot. "I don't understand anything about you."

He glanced down, trying to think how to voice his reasons for bidding on her ranch. "First of all, I want you to know nothing happened between me and that woman at Chantalle's place."

He watched her blue eyes spark with anger and knew his chances of making her believe he was innocent were not very good.

"You think I care what you did with your time in Galveston?" she asked, backing her Arabian into a stall, removing the bridal, and draping it across

Whit's saddle. When she turned to Whit, he was holding a bucket of water for the Arabian to drink.

"You may not care," he continued, "but I want you to know what happened all the same."

She grabbed a pitchfork and dug it into the loose hay, then tossed the feed over the stall to her horse. She propped the pitchfork against the wall and dusted her hands. "Do you saddle your horse, or do I?"

In that moment Mort came ambling into the barn. He stopped in his tracks when he saw Whit. "I never thought you'd show your face 'round here again."

"Mort," Whit said, holding up his hand, "Jackie and I are talking right now. Could you give your opinion of me later?"

"Jackie, you want me to stay?" Mort asked.

She glanced at Whit, and for the first time saw fatigue etched on his face, as if he hadn't slept in days. "No," she said. "Just let me have a little while alone with Whit so I can explain a few things to him."

Mort nodded and cast a warning glance at Whit. "I'll just be outside here if you need anything, Jackie."

Despite her anger at Whit, it was hard not to smile at Mort's protectiveness toward her. He'd looked after her since she was small, and she didn't know what she would do when he was gone. She shook her head and tried to ignore the ache inside her. Everything would change in a few days. Mort would be taking a stage to Wyoming to live with his sister. Ortega and Luisa would be moving to San Antonio to live with Selina, their eldest daughter. No one wanted to leave the home they'd known for so long, but that was the way it had to be.

Whit had been watching the different emotions

play across Jackie's beautiful face. She had such pride; she would always face life in her way and on her own terms. "Mort was ready to take me on," Whit said, smiling.

"Don't think just because he's up in years, he couldn't. Anyone who underestimates Mort is a fool."

"I'm sure you're right."

"Now," Jackie said in a determined voice, "let me set you straight on a few things."

He crossed his arms and leaned against the stall. "I'm ready to hear what you have to say if you'll listen to what I have to say afterward."

Jackie frowned as she thought about his offer. "I don't really care to hear anything you have to say." It still hurt to think of him touching that painted woman in Galveston with such tenderness. "Let's get something straight, Whit. You don't owe me any explanation, and I behaved badly toward you the last time we met. I have no right to interfere in your life, and I don't want you interfering in mine."

He noticed her words said one thing, and the expression in her eyes said something entirely different. She had been shattered when she'd seen him with Marian. "Jackie, I'm only here to help you save your ranch. I feel I owe you that much."

She tossed her head, her hair sliding across her shoulders in a curtain of red velvet. "Do you think I'd take help from you? You don't owe this family anything, and we don't owe you, either. You are just a stranger who crossed our path, and nothing more."

He read disillusionment in her eyes. She was tenacious. Life was caving in on her, and she was battling just to survive. "Tomorrow I hope I can hand you the deed to La Posada. Nada told me that Mort and Ortega were leaving—I hope that won't happen."

"I won't take anything from you." She stepped back several paces. "How can you think I would?"

"You can consider it a loan if you'd like. You were willing to take help from Miss Beauchamp; why not take it from me instead?"

Jackie shook her head, her eyes wide with denial. "I don't want your help. How many times do I have to tell you that? If you get the title to La Posada tomorrow, it will belong to you, not me."

Whit moved toward her and captured her hand. "I don't even know if I will be the high bidder, and I don't want to give you false hope, but if I do win the bid, I'll sign it over to Nada if you won't take it. Just think about that."

Jackie jerked her hand free of his and opened the stall. She tossed her saddle on her Arabian, tightening the cinch. "I don't have time to talk to you." She pushed the bit between the horse's teeth and shoved her boot in the stirrup, hoisting herself onto the saddle. "Today this ranch still belongs to me, and I have work to do."

Whit swore under his breath as he watched her ride out of the barn. He felt a tremendous sense of loss. She believed the worst of him, and nothing he could say could change that. His vision clouded for a moment, and he leaned against the stall. He was weary of fighting to get through each day. His search for Drew had led him nowhere. But Jackie . . . He could not walk away from her when her life was in shambles.

She would take his help. She had no choice.

*   *   *

Jackie turned the cattle into the south pasture for grazing, then reluctantly rode toward home. When she reached the river, she dismounted and sat on the bank. She had learned to swim in the river with her brother, Matthew. The family had picnicked along its banks. Her life was woven so tightly to La Posada, she didn't know what she would do when she could no longer call it home.

She tossed a stone into the river, remembering when she and Matthew had made a contest out of skipping stones. He always won, of course. She knew that people tended to make saints of those they loved after they had died, but Matthew had always been her hero. Three years older than her, her brother had never complained when she trailed after him, just wanting to be with him. He had patiently taught her how to bait a hook and fish. He'd picked her up when she'd been thrown from a horse and put her back in the saddle.

Jackie dipped her head, resting it on her bended knees. She missed Matthew so much today. Tomorrow would be worse. She didn't intend to be the object of pity or to be on exhibit when the crowds swarmed over her land—she would remain in the house until it was all over.

She heard a rider approaching, so she scrambled to her feet just as Hutch Steiner rode into view. Not wanting to be alone with him after the way he'd treated her the last time, she gathered her horse's reins with every intention of riding back to the house.

"Wait, Jackie," he said, dismounting and taking her reins out of her hand. "I need to talk to you."

Jackie glared at Hutch. "We have nothing to say to each other."

His jaw settled in a hard line. "But we do. I intend to be the new owner of La Posada tomorrow. And I still want you for my wife."

"Never!"

Hutch knew he'd approached her all wrong the last time they'd met, and he wanted her to understand he'd just lost his head. "I've loved you for a long time, Jackie. When I went away to the war, I was afraid you'd marry someone else before I returned. If you can forgive me for my bad behavior the other day, I'd like you to reconsider being my wife."

She shook her head.

He put his hand on hers. "Just think about it. You wouldn't have to leave La Posada. If you want to, we could wait to marry for a few months, until you became accustomed to the idea."

"I don't love you, Hutch. After our last meeting I don't even like you, and I sure don't trust you."

Hutch looked completely dejected by her words, and her heart softened a bit toward him.

"Jackie, you don't know what happens to a person when he wants someone as much as I want you."

She did know. She had loved Whit with every part of her being. But not now, not anymore. "I don't ever want to marry."

He smiled and touched her cheek. "I am going to dedicate myself to changing your mind."

Jackie saw some of the old Hutch in his smile. Reliable—a friend. "Don't ever try what you did last time, Hutch."

Hutch had always wanted her for his wife, had

235

never considered any other woman. But his father had pushed him into rushing Jackie. He wouldn't let that happen again. He knew why his father wanted him to marry Jackie—he'd come to Texas dirt-poor, with nothing to recommend him but hard work and a need to succeed. They'd never been accepted by the better families in Texas. The Douglas family had respectability. They were Texas royalty, and they'd never lost their standing, even now, when they were losing La Posada. Hutch's father wanted to leave a legacy that would be a tribute to him after he was dead, and he needed his son to marry well.

Hutch held his arms up as if in surrender. "I've learned my lesson. You'll find me to be a perfect gentleman from now on."

"I won't find you anything. I won't be here."

He had every intention of wooing her and treating her real nice so she'd soon agree to marry him. He was confident that before tomorrow was over, he'd own La Posada. Despite what she said, maybe she'd marry him just to have the ranch back in her family again.

Jackie merely nodded when he mounted and rode away. She was glad he was gone so she could be alone. She stared at the sunset, not realizing she'd been there for two hours. Moments later she heard the sound of a rider and drew in her breath, thinking Hutch might have returned. She didn't bother to look up as she heard him dismount.

"My answer was final—I'm not going to marry you, and that's it."

She heard a deep chuckle. "I haven't yet considered taking a wife."

She scrambled to her feet. "Whit. I . . . thought you were someone else."

"Obviously. Nada was worried about you because you hadn't come home. I said I'd look for you."

She watched him gaze at the dying sun, just as she'd been doing moments before. "And you knew exactly where to look for me."

The place where he'd first seen her was just over the hill. "As you see."

He turned to her, watching the sunset play across her hair, making it look like it was on fire. Instead of leaving, he leaned against the trunk of the tree, his arms crossed over his chest, observing her. He had intruded on her while she'd been saying good-bye to this land that was in her blood. "So someone was here and asked you to marry him." He felt uncomfortable with that prospect—he felt the stirring of jealousy. "But you turned him down."

She nodded, sitting down a little way from him. "Hutch Steiner is a neighbor. I don't think you've met him."

"No. And I don't think I like him."

She swung her head in his direction and stared at him, wondering why he would say such a thing. "He was my brother's best friend. He is going to bid on La Posada, but I don't think he has the money to actually walk away as owner."

"So," Whit prodded, "he wanted to give it to you as a wedding gift."

"Something like that."

His tone was harsh. "But you wouldn't sell yourself for the price of La Posada, would you?"

Jackie's brow furrowed. "You have the wrong

woman—I don't sell myself at any price. You need to go back to Galveston if you're looking for that kind of woman."

She stood, dusting her skirt. "We'd better go. You said my grandmother was concerned about me."

He stepped forward, towering over her. "She'll know you're safe with me."

He was standing so near, Jackie could feel the heat from his body. He smelled of shaving cream—spicy, male. She wasn't aware that she had gravitated toward him until she felt his hand clamp down on her arm.

"Jackie," he whispered, his tone a plea.

She didn't know how it had happened, but he was drawing her into his arms, and she was allowing it. Her breath was trapped in her throat as he dipped his head, brushing his wonderful mouth against hers.

He held her to him, closing his eyes, his hands going through her hair, bringing her closer to him. "I have needed to hold you like this. You don't know what torture it has been for me to stay away from you."

Her heart was racing, and Jackie thought it might be wise to leave before she lost her wits, like she usually did with him. "I'm going home."

He nodded. "Perhaps we should. I don't trust myself."

Jackie had no plan to do what she did; it just happened. She moved closer to him, her arms sliding around his waist, her mouth parting in invitation.

Whit gathered her in his strong arms, his mouth shaping to fit hers. His fingers slid into her hair, and he held her still while he plundered her lips. His kiss wasn't gentle; it was hard and masterful. He pried her lips open with his tongue, demanding entrance to her mouth.

Jackie had never had a man kiss her like Whit did, and she went weak, her body trembling, wanting more of what he offered. Hunger stirred, awakened, slamming into her like a tidal wave. She didn't object when he went to his knees, taking her with him.

Whit broke off the kiss, rubbing his lips along her cheek. "You took me to my knees with that kiss, honey." His mouth moved over her closed eyelids. "I never had that happen to me before."

Jackie threw her head back as his mouth moved down her neck. Her breasts ached and throbbed when he slowly began to unfasten her blouse. She bit her lower lip to keep from moaning when she felt him spread the blouse wide and dip his head, his lips moving over her breast to take the nipple in his hot, moist mouth.

"Whit," she breathed in a shaky voice.

He suddenly stiffened and started buttoning her blouse. "Forgive me, Jackie." His voice was low and ragged. "I lose my head whenever I'm with you."

She caught his hand, stilling it. When he looked into her eyes, he saw the same intensity in her expression that he felt. "You know what will happen if I don't stop now."

She laid her head against his shoulder. "Yes."

He raised her face and looked questioningly at her. "I can't do this to you, Jackie."

She pulled back, hurt. "I'm not really the kind of woman you desire, am I?"

He made her look at him. "I have wanted you since

the first day I saw you, and that hasn't changed. You are the kind of woman a man dreams of, but knows he can never have. In my case that is the truth, Jackie."

She turned her head away, feeling ashamed. She'd thrown herself at him again—there was no explaining why she would do such a thing when she knew he would only reject her. "You don't have to explain, Whit. I understand."

He gave her a shake. "No, you don't! I want you so badly, I'd give the rest of my life to bury myself in you right now. But I respect you enough to know I would only be hurting you."

"That's why you want a woman from Miss Beauchamp's establishment—you don't have to make a commitment to her."

With a strangled moan, he pulled her to him. "I never touched any of the women there in the way you think. I didn't want them—I could only think of you."

She wanted to believe him, but did she dare?

He forced her to look into his eyes. "I swear before everything I believe in, I have not touched another woman since the first day I saw you. I have no reason to lie. You know I'm telling the truth."

She did know. His eyes were honest, open, pleading.

Whit was watching her eyes and knew the moment she decided he was telling the truth. He was skillful at making love to a woman, and he used that skill now as he eased her onto the grass. She didn't understand what he was doing until he pressed his body on top of hers.

"I'm only human, Jackie," he said, kissing her

throat and then melding his mouth against hers. She felt the swell of him press between her thighs, and she rubbed against him, trying to get closer.

With a groan he joined her frantic movements—he was frustrated because their clothing was between him and his desire. He wanted to feel her naked skin against his. He needed her so badly he wanted to rip their clothing off so he could feel all of her.

Whit deepened the kiss as he slowly moved her skirt up her leg. His hand slid underneath and glided along her leg up to her smooth thigh.

She squirmed feverishly against his hand. His mouth found one breast, and then the other, and he slid his lips between them. He couldn't get close enough to her; he wanted all of her—if he didn't stop soon, he wouldn't be able to stop at all.

Jackie felt his finger slide inside her, and she momentarily stiffened. But he found a certain spot and caressed there, making her groan and toss her head. "Whit," she moaned.

She was wet, soft velvet. His voice was deep and husky. "Sweetheart, what are you doing to me?"

She fought to get closer to him, pulling at his shirt, wanting him to get rid of his trousers.

"Careful, honey," he breathed against her lips. "I know what you're feeling, but I need to stop now."

He started to withdraw his finger, and she shook her head. "No. I don't want you to stop." Her eyes gleamed as she pulled his head toward her and pressed her lips to his, arching her body, inviting him inside.

It was an invitation he was unable to refuse. With frantic urgency he unfastened his trousers, nudged her legs apart, and slid between her thighs. Pausing, he tried to control the desire that burned through him like hot lead.

Jackie felt the tip of his erection touch her intimately, and her breathing stopped, her heart stilled, and she waited.

Whit's mouth was ravaging hers, his breathing heavy. He pushed a little way inside her warmth. She was tight and he was big—he didn't want to hurt her. The thought that he might snapped his head up, and he gazed into passion-bright blue eyes.

Did he have the willpower to stop now that he was so near paradise? Her breasts glistened and beckoned to him, and he lowered his mouth, softly kissing one, then the other. He ran his tongue around a nipple and then took it into his mouth.

Jackie's body was rocking with emotions she couldn't understand. He was barely poised inside her, and she wanted him to bury himself deep.

Sanity returned to Whit in waves of guilt. His body trembled with the restraint he had recaptured just in time.

What was he doing to her?

He had no right to misuse her in this way!

Her eyes were filled with confusion when he shook his head. She wanted to cry out when he withdrew from inside her, leaving her feeling bereft and empty.

Whit's body trembled from the willpower it had taken to pull out of Jackie, when he'd wanted to lunge forward and bury himself deep.

His fingers shook as he fastened her blouse. He stared into sultry blue eyes, feeling like the lowest human being on earth for what he had done to her.

He was quiet for a moment as he measured each word before it was uttered.

"Jackie." His eyes were pleading for understanding, but she didn't understand at all. "There are no words that can vindicate what I've done to you—no way I can beg for your forgiveness." He drew in a painful breath. "At the time you needed me the most, I took advantage of you."

Chapter Twenty

Jackie lay silent and grave, looking up at Whit who had turned to fasten his trousers. "I'm sorry," she said achingly.

He turned to her and offered her his hand, pulling her to her feet. Then his hand dropped away, and he moved several steps from her, leaning against the branch of a tree and lowering his head. "Don't take any of the blame on yourself. How could you know I would . . . I would take advantage of your innocence. I went too far this time."

When Jackie swayed on her feet, Whit moved to her side and steadied her with both hands on her shoulders. "Honey," he whispered, brushing grass out of her hair. "You should be introduced to the pleasures between a man and woman in your marriage bed. Not like this."

Whit was being gallant, and Jackie knew it. A small whimper escaped her throat, and her gaze swept toward the ground. She was to blame for everything that had happened between them. And the worst part was that she wasn't sorry, and she was hurt that he was.

Whit raised her chin, forcing her to look at him. "Don't turn away from me. I am only doing what is right for you."

She was trembling on the inside, the sting of another rejection from Whit still ringing in her ears. Her fingers were trembling so much she had problems tucking her tangled hair behind her ears. "I'm going now."

He saw the dejection in her eyes and wanted to hug her to him, but he didn't dare because it wouldn't stop with a hug. "Don't feel bad, honey—you didn't do anything wrong. It was all me." He took a step away from her. "I want you so badly I lost my head for a while. You'll never know what it cost me to let you go tonight."

Her eyes filled with frustrated tears that brimmed over and trickled down her cheeks. She hated herself for crying—it was a weakness she had hardly given in to before she met Whit. "I am a shameless hussy. You have every reason to detest me."

Her tears were killing Whit. He pulled her to him gently and kissed each tear away, holding her as if she were the most precious person on earth—and to him she was. "I hope you will understand what I'm going to say to you. It's important that you do."

She pulled back and wiped the tears away with her hand. "You can save your breath if you are going to try to make excuses for me once again." She looked him straight in the eyes. "I'm going to go back to the house now."

He held her when she tried to move away from him.

"Not until you hear what I have to say." He tilted her chin up when she tried to lower it. "Sweetheart, sometimes there is this . . . attraction between a man and a woman. I felt it for you that first day we met, and I believe you felt it too. My feelings are different from what most men feel for a woman. Some might call it love." He was thinking of his mother and father, and how they had once thought they'd loved each other, and how she had left him in the end. "What I feel for you will last for the rest of my life. I would never tire of you—if you were mine." He looked deeply into her eyes. "I know when you are hurt; I'm hurt for you. When I see your tears, like now, it rips at my heart. But you are not mine. Do you understand?"

"No. I don't."

He drew in a deep breath. "Jackie, I have nothing to give you. I have lived my life with only one purpose. But then you came along and changed everything."

"Are you saying you don't love me?"

"I put it all wrong. What I'm saying is what I feel for you is more than the love some people think they feel for each other. For those people, the feelings burn out, and they are left with only the memories of when they desired each other. That would never happen with you and me."

She pushed his hand away. "What are you saying?"

He could not make a commitment until he saw how the bidding went in the morning. He had nothing to give her, no security—but if he could give the ranch back to her, maybe they could have some kind of future together. If he lost, he'd ride away. He gently touched her cheek, allowing his finger to drift across her full lips. "I think I've said enough for one night. We'd better get you back to your grandmother before she sends Mort after me. He's already threatened to beat my hide."

It was a silent ride back to the ranch. Whit allowed Jackie to think about what he'd said. Right now she felt rejected because he had not taken advantage of her. To Whit, it was the most honorable move he'd ever made. He had been so close to heaven, and he had let it slip through his fingers.

When they reached the house, he spoke. "I'll unsaddle your horse. Go on in, honey. And try to get some rest. Tomorrow is going to be difficult."

She held her spine straight as she walked away from him. Her heart was in shreds, and her self-respect had been shattered. She was ashamed of her actions, embarrassed that she had repeated the same pattern with Whit. Only this time she'd gone further. He'd lost his head at first, but what man wouldn't if a woman threw herself at him so wantonly?

She wanted to die.

She wanted to feel the touch of his lips on hers once more.

She wanted to hide so she would never have to face Whit again.

Nada heard Jackie close the back door and nodded in satisfaction—Whit had found her and brought her home. "Come on in the kitchen, child. I saved supper for you."

"I'm not hungry."

Nada came into the parlor, where Jackie stood at the window, staring toward the barn. "I know tonight's hard, and tomorrow will be harder still. But we have been through worse and survived, and we'll survive this as well."

"I don't want to survive."

Nada strode purposefully toward Jackie. "That's nonsense. You have your whole life ahead of you." She saw the tears on Jackie's cheeks and misunderstood the reason for them. "La Posada is lost to us, but we'll still go on."

Jackie shook her head, burying her face against the lace curtains. "That's not what I'm thinking about." She turned tear-bright eyes to her grandmother. "I'm a shameless hussy."

Nada was drying her hands on her apron, and she jerked her head up in shock. "What are you talking about?"

"Gram." Jackie looked at Nada sorrowfully. "I did it again. I threw myself at him."

"Whit?"

She nodded.

"Do you want to talk about it?"

Jackie drew in a steadying breath and gave a half nod. "You will be so ashamed of me, but I have to tell you anyway."

Nada took Jackie's hand and led her to the sofa, settling them both on the rough texture. "You talk, and I'll listen."

It was hard for Jackie to look into her grandmother's clear, honest eyes, so she stared at the curtains that were being stirred by the wind. "I wanted Whit to make love to me tonight. I let him kiss me . . . and touch me." A single tear rolled down Jackie's cheek. "You have to know I would have given him

248

anything he wanted." Her head fell forward on Nada's shoulder. "I *am* a hussy."

Nada blinked back tears, hoping that what she feared had not happened. "What did Whit do to you?"

"He told me I should only be with a man in my marriage bed."

Nada drew in a relieved breath, her faith in Whit renewed. "He's right about that, child."

"He said what we felt wasn't love—and I don't understand this part: he said what we felt was beyond love."

"I'm not sure I understand that myself. It seems to me that you either love someone or you don't."

Jackie's grandmother smelled of lemon and vanilla, like she always did, and the comfort of her arms soothed Jackie's pain. "He doesn't want me, and he was trying to be kind."

Nada knew that wasn't so. She was proud of Whit. He'd seen that Jackie was at her most vulnerable tonight, and he'd done the honorable thing by her.

Jackie didn't want to talk about Whit anymore; she concentrated instead on the bleakness of their future. "I don't know what we're going to do, Gram. With what little money we have, we can't even maintain the house in Copper Springs for more than a year or so."

"Child, the future is like looking in a mirror—we can see the here and now; we can see what's behind us; but we can't see what will be reflected in the mirror when we walk away. Tomorrow is going to be hard to get through, we know that—but trust that the future will only get better."

Jackie raised her head from Nada's shoulder. "How can I believe that?"

"Have faith."

Jackie's eyes widened. "What are you saying?"

"Look for what's beyond the reality you see today. Trust. Whit didn't come back here just to return your horse."

"You really think that?"

Nada felt the weight of tomorrow heavy in her heart, but she had to remain strong for Jackie. Nada had survived the death of her husband, her only son and his wife, and her grandson—she could surely survive this day's work. She had to see her granddaughter settled with a good man before she died. "I certainly do. If Whit had cared less about you, he'd never have stopped tonight." She patted Jackie's hand. "I also see something else in him. I see a man who has little hope for his own future—a man who has suffered a great deal and only became stronger for it. I don't know what force is driving him. But I've never seen a man so alone, or who needed someone to believe in him as much as Whit does."

Jackie stood slowly. "You're right. I've been so buried in my own selfish needs that I haven't noticed anything else around me." She turned to Nada with a questioning expression. "How can I help him?"

"Believe in him."

"I'm having trouble doing that right now. Did you know he's going to bid on La Posada?"

"He told me that."

"I don't know what his motives are. I really don't."

"Then you are not ready to believe in him."

Jackie had no answer. Sometimes she thought Nada

was too good for this world and saw only the best in others. Jackie kissed Nada on the cheek. "Good night, Gram."

Lying back on his bedroll, Whit heard one of the horses kick the door of its stall. A barn owl hooted from its perch on the fence just outside the door. The wind stirred the leaves on the huge oak tree near the house. It was cloudy, a dark night to match Whit's dark mood. He couldn't win that auction tomorrow morning—he didn't have enough money. La Posada was a jewel, with twenty miles of river running through the property. The auction was sure to draw people from all over the state.

He turned over on his side, propping his head on his arm. He wanted to see Jackie smile, to be light-hearted, as she had been the first day he'd seen her. He wanted to give her the ranch, but he would probably be outbid.

Whit closed his eyes, knowing he wouldn't sleep at all. He also knew that inside the house was a young woman who was troubled by what had happened between them tonight. She would not sleep either.

Chapter Twenty-one

The atmosphere at the ranch house was more like a neighborhood festivity than the ending of the Douglas dynasty. Carriages, farm wagons, and horses lined every available space between the house and the barn. Some people had even brought picnic lunches and were helping themselves to the springwater from La Posada's well. Children of all ages were dashing about, playing games, some climbing trees, others wrestling on the grass.

Whit watched two boys try to sneak food from a picnic basket. Twin boys, not yet in their teens, were swinging on the gate that led to the corral. Mort scolded them and sent them in a different direction while he fastened the gate, planting his body in front of it as if he were standing guard. A short time later, Whit saw Mort chase the same two boys out of Nada's garden, threatening to tell their ma and pa if they didn't behave.

Whit's gaze swept to the house, where the curtains were drawn together, Jackie deliberately shutting out the sight of the people tramping about. He imagined that the most humiliating part of the day had been when the auctioneer had shown people through the house. Whit had stood in the shadow of the barn watching the long line of people going through the front door and coming out the back. He imagined that Nada, with her natural kindness, had been gracious to every person. He figured that Jackie had resented the intrusion into their privacy. He could only imagine how much they were suffering because of the chaos going on around them. Strangers and friends alike were tramping through their yard; those who hadn't come to bid on the ranch had probably come out of curiosity.

Men in work clothes mingled alongside women in fancy gowns and lace parasols. Whit had never expected the auction to draw such a crowd. He had a heavy feeling in the pit of his stomach. His five thousand dollars would not be the high bid today.

Whit's hope had been that most people who had showed up wouldn't have the money to buy the ranch and were there only out of idle curiosity. Now that seemed like a futile hope.

The auctioneer, a short, balding man who had a booming voice, waved his hands in the air and called for silence.

"Gather around, folks. The bidding will begin in twenty minutes. To claim the winning bid on La Posada, the high bidder will be expected to provide either cash money or a bank draft for the settled amount. After that is concluded, those of you who wish to bid on the stock will be given a list of cattle and horses by my assistant, Verge Brown."

Whit was preoccupied by his troubled thoughts—
before the afternoon was over, La Posada would no
longer belong to Jackie. And it wouldn't belong to
him either. He'd been a fool to think he could buy a
ranch the size of this one. Whatever had he been
thinking?

Silence fell across the crowd, and people began to
drift toward the auctioneer, some elbowing their way
to the front row.

A latecomer arrived, and folks scattered to get out
of the way of the two prancing grays that pulled the
fancy carriage. Whit watched Simon Gault hop out of
the carriage, smiling and speaking to people as he
walked along.

Things had just gotten a lot worse. Simon's voice
grated on Whit like broken glass as he tipped his hat
and stopped to speak to a lady in a bright blue gown.
Whit let out his breath as Bruce climbed out of the
buggy.

Simon's eyes darkened with hatred as he pushed
past Whit without a word.

"Find me a chair, and put it in the shade," Simon
told Bruce while wiping sweat from his face with a
handkerchief, which he then shoved back in his
pocket. "I don't intend to stand among this rabble."

Whit tensed. He knew why Simon was there, and
Whit knew he could never outbid the man. He felt his
heart being chipped away piece by piece. He turned to
glance at the house and saw the curtains move.

Jackie.

His broad shoulders straightened, and he felt as if
the ground had just fallen out from under him. He'd
let his family down, and his sisters had died as a re-

sult. Now he was letting Jackie down, and she would lose her ranch.

The podium was nothing more than a tall wooden crate placed on its side. The gavel came down, and the auctioneer's voice was loud enough to reach the crowd at the far end of the yard.

"Let the bidding begin!"

The first bidder, a rancher Whit knew from near San Angelo, Bud Hargroves, called out, "A thousand dollars." Whit stood back, feeling the ranch slip through his fingers like grains of sand. He could not compete with wealthy ranchers like Bud who coveted La Posada.

"Three thousand dollars," Whit called out.

"Four thousand dollars." A new voice was added to the fray. Hutch Steiner was beginning to suspect that he didn't have enough money to buy the ranch. He would stay for another round, and then he'd have to drop out.

"Five thousand dollars," Simon called out from his perch on a wooden barrel under the shade of an oak tree. His hate-filled gaze met Whit's, and he smiled. Simon was not about to let Whit have the ranch. In his mind he had somehow related this incident to the gold mine Hawk's pa had stolen from him. He had gotten the better of the father, and he was about to get the better of the son.

Leaning back against a fence, Whit felt the weight of defeat. He only half heard the following bids.

Jackie.

Simon narrowed his eyes as he watched Hawk's shoulders flex. The expression on Whit's face told

Simon the whole story. Hawk could not be the hero for the Douglas woman. Simon felt excitement stir within him. This was even better than having Hawk killed outright. Now the man would suffer and struggle for years—decidedly better than his death would have been.

Simon sent Bruce to fetch his canteen while he watched a rancher up the bid. With a snarl on his lips, Simon topped the man's bid. Whit had stepped back, his hard gaze unreadable, but Simon knew Whit was a defeated man. He watched some of the crowd move away, mumbling, and soon there were only seven bidders left. Others were watching with interest from the sidelines.

Simon felt something poke him in the back, and before he could turn around, Chantalle spoke to him.

"This is a derringer you feel. Don't move and don't make another bid."

"Chantalle, what in the hell do you think you're doing?" He started to turn around to face her, and she moved the gun upward and pressed it into his neck until it hurt. He licked his lips. "I'll kill you for this." He started to turn around again so he could look her in the eyes, so she would know he was serious.

"No, no—don't turn around. Act like everything is normal. But do as I say—don't make another bid."

"Why in the hell not? What interest do you have in this matter? And I won't believe you if you say you want the ranch for yourself."

"That is none of your business. I'm going to move away now, but if you don't heed my warning, I'll tell all of Galveston about your dirty little secrets and the room you maintain at my place. I see Bruce coming now. This is what I want you to do: get in your buggy and head out. I want you gone."

Simon shook his head. "You won't tell anyone about me," he asserted.

Her voice had an edge to it. "I promise you I will. You know I always keep my promises."

She was serious, and he knew it. "I'll get you for this, Chantalle," he warned. "No matter how long it takes, I'll get you."

Chantalle laughed. "No. You won't. I have enough dirt on you to sink you like an iron-bottom ship." She slid the gun into her drawstring bag and waited. "You need to leave now," she said with a hiss. "Or would you like me to make an announcement about you to the good folks gathered here today? If you think I won't, just put me to the test."

Chantalle meant it, all right. She'd do it, Simon thought. But he didn't know why she was interfering here today. No matter—he'd figure it out. Simon prized his good name above everything else, because he'd worked so hard to establish himself in Galveston.

Chantalle watched him stalk away, and Bruce fell in behind him. She tensed as Simon stopped in front of Whit.

"Don't think you've won. I'm not through with you yet."

Whit stared into cold, ruthless eyes, not understanding Simon's meaning and wondering why he was leaving. "If I could prove that your little shadow there," he said, nodding at Bruce, "was the one who came to my hotel room the night before I left Galveston, you'd have to deal with me right now. Don't make threats unless you're prepared to live with the consequences."

Simon's fists balled at his sides, his eyes dark pools of depravity. "We'll meet again, Hawk," he said tersely, his gaze issuing a threat. "I promise you that. And I always win in the end."

Whit's gaze turned to Bruce. "I'm trembling in my boots, Simon."

With a loud curse, Simon stalked away. There were too many people around to retaliate at the moment. His hatred for anyone bearing the Hawk name escalated.

Chantalle didn't move from her position under the shade of the tree until Simon's buggy was out of sight. Then she walked toward Whit, her red parasol standing out among the more subtly-colored sunshades. She was wearing a simple high-necked gray gown with a white lace collar, looking matronly rather than like the astute businesswoman she actually was.

When Chantalle approached Whit she smiled, and he returned her smile. He could see that her face had been scrubbed clean of makeup, and she wore only a dab of color on her lips. He thought she looked prettier this way. "I didn't expect to see you here today, Chantalle. It looks like everyone in three counties showed up for the auction."

Chantalle read aching disappointment in Whit's eyes—he thought he'd failed to save the ranch for Jackie Douglas. She was about to turn his disappointment into triumph. It felt good to do something for a person as worthy as Whit. It also felt good to get the best of Simon. She paid no heed to the startled glances, the whispers and nods in her direction, or the snide remarks that were spoken loud enough for her to hear.

"Chantalle," Whit said, taking her hand in a friendly gesture, ignoring the shock on other people's faces. "Whatever lured you out of Galveston?"

Chantalle knew that Whit was taking her under his protection by acknowledging her. It would never occur to him to ignore a friend, no matter what the circumstances. "I came to see what all the excitement was about."

"I saw you talking to Simon. Are you the reason he left?"

She chuckled. "If you're talking about the derringer I had at his back, then yeah, I made him leave. Simon knows that when I tell him something, I mean it."

Whit's dark brows met in a frown. "Why would you do that? You're the one who's always warning me he's a dangerous man."

"Oh, he'll try to retaliate. But I know just how to handle him."

"And why would you place yourself in a position so he would want to retaliate?"

"I came to loan you some money."

His mouth flew open, and for a moment all he could do was stare into Chantalle's twinkling eyes. "What?"

"Go on up there, Whit. Bid on your lady's ranch. I'll loan you whatever money you need to be high bidder."

He stared at her, afraid to believe she was being so generous. "Why would you do that?"

Chantalle winked. "Let's just say—and I've told

you this before—that I have a soft spot in my heart for gamblers."

Whit felt hopeful, and then uncertain. He thought of the night Simon had hurt Marian. Maybe this was Chantalle's way of getting even with Simon, but it was an expensive way to do so.

"The bid is already up to nine thousand dollars, and it's going to go much higher. How will I ever be able to repay that much money?"

"You'll make this ranch successful and pay me as you can. It's high time you put aside that deck of cards and became a cowboy." She gave him a little shove toward the other bidders. "You don't have time to talk to me—go buy yourself a ranch."

Chapter Twenty-two

Whit stood beside Chantalle, and they both watched the last wagon pull away while Chantalle's hired man, Will, waited near the buggy for her. Whit clutched the deed of La Posada in his hand, still unable to grasp the fact that Chantalle had helped him save the ranch for Jackie.

"You don't know what this means to me. I don't even know how to begin to thank you."

"Maybe you can name your first daughter after me." She smiled and shook her head. "Probably not a good idea. I don't think your little redhead would like that. If you don't think she'll be jealous of me, how about a kiss on the cheek?"

Whit bent and kissed her as she laughed up at him. "I think when Jackie finds out about your generosity, she'll bless your name from this day forward, Chantalle."

She had her doubts. "Don't put that to the test."

"You have my word: I'll repay every penny of the

loan," he said earnestly. "I don't want you to worry about that."

"I'm not worried. I know I can trust you." She touched his shoulder. "You are a very fine man, Whit. Jackie Douglas is a fortunate young woman."

He watched Chantalle with a doubtful expression, his dark brows meeting in a frown. "I doubt Jackie would agree with you."

Chantalle gave a knowing laugh. "Oh, I think she will. Just have patience with her for a while—she will come around."

He glanced toward the house, where the curtains were still drawn over the windows. "She's the kind of woman who makes me want to be patient—something I've never been in my life." He glanced back at Chantalle. "We need to make arrangements for my payments to you."

"That's easy," she said, moving her sunshade so she could block out the late-afternoon sunlight. "I'll expect you to give me the first payment exactly one year from this date."

Whit looked astounded. Chantalle was a shrewd businesswoman, and he had expected her to want her payments starting next month. "And what will the interest be if I wait that long to make the first payment?"

"For you, less than the bank charges, Whit. Get the ranch in working order, hire more men to help out, buy more cattle. I'll leave word with the bank in Copper Springs that you are to be extended extra credit."

He was so overwhelmed by her kindness, he didn't know what to say. "Has anyone ever told you what an exceptional woman you are, Chantalle, and what a generous one?"

She shrugged and winked. "But of course. There have been many men who have thought well of me. But not so many that I thought so well of." She smiled. "I think well of you."

"And how does your captain deal with all those admirers?"

She gazed into the distance with a serious expression. "Joshua does not worry that anyone will turn my head but him."

Whit could have sworn he'd seen the glistening of tears in her eyes, but it must have been only the reflection of the sun. "I think it might be a good idea to make you a partner, Chantalle. I feel sure Jackie will agree."

She touched his arm. "No. Don't even think about that. If I read that beautiful young lady right, you're going to have trouble convincing her to take anything from you, let alone with me involved in it. Maybe it would be wise for you to convince Miss Douglas to become your partner. That way she'll have to stay on and help you," she hinted. "If you don't, she'll probably leave."

"You are very wise when it comes to human nature."

A smile transformed her face, and she was almost beautiful "I have to be—it goes with my profession."

Chantalle hadn't made her remark flippantly, and Whit knew that, like a true gambler, she could judge a person's character.

"There is another reason I wanted to help you, Whit. That night when you came charging up the

263

stairs to Marian's rescue . . . you didn't have to. Many men would have just thought she deserved what Simon did to her, but not you."

His expression became serious. "I have traveled for much of my life in search of my father, and then my brother, and in all that time I have never had a friend like you." A knot formed in his throat. "Because of you I can go in that house and tell Jackie to unpack her belongings. I can tell her she doesn't have to send away the elderly cowhands who have worked on this ranch since before she was born."

Chantalle started toward her buggy with her head lowered so he couldn't see how affected she was by his words. "I don't expect we'll be seeing you in my gambling room from now on."

"No. I have turned my last card." He lifted her into the buggy. "But if you should ever need me for any reason, I'll be there as fast as I can."

She chuckled. "Go use your pretty speeches on the woman who has your heart. Mine's too old to take such talk."

He tipped his hat to her and stood there while Will drove her away. Chantalle had come to his rescue. He smiled, feeling happiness for the first time in many years.

Jackie.

Jackie had spent the day sorting through the things she'd collected over the years, hoping to ignore the loud voices outside. The house they would be moving to in Copper Springs was much smaller than this one, so they had to dispose of furniture and treasures that had been in the family for many generations.

Nada entered and moved a pair of boots off a chair so she could lower her body onto it. "It's a shame to say good-bye to all this." She wiped her eyes on her apron. She hadn't intended to let Jackie see her cry, but today had been hard. "How are you coming along, child?"

"I don't know what to keep and what to get rid of. I should have done this weeks ago—but I had always harbored the hope that we wouldn't lose La Posada."

"I know. I don't know what we are going to do with everything."

"I heard everyone leave. I expect the new owner to come calling anytime, wanting to know how soon we can vacate the house."

Nada nodded. "I suspect you're right. I wonder who the new owner is." Nada moved to the door. "I have stew on the stove. Come on in the kitchen and have a bowl. You haven't eaten all day."

There was a knock on the door, and they both froze, glancing at each other. "I suppose that's the new owner," Nada said, running her hand over her hair and removing her apron.

Jackie wrapped paper around a beautiful pearl-handled brush and mirror set that had belonged to her mother and placed it in a crate. Then, with a sigh, she followed her grandmother to the front room.

Nada opened the door and stepped back. "Oh, it's you, Whit. I wasn't sure you were still here. We were expecting the new owner."

Whit removed his hat and stepped into the room. "I am the new owner."

Chapter Twenty-three

Nada's hand went to her throat. She had not really expected Whit to be the high bidder. She felt Jackie beside her, stiff and silent, no doubt shocked into stupefaction. "I'm glad it belongs to you, Whit," was all Nada could think to say.

"You will have to give us a few more days to vacate," Jackie said, exhaustion in her tone. "We don't have too much more to pack."

Whit took Nada's arm, but his gaze was on Jackie. "Something smells delicious. May I join you for supper? Then I'll tell you my plans."

Nada looked at him with wise eyes. "Jackie and I were just about to sit down. You are welcome to join us."

"I'm not going to eat," Jackie stated scornfully.

"Then sit with us," Whit said, leading Nada toward the kitchen. "You'll need to hear what I have to say." He knew Jackie's curiosity would win out over her stubbornness.

When Whit was seated at the table, Nada placed

a bowl of steaming stew in front of Whit and set a platter of biscuits within his reach. Jackie sat across the table from Whit, her gaze following her grandmother around, because she didn't want to look at Whit.

Whit reached into his breast pocket, withdrew a paper, and spread it out on the table. "This is what I want to talk to you both about."

Jackie's eyes dropped to the deed she had coveted for so long. "How did you get the money to buy the ranch?"

He met her gaze. "Miss Beauchamp was here today. She covered my bid."

Jackie propped her chin on her fist and shook her head, anger eating away at her. "Of course. I should have known she'd help you, since you are such a *good* customer at her place. She turned me down flat when I asked for a loan."

Whit heard Nada hiss through her teeth and saw her frown at her granddaughter. "Jackie, let's hear Whit out before we go rushing to judgment."

Feeling the heat of Whit's gaze on her, Jackie picked up her fork and pushed a chunk of meat around in her bowl. She had plenty to say, but she'd just keep her mouth shut for the time being. It was difficult, though, to hide her irritation, and angry words begged to be spoken.

Whit was having a hard time keeping his gaze from remaining on Jackie. He'd noticed how pale she looked, and how beautiful. "Now," he said, leaning forward in his chair, "I told you both yesterday that I was going to try to help you."

"Bighearted of you," Jackie stated haughtily, at last able to voice her displeasure.

Nada was ready to scold Jackie again, but Whit held up his hand. "There is nothing bighearted about my buying La Posada. I'm asking for a business arrangement between us, Jackie, nothing more." He flipped the deed over to the back so both women could see what it said. "If you notice, you are a joint owner, Jackie. We are partners."

She looked up from the deed into his eyes. "I don't understand."

"I want you to unpack and put everything back the way you had it before. I'm going to tell Ortega and Mort that they'll be staying on. Nothing has changed today except that now every stick of furniture and every head of cattle on this ranch belongs to you."

"To you," Jackie corrected.

"To us."

"And what do you expect to get out of such a partnership, Whit?" Nada asked, already knowing the answer.

"I get the chance to accomplish something worthwhile in my life. I want to hire more men and buy more cattle." Excitement thrummed through his words. "I want La Posada to be what it once was." He could have added that he'd like to see Jackie smile again, but he didn't.

Jackie still wasn't satisfied. He was offering her a way to stay on the ranch she loved, but she didn't know why. "If you have all these plans and the money to follow through with them, why do you need us?"

His gaze settled on Jackie. "I want more than you

268

may be willing to give." His tone deepened. "I want respectability."

Jackie shook her head. "I still don't understand."

"I haven't had a place to call home in a very long time. I want to watch La Posada grow and thrive, and I want to be a part of it. The Douglas name is very much respected in these parts. I'll hope to earn respectability by being associated with this family."

Nada watched Whit closely. He wasn't quite telling the truth. She knew he didn't care anything about what other people thought of him—he wanted Jackie. She lifted her coffee cup and observed her granddaughter over the rim. Whit might not know it yet, but he loved Jackie. He already knew that he wanted her, but Nada wasn't sure Whit realized just how deep his feelings for Jackie went. A smile touched her lips. Whit hadn't seen Jackie at her best yet. When he first came along she'd been fighting for their very existence. Nada wanted Whit to get to know the playful side of her granddaughter, the tenderness, the loyalty that beat in Jackie's heart. She wanted Whit to see Jackie smile and to know he was the reason for her smile.

"Say we did take your offer," Nada stated. "You couldn't go running off to Galveston when you got bored. Ranching is hard work."

"Yes, ma'am, I know that. I'm prepared to do my part."

Jackie crossed her arms over her chest and glared at him. "And if I don't agree, will you kick me and Gram off the ranch?"

"No." Whit knew he was about to win, and he had never played for higher stakes. "If you decide you don't want me here, I'll cross *my* name off the deed and ride away, leaving everything to you."

Jackie's heart slammed inside her. He would do it. She could tell by the look in his eyes that he meant every word he said. Whit had always been kind to her—and now he was offering her a way to keep La Posada. Mort and Ortega could stay on in their homes. She wanted to say yes. She wanted to walk into his arms and let him hold her. She wanted to tell him how much she respected him. "Will you give me time to think about it?"

He smiled, and Nada caught her breath at the warmth that lit his eyes. Her prayers had been answered. Jackie was going to be all right. Although Whit had a troubled past, he would take care of her, treat her tenderly, and love her to the end of their lives. She saw a man burning with love for her granddaughter, and yet one who was not quite sure how to handle the little hellcat who had probably caused him many sleepless nights.

"For what it's worth, I'm not too proud to take your offer," Nada stated with a smile. "Now, can we eat before everything gets cold?"

Whit reached for a biscuit with an uncertain expression on his face. "I believe both of you need to know something about my past. You may not think well of me when you hear everything I have to say."

Nada gave her granddaughter a piercing glance, but her words were for Whit. "I don't need to know more than I know right now. I'm obliged to you for what you've done to help us, and I know Jackie is, too."

Jackie dipped her head as if she were studying the

pattern on her fork. "Yes. I am. It's just that I thought we'd lost everything, and now . . ."

They all fell silent as each of them was lost in his own thoughts. Whit was certain Nada wouldn't have such a high opinion of him when she learned that he was responsible for his sisters' deaths. And Jackie— what would she think of him when he told her the truth?

Jackie was aware that Whit was staring at her. She wouldn't be able to swallow another bite if he didn't focus his attention on something else. She met his gaze, wondering what he wanted to say about his past. Whatever it was, it wouldn't change the way she felt about him. She loved him, and she always would.

Whit stood. "Nada, thank you for the delicious meal. Your biscuits are the best I've ever tasted. Mort and Ortega are waiting for me in the barn. I told them I wanted to talk to them after I talked to the two of you."

"I'm afraid you're going to have to sleep in the barn again tonight," Nada told him. "We would put you in Matthew's room, but with everything strewn around and crates everywhere, you'll have to wait until we make the room livable again."

He grinned. "I've grown sort of accustomed to the barn." His gaze fell on Jackie, who looked like she'd just lost her best friend. He picked up the deed to the ranch and handed it to her. "You need to put this in a safe place. You'll have to get it recorded as soon as possible."

She took it, holding it against her chest.

"Later I would like a word with you, Jackie. Would that be all right with you?"

She nodded.

After Whit left, Jackie turned to Nada with a stunned look on her face. "I can't believe any of this."

Nada patted her hand. "Well, I for one prefer living here to moving to town. And so do you."

"I don't know what to think. Why did Whit put himself in debt to buy our ranch? And I'm bothered by his dealings with that woman—that Miss Beauchamp. Why would she help him buy the ranch when she wouldn't help me? And remember I told you she charges a very high interest on the money she loans to people?"

"Those are things you'll have to ask Whit."

"I'm confused."

"Take each day as it comes, Jackie. And take Whit's offer. He wouldn't have gone to such great lengths unless he wanted something."

"La Posada."

"I don't think so. Anyway, you have no choice but to agree to his terms, unless you want to see him ride out of your life."

"I know." Jackie started stacking dishes. "I don't know if I can trust myself around him. You know how I've behaved in the past."

Nada had to turn away to keep from laughing out loud. Tonight Whit couldn't keep his eyes off Jackie. She wondered how long it would take him to ask her to marry him.

Ortega watched Mort lug a bucket from stall to stall, watering the horses. Ortega tossed hay to the animals, and then waited, arms crossed over his chest, to find out what the new owner of La Posada had to say to him and Mort. He figured he already knew—they would be asked to leave. Ortega was about to find out the answer, because Whit Hawk was walking into the barn.

"Good evening," Whit said, leaning a booted foot on the lower rung of the stall. "By now you probably know what I want to talk to you about."

"Yeah, likely we do," Mort said, setting the bucket down and giving his full attention to Whit. "You want us to move on so you can put younger hands in our places."

"That couldn't be further from the truth. Though I've worked at various ranches over the years, I don't know how to run a place. Both of you have stores of knowledge I need. I want you to go on with your same jobs, just as you always have, only with a few differences: I'll need both of you to advise me. We want to buy more cattle and hire more men. Ortega, I'll want you to be foreman—hire the men. Mort, I'll want you to go with me when I buy cattle. You know what to look for; I don't."

Both men were stunned into silence. They didn't have to leave—they still had a home, and they were going to be useful.

Mort was the first to speak. "You sure got taken when you bought that gelding, although he turned out to be a right nice horse when we got his hoof cured."

Ortega glanced at his new boss, wondering if he'd take offense at Mort's ribbing. He watched Hawk smile, and Ortega relaxed.

"That's the very reason I'll need to depend on you,

Mort. I want you at my side to make sure no one sticks me with diseased stock."

For the last few years Ortega had been the unofficial foreman of La Posada, but there had been no money to hire riders or to buy cattle. He and Jackie had done most of the heavy work. "What about Jackie and Nada?" he asked, not ready to throw his lot in with Hawk just yet.

"Nothing will change there. Jackie is my partner. She will have the final say on everything. I respect the fact that she knows more about ranching than I'll ever know."

Both men had expected to hear bad news tonight, and they didn't quite know how to react.

"What do you say?" Whit asked, looking from Mort to Ortega. "Are you willing to help us?"

Mort grinned and walked over to shake hands with Whit. "I'm sorry if I shot off my mouth at you the other day. I do that a lot."

"I admire your loyalty to Jackie. Don't apologize for that."

Ortega hung back, not ready to comply. "You know I'm on up there in years. Are you sure you do not want a younger foreman, Señor Hawk?"

"I want your knowledge, not your youth. Hire good men who are willing to work hard so you don't have to do all the work yourself."

"If we hire more men, we'll need a bunkhouse," Mort stated practically.

"Then maybe you can hire someone to build one for us, Mort. I think we should get started on that as soon as possible."

"I'll take the wagon and go into Copper Springs tomorrow." Mort looked concerned for a moment. "Do we have the money to do all this?"

Whit grinned. "Thanks to a certain lady with a red sunshade, we have whatever money we need."

Ortega and Mort both looked puzzled, but they didn't ask questions. Mort had coffee on the stove and wanted to eat and have a cup before he went to bed. Ortega wanted to get home and tell Luisa the good news. She'd been crying for days because she did not want to leave La Posada.

"I want to thank you for what you've done," Mort said, his faded eyes tearing.

"I as well, Señor Hawk. You will not be sorry you put your trust in us."

"I know that. I have seen your loyalty to the Douglas family. I look forward to the day when you will show me the same respect."

Chapter Twenty-four

The night was strangely peaceful after the uproar of the crowd that had tromped through Nada's flower beds and picnicked on the grass. There was only the light from a pale quarter-moon spilling through the open barn door. Whit lay on his bedroll, his arms folded behind him to pillow his head. So much had happened today he could hardly sort it all out in his mind.

He thought of Simon, wondering why he'd come to bid on the ranch. Whit had a feeling Simon had somehow found out about Jackie, and Whit's feelings for her. For some reason that Whit would never understand, Simon had a grudge against him. He tried to think why. It wasn't what had happened at Chantalle's, because Chantalle had warned Whit that Simon was after him before that incident.

Whit wondered if Simon might have been an enemy of his father's and was somehow carrying his vendetta to the son. But that couldn't be—Simon had not arrived in Galveston until long after his father had left.

His eyes drifted shut as he thought of Chantalle. She was a businesswoman, but she had a heart. For some reason she liked him and wanted to help him. He'd see that she was repaid as soon as possible.

His eyes snapped open. Someone had to have told Simon that Whit was interested in La Posada. That was the reason Simon had shown up for the bidding. If that was the case, Chantalle had someone at her place who was reporting to either Bruce or Simon.

He considered all the possibilities and came to one conclusion—it had to be Angie. He would have to make a trip to Galveston as soon as possible and warn Chantalle. Not tomorrow, because they had work to do. But he could leave in two or three days.

His thoughts of Jackie were somewhat more complicated. He wanted something from her that was just out of reach, something she might not be willing to give him. For now Whit had to be satisfied that Jackie and Nada would sleep in their own beds and not have to move to the small house in Copper Springs. And Jackie could keep the ranch she loved so much. Whit would see that they were settled—it might take a year, or even two; then he'd probably go looking for Drew once more.

A soft voice came out of the darkness. "Whit?"

"I'm over here." He rolled to his feet as Jackie appeared in the doorway. He struck a match and lit a lantern.

She advanced hesitantly, her arms loaded with quilts and a pillow. "Gram thought you'd be more comfortable with these."

"Your grandmother is one of the kindest women I've ever known."

She held the quilts and pillow out to him. "I've decided."

He tossed the quilts onto his bedroll and gave her his full attention. "You are going to become my partner, aren't you?"

"Yes." She was rubbing one hand nervously down the side of her skirt. "Today when you made your offer to us, I must have sounded ungrateful, and I apologize for the way I acted. It's just that you took me by surprise."

"Jackie, I understand what you had to go through. You don't owe me any explanation."

"I think I do." She lowered her head, her heart beating wildly inside her. He was standing a good distance from her, and she knew why—he was afraid she'd throw herself at him, as she had before. "You deserve much more credit than I've given you. Yours was an act of kindness, and I reacted badly."

He raised his head and laughed softly, wishing he had the right to take her in his arms and kiss those lips into submission. "Do you remember something I said to you when we first met?"

"You said a lot of things that day."

"I told you that I wanted to dance with you."

"Here? Now?"

"No." Humor ran through him like a cleansing wind. "Mort told me Copper Springs is having a Founder's Day get-together in two weeks. He said there would be dancing. How about if I collect my dance then?"

"I hadn't planned on going to the celebration, but then, I thought Gram and I would be mourning the loss of the ranch."

"I hope you will reconsider."

She saw his chest rise and fall as he waited for her answer. "Yes. I would like that."

"Now that's settled, and I can talk to you about something Mort and I wanted to do tomorrow—with your approval, of course. Mort told me that you had always wanted to buy stock from the Granger ranch to breed with your longhorns."

"It was simply a wish, nothing more." She watched him closely. "Do you have that kind of money after today?"

He still had the five thousand dollars he'd won in the poker game and the credit Chantalle had arranged for him at the bank. "Money is not a problem. What do you think?"

"Mr. Granger has hardy stock from some experimental breeding he's done over the years. I think they would breed well with my . . . with our longhorns."

"Then Mort and I will ride over there tomorrow and talk to him. I also made some other decisions that I was going to speak to you about in the morning." He ran his hand through his hair. "I asked Ortega to be your foreman. He's loyal, and he stayed even when you couldn't pay him. He seems to be in good health, and he knows everything there is to know about this ranch."

She tried to ignore the tightening in her chest. "Ortega is the perfect man for the job. We had a foreman when my brother ran the ranch, but he joined the war with Matthew." She shrugged. "After that, there was no need for a foreman—we had no cowhands left."

"I asked Ortega to start hiring more men. We'll need them when we buy more cattle. The way I see it, we have to spend money to make money. What do you think?"

"In ranching that's exactly what you have to do to succeed." She looked bewildered and worried. "Are you sure we have the money to hire more men?"

"I'm sure."

Jackie nodded, not really understanding where all his money was coming from. Surely Miss Beauchamp hadn't given him money for hiring men and buying cattle. "Gram said to tell you that she would have Matthew's room ready for you tomorrow. You can't go on sleeping in the barn."

"Tell Nada I said thank-you."

It seemed intimate in the barn with just the two of them in the half light. Jackie watched the light from the lantern flicker across Whit's chiseled face. His eyes seemed to hold an invitation for her, but she dared not do anything rash again after telling him she wouldn't. Jackie knew she should return to the house before she did something she'd be sorry for.

"I'll say good night now."

"Good night, Jackie."

He watched her move away, his gaze on the swinging of her hips. She was driving him crazy.

Chapter Twenty-five

Whit knocked on the kitchen door, then waited for either Nada or Jackie to answer.

It was Jackie who held open the screen door. "You don't need to knock; just come on in," she told him.

"I wasn't sure."

Jackie felt the heat of his amber gaze and stared over his shoulder, knowing she'd be lost if she looked into his eyes. "Gram fixed Matthew's room for you. She said to tell you to bring your things in."

"Thank you." He removed his hat and stepped inside. "I have something I want to show you in the corral. Do you have time to come with me?"

To the ends of the earth, she thought, finally meeting his gaze. She glanced out the screen door, but the view of the fenced-off remuda was obstructed by the barn. "What is it?" she asked curiously.

"You'll just have to come and see, won't you?" He nodded at the water pitcher on the table. "But first, do you mind if I have a drink?"

She stepped to the table, poured a glass, and

handed it to him. His fingers brushed hers, and she drew back so quickly she almost spilled the water. His sensuous gaze made her heart beat twice as fast as normal.

"Mort seemed mighty pleased with himself when he was here this morning, but he wouldn't say why. Would it have anything to do with Mr. Granger's cattle?"

"My, my, but you are inquisitive. Why don't you just come and see for yourself?" He held the door open and swept his hand forward, indicating she should precede him. Placing his hat on his head, he followed her across the backyard toward the barn.

They walked side by side, both lost in their own thoughts. Whit wondered how he would ever break down the barrier that stood between him and Jackie. Jackie wondered why her knees went weak every time she was near Whit. Even the sound of his long strides as his boots scattered the gravel they walked through caught her attention. She was so attuned to every move he made and so aware of him as a man.

When they went past the barn and approached the corral, Jackie clasped her hands, and joy washed over her.

"It's my bull!" She turned to him with happiness dancing in her eyes. "Whit, you brought him home!"

He loved seeing her eyes sparkle with happiness. She'd had so little pleasure in her life, he wanted to make her smile every day. He wanted all of her days to be carefree, like now. "You seemed to be partial to him, and since you risked your life to save his, I thought he should be with you."

With as much gracefulness as she could manage,

she scrambled over the fence and made her way to the young bull. Running her hands through the thick coat of hair, she bunched it at the animal's nape. "I never thought I'd see him again." She turned to Whit, filled with gratitude. "Thank you."

His tone was deep, and there was a tightening in his throat as he replied, "It was my pleasure."

Jackie realized she was staring at Whit, and she lowered her head, rubbing the bull's ear. She didn't have the words to thank him for all he'd done for them.

"He hasn't been fed yet. Ortega just brought him home. I'll get him some hay." Whit moved toward the barn, and Jackie stared after him, watching the way his shirt stretched across his broad back. He was almost beautiful, if a man could be called that and still be manly. Whit was very manly. She ached with longing, wanting him and knowing it could never be. He'd certainly made that clear—several times. She had to remind herself that just because he was helping her, it didn't mean his heart was involved in the least.

After he'd returned with a pitchfork of hay and tossed it to the bull, Jackie climbed back over the fence, and they both watched the bull for a moment.

"He's a wonderful animal," Jackie said.

"He's a nuisance," Whit reminded her. "Mr. Booth was more than happy to sell him back to us for the same price he gave you. That devil broke down two of Mr. Booth's fences, wandered off twice, and destroyed most of Mrs. Booth's garden."

Jackie smiled and then laughed aloud. "He didn't!"

"I can assure you he did." A smile touched Whit's lips. "I have a message to you from Mr. Booth. He

said I was to tell you he'd never buy any cattle from
you that was spawned by Lucifer."

"Lucifer?"

"That's the name they gave him. And from what
I've seen of the little beast, it's a name he deserves."

Jackie laughed again, settling her chin on the folded
arms she'd propped on the top rail of the fence. "Lucifer. I think he can keep that name."

"A good idea, so no one will expect anything but
mischief from him."

Jackie watched Whit remove his hat and blot his
forehead on his sleeve. "Nevertheless," she said, "I'm
glad to have him home."

He walked back to the barn to return the pitchfork,
and she trailed along behind, reluctant to leave him.
"Whit," she said, trying to think of a reason to keep
him with her longer, "will you tell me about yourself?
I don't really know much about your life before you
came here."

He took her hand and seated her on a wooden keg,
then leaned against a post. "You deserve to know
about me, and I said I'd tell you if you wanted to
know."

"I do."

"Where shall I start?"

She held her hands demurely in her lap. "Tell me
about your childhood. I know your family was once
prominent in Galveston society."

"At one time we were, yes." Whit had not told anyone about his past, other than the bits and pieces he'd
told Chantalle. He wanted Jackie to have the full
picture. She would probably despise him when she

learned how he'd deserted his young sisters, and how they had both died as a result.

"My story isn't a pretty one. My mother left my father and went off with another man to New Orleans, I think."

He waited. Jackie said nothing.

"I can never remember if my father gambled away the shipping business before or after my mother left. I was just nine at the time, so my memory of the events is quite vague."

"It couldn't have been easy for you."

"It was very hard. I was the eldest of my family. Drew is one year younger than me; my sister, Laura Anne, was only two at the time; and the baby, Jena Leigh, was only a year old." He took a deep breath. Saying the names brought back the ache inside him. "My father took us to my aunt and uncle near Pecos, where he left us. He went off to California, or so he said at the time."

Whit watched Jackie's face, dreading the moment when he would see the curiosity in her eyes turn to pure scorn. "I won't go into any of the details about the time we spent with our aunt and uncle, except to say that when my aunt died, my uncle took us to an orphanage in El Paso."

Whit watched the curiosity in Jackie's gaze turn to pity, and he didn't want anyone, especially her, to pity him. She sat there, so prim and proper, with her untamed red hair falling about her face in wild disarray.

"You haven't had an easy life, have you, Whit? I know you have been searching for your brother, but where are your sisters? You have never spoken of them before now."

He lowered his head, wondering if he could tell her about the darkness that had been eating away at him for years. "They're both dead."

He watched a lone tear trail down her cheek. "Whit, I'm so sorry. What a tragedy."

"Don't waste any of your pity on me, Jackie. I don't deserve it. It's because of me that Laura Anne and Jena Leigh are dead. It's my fault that I lost touch with Drew."

"I don't believe you," she declared loyally. "None of what happened could be your fault."

"But it is."

She tried to think of something to say, something that would take the conversation in a different direction. "What was it like when you lived at the orphanage?" After the words left her mouth, she wished she could call them back. That couldn't have been a good experience for Whit.

"As strange as it may sound, it wasn't so bad there. Mrs. Kingsley, who was the matron, was one of the kindest women I've ever known. She saw that we all had a fine education. She was patient and caring, and she left her mark on my life. As a matter of fact, when I came to know Nada, she reminded me of Mrs. Kingsley."

"Do you visit her often?"

His head dropped as if she'd just delivered him a mortal blow. "Mrs. Kingsley died in the fire, probably trying to rescue the children."

Jackie reached out her hand to him, and then let it fall back to her lap. When he raised his head, his eyes were shimmering, and she could see that he was still

286

suffering over what had happened. "We don't have to talk about this any more if you don't want to."

"I want you to know everything." His voice was gruff, and it took him a few moments to speak. "I left the orphanage when I turned eighteen and went to California in search of my father. I won't bore you with any of the details of that search. I didn't find him. And I can only assume he didn't want to be found, or else he's dead."

"Maybe he's looking for you," she said with hope in her voice.

"I don't think so. I haven't been that hard to find."

Jackie lapsed into silence.

"By the time I returned to El Paso . . ." He paused and stared up at the loft, not wanting her to see the despair in his eyes. "When I returned, I discovered the orphanage had burned down, and my sisters had died in the fire."

Jackie's hand flew to her mouth to smother a sob. Whit was hurting, and she wanted to take him in her arms and hold him until the sadness passed. "Whit. How can any of that be your fault?"

He glanced back at her, expecting to see the disgust he'd dreaded. Instead her eyes were shining with unshed tears, her expression one of horror. "It's my fault because my father trusted me to take care of my brother and sisters," he explained. "I should have been their protector, and I wasn't there when they needed me the most."

"Your father put a terrible burden on you at such a young age. You have become judge and jury, convicting yourself, when none of what happened was your fault. A mother and father are supposed to care for their children—the child that you were could not have been . . ." She had to stop for a moment, because she couldn't speak past the lump in her throat. She swallowed several times, now understanding the anguish she'd often seen in Whit's eyes. His tragedy only made her love him more. "Someone should have been taking care of you. Don't carry the guilt that by rights belongs to others."

He wanted to believe her. He yearned for the day when he could cast off the burden he'd carried for so long.

"For good or bad, Jackie, you know the worst of me. I don't ask you to understand. I only thought you should know."

She was fighting the urge to go to him, to pull his head onto her shoulder and make the pain go away. "I don't think less of you after what you've told me—I think more of you. I have seen your determination to find your brother. I hope you do find him, Whit, so he can convince you that none of what happened is your fault. I do so hope you find him."

He turned away from her under the pretense of trimming the wick on a lantern. "I have never told another living soul that story, Jackie."

She slowly stood. "Thank you for telling me. I should go in now."

He took a deep breath and watched her leave. When she thought over what he'd told her, she'd come to the realization that the guilt was his. If he'd been at the orphanage when it burned, he could have saved his sisters—or he could have died with them.

*   *   *

The day had been long for Jackie. It had started out joyously, with Whit taking her to . . . Lucifer. But then learning about his past had taken the heart right out of her. She had hoped to see Whit at supper, but Mort said Whit had ridden out to see about the cattle that had been delivered that day.

She walked down the hallway and entered her bedroom, quietly washed her face and dried it, undressed, and slipped into her nightgown. She climbed into bed and buried her head in her pillow, finally allowing the tears to flow. "Whit," she whispered. "You didn't do anything wrong."

The fact that he'd suffered grievously over the death of his sisters wasn't fair. His father had put an onerous burden on the shoulders of a very young boy—but Whit, being the kind of person he was, assumed the obligation, proving his honorable character. It was unfair that he should have been made to feel responsible for his brother and sisters.

Jackie wondered if Whit had ever had anyone to look after him. She wanted to be the woman who made him smile again—not just a superficial smile, but one that would go all the way to his heart.

But so far, knowing her certainly hadn't made his life any easier. She knew now why he'd help them save the ranch. Whit seemed to feel that if he could do something for someone else, it would help take away part of the guilt he carried around with him.

Jackie pounded her pillow in frustration.

He hadn't done anything wrong—why couldn't he see that?

Jackie had made a decision: after today she would no longer go around mooning over him, making him want to bolt because of her boldness. And when he did leave to continue the search for his brother, she wanted him to go on his way without carrying guilt on his shoulders for any reason.

That was what it meant to love someone—to be able to let them go when they no longer wanted to stay.

Jackie could only imagine the torture Whit had lived with every day of his life. There was nothing she could do to make it better for him.

No one could give him back the family he'd lost.

She closed her eyes and said a prayer that Whit would someday find peace within himself.

Chapter Twenty-six

It was a hot day without a cloud in the sky when Whit dismounted and walked toward Ortega. Both men stood at the fence watching the two wranglers Ortega had hired to drive the new cattle into a pen to be branded.

"I think those men will make good hands," Ortega told Whit. "The tall one is Bob Forester; he worked at the Diamond S for ten years. The short man is Manuel Garza—he is my cousin. We still need a dozen more riders."

"I trust your judgment. Do whatever you think best." Whit grinned at the foreman. "I had to vacate the barn so those two could sleep there until the bunkhouse is finished." He shoved his hat back. "By the way, what happened to the original bunkhouse? A ranch this size must have had a big one to hold all the hands."

Ortega nodded. "There was a long cold snap two years back. It came early and stayed late. The old building was rotting and falling down anyway, so we used the lumber to keep warm all that winter."

He grinned. "I was not sure which was going to hold out the longest, the wood or the winter."

Whit watched the man called Bob close and fasten the gate while Manuel cut out one of the calves and threw a rope around its neck.

Whit pulled on his gloves and vaulted over the fence in time to grab the calf and flip it to the ground. He braced his knee against the animal's legs while Bob applied the branding iron.

It was late afternoon when the branding was finally finished, and the sun was touching the western horizon, throwing out colorful streaks across the heavens. Whit dismounted at the barn, and Mort hurried forward to take his horse.

"How'd the branding go?" the older man asked, unsaddling Whit's horse.

"All finished."

Mort was grinning. "It's looking like a working ranch 'round here."

Whit was hot, tired, and dusty. "My mouth feels like I swallowed half of the dirt on La Posada."

"I was to tell you when you got here that supper's waiting for you up to the big house."

Whit slapped his hat against his leg, sending dust flying. "Do the new hands have a place to sleep tonight?"

Mort nodded at two cots that had been set up in the barn. "Yeah. It ain't fancy"—he grinned—"but it'll be their home for a spell."

Whit removed his chaps and carried them to the tack room, hung them on a peg, then went outside to the water trough and pumped water, dousing his head, then washing his face and hands. He rubbed his boots on the back of his trousers in an attempt to remove most of the dust. His stride was long as he moved toward the house.

Jackie would be there.

Something had been missing when Whit awoke that morning.

Guilt.

Usually his first thoughts of the day were of Laura Anne, Jena Leigh, and Drew. But last night he had dreamed of Jackie, and when he awoke she was still on his mind. She had believed in him, and because she didn't think he was guilty of neglecting his sisters, he was beginning to believe it himself.

Could that be right?

Whit had no time to examine his feelings, because the object of his thoughts was standing at the back door waiting for him. It flashed through his mind that if he were her husband, she'd be waiting for him every evening when he came in from work. That thought almost sent him to his knees.

Jackie saw that Whit's hair was wet, and she knew he'd washed outside the barn. She took his hat. "You look tired, Whit."

"It's a good tired."

Nada was standing at the stove. "Sit yourself down and eat." She grinned at him. "It feels right to have a man come home covered with good, honest dust."

"I'll take a bath before I eat," he said apologetically.

Nada set his plate on the table. "No, you won't. If you want a bath, you can take it after you've eaten."

293

Constance O'Banyon

He sat down and watched Jackie working beside her grandmother. She wore a green gown with lace at the collar. Her hair was tied back with a strip of the same material as her gown. He'd never noticed what a woman wore until Jackie. He noticed everything about her.

Nada passed Whit a platter of steak and, once he was served, took a thick slice for herself. "The workmen came today to deliver the lumber for the new bunkhouse. They said they'd start work on it tomorrow. I told them you would let them know what you wanted done."

"I would imagine it should be built along the same lines as the old one. What do you think?"

Nada nodded. "I think I still have the plans up in the attic. I can take care of that for you. You have other things to do."

"I'll be leaving early in the morning for Galveston." He looked at Jackie and recognized the suspicion that flashed in her blue eyes "I have business there."

Jackie had very little to say for the rest of the meal, but Whit could read her like a book—she thought he was going to see a woman; and he was, but not for the reason she thought. He had to let Chantalle know that Angie was spying on her. It could be that Chantalle had already figured that one out, but he had to make sure.

After the meal, Whit had excused himself to take a bath and put on clean clothing. Nada and Jackie had moved his few possessions to the bedroom that had belonged to Jackie's brother. Now he pressed his hand

294

down on the mattress, thinking how good it would feel to sleep in a comfortable bed.

He was restless—too restless to go to sleep—so he walked quietly down the hallway, not wanting to awaken the women. He went out the front door, taking care that the screen door didn't slam.

The sky was alive with stars. He took a deep breath. He was beginning to think of this ranch as home, and that could be dangerous. Jackie was attracted to him—he knew that much—but he wasn't sure if her feelings went deeper than the pure lust that flamed between the two of them. He thought it did, but he could be wrong.

He heard the screen door open and knew it was her. "It's a nice evening."

She came up beside him. "Yes, it is." She glanced up at him. "I just wanted to tell you to be careful in Galveston."

"Why would you say that?"

"I know you had some kind of trouble there. Mr. Granger said a man named Simon Gault was asking him questions about you when he was in town last week. He said Mr. Gault didn't have a friendly attitude toward you."

"That's true." A breeze picked up a strand of her hair, and it fell across Whit's face. He paused in what he was saying. "I can't tell you why he wants to see me dead, because I don't know."

"But surely—"

He turned to her, his gaze dropping to her lips. "Jackie, the reason I am going to Galveston is to warn Chantalle about Simon. I think he has a spy in her house. He is a very dangerous man, and he may resent her for giving me the money to bid on La Posada."

"Then you must go and warn her." She touched his arm. "But please be careful. I wouldn't like it if anything happened to you."

He touched her cheek. "Do you worry about me, little redhead?"

"Someone has to."

"And you have appointed yourself as that person?"

"Yes. I think I have."

He drew her into his arms, unable to stop himself, and she allowed him to hold her close. "What are we going to do about us?"

Her voice shook with emotion. "I don't know."

Whit tilted her chin so he could see her face. "Right now, although I shouldn't, I'm going to kiss you."

Her eyes fluttered shut, and she gave her lips up to his skillful manipulation. Desire sizzled between them as he pulled her against him, and she felt him harden. Her lips opened, and she groaned when his tongue caressed and played tag with hers.

With a sharp breath, Whit raised his head, pressing his face against hers. His voice was deep, and he was breathing hard. "I needed that to carry me through the next few days, when I won't be able to see you."

"Oh, Whit. What is this feeling between us? Is it what you said it was before, or will it burn itself out?"

"It will never burn itself out." He touched his mouth to her cheek, and against his will his hand went up to cup her breast, bringing a gasp from her. "I know because it's such a powerful feeling. I've never felt anything like it before you."

She closed her eyes as warmth spread through her

body. His hand had slipped between the buttons on her blouse, and he was softly caressing her nipple. "I swore I wouldn't let this happen again," she said breathlessly.

"Nothing in this world can keep me from touching you, unless you don't want me to."

She placed her hand over his. "I want you to."

His body was trembling with need, but he withdrew his hand. "As you know, I can't keep my hands off you. I don't seem to have much willpower where you're concerned."

She touched her lips to his cheek. "Take care of yourself, and come back soon."

"I will see you Saturday night. We have a dance, remember? Wear your prettiest gown for me."

Jackie backed toward the door. "I will."

Whit watched her disappear inside, and he turned back to gaze to the heavens. Happiness was almost within his reach. If he was lucky, he'd win the highest stakes he'd ever wagered.

Jackie.

There was a sharp breeze blowing in off the gulf, making the air smell like salt. Chantalle gripped a pair of shears and was clipping roses and placing them in a basket so she could display them on the piano.

"A flower among roses," a deep voice said from behind her.

She spun around and smiled brightly at Whit. "A faded bloom among rosebuds," she said with humor.

"Not you. You'll never fade."

"Enough flattery," she said, leaning forward and kissing his cheek. "What brings you to Galveston?"

He saw Will walking toward them. "Can we talk somewhere?"

She handed her basket of roses to Will. "In my office. But let's go up the back stairs so no one will see you."

Moments later Whit was seated in a chair, with Chantalle behind her desk. "You handsome devil, what are you doing here? I thought nothing could pry you away from that beautiful little redhead."

He frowned. "I had to come. I think you might be in danger."

She sat forward in her chair. "What do you mean?"

"I think Angie is reporting everything you do to Simon. Who else could have told him I was planning to bid on La Posada? I'm afraid she's become a danger to you."

Chantalle nodded. "I know she's spying. And Simon hasn't been here since he returned from the bidding. If I know him, he's sulking. But his needs will soon drive him back to his room down the hall."

"Will ought to start sleeping in the house—you need to lock your door when you go to bed. And I'd feel better if you'd hire a couple of guards."

She sat back and smiled warmly. "You rode all the way here because you're worried about me?"

"I'm worried about a dear friend who came to my aid when I needed help."

His softly spoken words went right to Chantalle's heart. "I don't want you to worry about me. Simon is not a threat to me, because he needs the services I can provide him. The time may come when that will change, but not yet."

"You mean to allow him to come here after all he's done?" Whit asked in disgust.

"It's a way to keep an eye on him. You are in more danger from him than I am."

"You're sure he won't come after you?"

"As sure as I can be." She grinned. "Since you came riding to my rescue, I'm going to feed you the best dinner in town."

"What about Angie?" Whit wanted to know.

"There again, it's better to have her where I can watch her."

Whit saw Chantalle's eyes darken. "I've learned that it is in my best interest to feed Angie misinformation. After a while, her benefactor will turn on her. When Simon realizes she's giving him false information, she'll be in trouble with him. He'll think she's making it up just to get his money."

"You're cunning, Chantalle." A grin curved Whit's lips. "You have a devious mind. I'm glad you're on my side—I wouldn't want you for an enemy."

"Someone as handsome as you, my enemy? Not in this lifetime."

Whit became serious again. "Nonetheless, promise me you'll be careful."

"I promise." She stood. "Now about that meal I promised you . . ."

Chapter Twenty-seven

The community building was bursting with people. Music filtered through the town, and red-white-and-blue banners were draped beneath ropes strung across the streets. Speeches had been delivered commemorating Founder's Day, and fireworks lit the sky near the fairgrounds.

Although Jackie's gown, a yellow calico with puffed sleeves, was hopelessly out of fashion, it was her favorite. She had swept her hair up and away from her face, allowing one long winding curl to hang over her shoulder.

Jackie knew everyone in Copper Springs, and they all had questions about the auction. Jackie and Nada had known the questions would come up, and they decided simply to tell everyone that Whit Hawk was a partner who had invested in the ranch. It was the truth.

Jackie had danced with several partners, but she was worriedly watching the entrance. Whit had said he'd be there, but it was getting late.

Suppose something had happened to him?

What if that man, Simon Gault, had hurt Whit in some way?

She had almost worked herself into a state, just thinking of the possibilities of what could have happened to Whit.

There would be only two or three more dances before midnight, when the planning committee would bring the festivities to a close. Whit would come—he'd said he would.

Hutch tapped Jackie on the shoulder, and she spun around, thinking it was Whit. He must have read the disappointment in her eyes.

"I couldn't get close enough to you before now to ask for a dance. This one's mine."

She nodded, not really wanting to dance with Hutch. The music started, and he swung her around in a lively jig. There was no chance for conversation, because they had to change partners and then dance back together again. When the dance was finally over, Hutch kept Jackie beside him.

"Everyone's saying you are going to marry Hawk." His voice had an edge to it. "Is that true?"

"Hutch, who I marry is none of your business."

His grip tightened on her arm. "I want an answer now! I think I deserve one. Are you going to marry Hawk or not?"

Whit walked into the hall, his gaze roaming over the crowd, looking for his little redhead. When he saw her, she was with a man he didn't know and already didn't like. His jaw tightened in displeasure, and then he smiled. Jackie was breathtaking in her yellow gown. Even from this distance he could see how

301

creamy and smooth her shoulders were in the off-the-shoulder dress. He pushed his way through the crowd, moving in her direction.

"You haven't answered me, Jackie," Hutch said.

A shadow fell across Hutch's face. "I believe this is my dance," Whit said, his eyes like winter ice. "Remember, Jackie?"

Hutch hadn't yet released Jackie's arm, and the music had already started.

"Let go of her," Whit said in a cool voice that held the promise of retaliation if Hutch didn't comply with his demand.

Hutch's defiant eyes stared into cold amber ones that held a decided threat, and his hand dropped away from Jackie's shoulder.

Whit immediately swept Jackie into his arms. Not even on the day when she had danced in the meadow alone, dreaming of a man who would love her, could she have conjured up a more perfect dancing partner than Whit.

His breath stirred a curl near her ear, and she had to fight the urge to melt into him. "I am dusty from the road," he apologized. "If I'd taken time to go home and bathe, I'd have missed our dance."

Jackie saw the tired lines under Whit's eyes. "You rode all the way without stopping, didn't you?"

"Yes. Tonight belongs to me." Whit closed his eyes as Jackie followed his lead, turning when he turned, stepping sideways when he did; each move they made was in perfect unison. Whit knew she was the only woman for him. He wanted her as his wife, as the mother of his children, to be beside him in good times and bad. He'd known that from the first day; he was now ready to make a commitment.

He glanced at Jackie's soft, inviting lips and then raised his gaze to the eyes that haunted him even in his dreams. "I suppose that man I had to wrestle for this dance is the same one who proposed marriage to you."

"That's right. His name is Hutch Steiner. His father wants him to marry me so he can gain the respectability of an alliance with the Douglas family."

"I somehow don't think that was his only reason for asking you to marry him."

"Well, it's the most important reason to Hutch."

Whit remembered the possessive way Hutch Steiner had held Jackie's arm, and jealousy shot through him. Jealousy was a new experience for him, and he didn't like the feeling. Jackie had no idea how beautiful she was or what effect she had on the men around her. Even now, as he glanced about the room, most of the men were tracking her with their gazes. She was a seductress, with beautiful red hair and a face that would make the angels cry with envy.

Whit had not been able to concentrate on anything today but Jackie. After the night he'd told her about his past, it had seemed as if a floodgate had opened, washing away all his guilt, making him want to look toward the future and put the past where it belonged—in the past.

His mouth touched her ear, and he didn't care if everyone was watching. "Marry me instead, Jackie," he said, his grip tightening on her hand. "Say you will be my wife." His fingers slid across the top of her hand, caressing, touching. "I need you with me."

She wanted to cry—she wanted to shout to the world that the man she loved, loved her. "Yes," she said without even hesitating. She would not pretend to be coy with Whit. She wanted only truth between them. He was the man she loved, and she wanted to be his wife. "I will marry you, Whit."

The music had stopped and yet the two of them stood there holding hands, gazing into each other's eyes, unaware that everyone was speculating about what they were saying to each other.

Nada, who had been talking to Edith Steiner, laughed and nodded toward her granddaughter and Whit. "It looks like Whit has finally asked Jackie to marry him. If I'm any good at guessing, I say there'll be a wedding in the family before long."

Edith looked peeved and grasped her fan in her slender hand, stabbing the air. "My husband had hoped Jackie would marry our son, Hutch. They always got along so well together."

Nada shook her head. "I don't think that's even a remote possibility now."

Whit badly wanted to kiss Jackie, but he was suddenly aware that they were the center of attention. "Let's get Nada and go home. I need to be alone with you."

Jackie's eyes were sparkling with tears as Whit led her to her grandmother. "We're ready to go home, Gram," Jackie said, still staring at Whit.

After they had worked their way through the crowd, saying good night to everyone, Whit tied the reins of his horse to the buggy and then helped Jackie and her grandmother inside.

"I'll drive you home," he said, sliding onto the seat.

Nada planted herself between Whit and Jackie. She knew the two young people had just admitted they loved each other, and they would have a lot to talk about when they arrived at the house. But in the meantime, Nada would direct the conversation in the way she wanted it to go.

"Sure is a nice evening," Nada remarked as Whit took up the reins.

"Yes, it is," Jackie replied, unable to contain her happiness. She wanted to be in Whit's arms; she wanted to feel his lips on hers. She sat with her hands clutched together in her lap.

"How was your trip to Galveston, Whit?" Nada asked.

He was distracted and hadn't heard her. Nada smiled and said, "Whit?"

"I'm sorry, Nada; I didn't hear what you said. I was thinking about something else."

She chuckled to herself. "I was just asking about your little trip to Galveston, and how that went."

The moon was bright, and there were several buggies ahead of them; one turned off into a lane that led to a ranch. "Everything went fine," he said, guiding the buggy around a bump in the road. "I hurried back as quick as I could. My business didn't take long." He didn't tell Nada that he'd ridden like hell to get to Copper Springs in time to dance with Jackie tonight.

The trip continued with Nada asking questions, and Whit and Jackie answering. At last she decided to get right to the point. "Have either of you got anything you want to tell me?"

They had drawn up to the house, and Whit turned to Nada. "I do. I have just asked your granddaughter to marry me, and she's said yes. Do we have your blessing?"

Nada said nothing until Whit had helped her and Jackie out of the buggy. "You have my blessing, Whit." She reached up and kissed his cheek, and then clutched her granddaughter's hand. The two women stared into each other's eyes in understanding, and then Nada smiled. "I guess you know what you're doing, Whit—she's going to cause you nothing but trouble."

"I already know that," he replied, smiling tenderly at Jackie.

Nada started for the house. "Although I know the two of you have a lot to talk about, don't stay up too late. This is a working ranch."

Jackie and Whit watched Nada disappear into the house, and then he turned to her, taking her hand and placing it over his heart. "I did hear right. You did say you would marry me?"

She moved closer and laid her head against his chest. "Yes. I can't think you would ever have had any doubt."

He broke away for a moment and untied his horse from the back of the wagon. He then took her hand and led her and the horse toward the barn, needing to be alone with her. Bob and Manuel had not yet returned from the dance. But when they entered the barn, to their disappointment, Mort was there. He came forward and took Whit's horse and backed it into a stall, then went about unsaddling the animal.

Jackie and Whit stared at each other, waiting for him to leave.

"I'll just go get the team and put them in the corral.

Night," he said at last, looking from one to the other, smiling and walking toward the door. He'd known Whit had something important he wanted to say to Jackie. He ambled toward the buggy to unhitch the horses. Everything was settling down around the place. Whit had come into Jackie's life and made it good for her.

Whit pulled Jackie into his arms. "Now I'm going to kiss you the way I've wanted to since that first day."

She touched his face, loving him in every way. "You talk too much, cowboy."

Her lips were soft and parted under the insistence of his mouth. Desire spread through him like a hot knife through soft butter. He clasped the small of her back to bring her closer, but it would not be close enough until he had nothing between them but bare skin.

He raised his head. "How do you suppose Nada knew I was going to ask you to marry me?"

Her laughter bubbled out and warmed his heart. "Gram is a very wise woman. And she already knew how I felt about you."

"Did she now?"

"From the very beginning."

Whit touched his lips to her cheek. "Mmm. I want you." His voice was rough, but his lips were gentle when he took possession of hers. His breathing was heavy when he finally raised his head.

"That day you came dancing into my life, you were brighter than the sun to me. You made me think of settling down and having a home."

Happiness burst through Jackie. "I never thought

you saw me that way. I was so embarrassed that you caught me dancing barefoot."

"I could hardly concentrate on anything we said as we walked to the house that day. I had never felt that way about a woman before, and I didn't know what to do about you."

"I felt the same way. I knew that day that you were the one I had been waiting for. The one I was dancing for."

He smiled down at her. "Am I?"

"Yes." She framed his face with both hands and tip-toed to reach that wonderful mouth. When Jackie touched his lips, she put all her tender feelings in the kiss.

Whit's heart was about to burst out of his skin. He kissed her eyes, her cheek, brushed her lips, and then his mouth moved slowly down her neck. Her fingers splayed through his hair as his mouth touched the curve of her breast.

Suddenly he raised his head and stepped back. "I lost my head again. I always do with you."

She no longer had to dream and hope that the right man would wander into her life—he already had. Whit hadn't said he loved her yet. But that was only because he hadn't trusted many people in his life, and it was hard for him to open himself to love.

Jackie watched a muscle contract in Whit's throat, and she wondered if tonight was as magical for him as it was for her. "I want to make you a good wife, Whit."

"You will, sweetheart," he said, pulling her closer. "I never had any doubt of that." He touched his lips to the top of her head, and she smelled of vanilla and honey. He wanted to release her hair so it would tumble down her back. He wanted to bury himself in her body and make love to her all night. His body swelled and ached. "How soon can we be married?" His voice came out in a whisper.

Jackie had never been a demure young woman. Nada had brought her up to be honest and to state her true feelings—to speak her mind. "I hope it will be very soon."

There was an urgency in his voice. "Talk to Nada—tell her we don't want to wait."

She pressed her head against his chest, feeling the powerful thundering of his heart against her cheek. "I will. Gram will understand."

He took her arm and led her toward the house. "You go on in. I need to get you a safe distance from me."

"I trust you. You have always been the one to stop us when we would have gone too far."

He gave her that slow smile that melted her bones.

"The danger is that I now have the right to touch you." He pulled her back against him, his laughter deep. He felt real happiness for the first time since he could remember. "You belong to me now, my little redhead."

"And you belong to me," she answered.

Whit looked astonished for a moment. He had never belonged to anyone, and the feeling sent a jolt through him.

Looking into his glorious golden eyes, which seemed to have captured the moonlight in their depths, she said softly, "I want sons with your amber eyes."

He grabbed her so quickly she couldn't catch her breath. "And I want daughters with your glorious hair."

Whit suddenly became quiet, and then he said earnestly, "You have my promise that you'll be safe in my care, Jackie."

She knew in that moment that he was thinking about his sisters—and she knew he was thinking they hadn't been safe in his care. "I know I will." She raised her head, her tear-bright eyes glistening. "I will love you until the day I die."

"Jackie," was all he could manage to say.

She touched his cheek and then moved up the steps to the house. With a mischievous smile, she said, "Tomorrow I'll see if you have changed your mind about marrying me."

"Not a chance," he told her.

Whit stood there in the shadow of the house long after she had gone inside. "Jackie," he said with feeling, his eyes misting a bit.

She had brought him out of the dark into the light.

Chapter Twenty-eight

Nada placed coffee cups on the table while she listened to Jackie happily explain that she and Whit wanted to be married as soon as possible. Nada nodded, knowing it would be prudent to do just that, considering how the two of them felt about each other.

So far Whit had been the strong one. But with Jackie beaming and declaring her love for him, Nada didn't know how much longer he could hold out. She thought it was better for them to get married as soon as possible.

"Mort is going to take me to Copper Springs this morning for supplies. I'll make it a point to stop by to talk to Reverend Witherspoon and see if he can perform the ceremony next Saturday." She smiled at Jackie. "Will that be soon enough to suit you and Whit?"

"I wish it were today," Jackie said wistfully, pulling the curtains aside and looking toward the barn, watching for Whit to appear. He'd gotten up early and eaten while she still slept. She'd meant to make breakfast for him, but instead her grandmother had.

"Anyone who saw you and Whit together at the dance last night won't be surprised by the quick wedding."

Jackie was thoughtful for a moment. "Whit doesn't know many people in the county. Would it be all right with you if just Mort, Ortega, and Luisa are invited to the wedding? I would like to wear my mother's gown, and I'd like to be married here in this house, just as my mother was."

Nada was so happy, her heart was barely big enough to contain all she felt. "I was hoping you'd want to be married here. Virginia stood under the archway in the parlor when she married my son. I think about them every time I pass through that arch. Virginia was a good woman, and she made my son happy. Your grandfather married me when I was a young girl with very little family and no money at all. You and Whit will have some hard times ahead of you, but I'm not worried about either one of you."

"Grandpa was quite a catch, wasn't he?"

"The most sought-after bachelor in three counties. He was beautiful, and he had a big ranch and plenty of money." Nada hugged Jackie to her. "Your man is quite a catch, too. I saw a lot of women staring at him last night."

"Whit is perfect!"

A deep-toned voice spoke up behind Jackie. "Nada, you are my witness—if the time ever comes when your granddaughter finds a flaw in my character— which surely she will—you are to remind her that I'm perfect."

Jackie spun around. She felt awkward at first, wanting to walk into his arms, but their love was new, still untested. His expression was so soft as he looked at her, she could not find her voice.

"Nada, you didn't answer me," Whit said, his smile for Jackie. "You will bear witness that my bride-to-be just declared me to be perfect?"

Nada snorted. "Lovesickness. That's all it is. She'll get over it."

Whit drew Jackie into the circle of his arms and rested his chin on the top of her shimmering red hair. Neither said anything, because their hearts were too full. Nada bustled about the kitchen, trying to finish breakfast.

"Sit down and eat, both of you. You can't live on love alone."

Whit laughed softly, pulling out the chair for Jackie and then one for Nada. "I confess I'm hungry." His gaze fell lightly on Jackie, and she blushed, ducking her head, a trait he found very endearing in her.

Nada filled Whit's coffee cup with steaming brew. She had never seen his eyes sparkle quite so brightly. "I assume you still want to marry my granddaughter after having the night to think it over?"

"Yes, ma'am, I surely do."

Nada laughed. "Things are about to get interesting around here—we have a man in the house again, and soon we'll have little ones running around, getting underfoot. I sure have missed children. Every time I see Susan Gerrard bouncing her new great-grandchildren on her knee, I turn green with envy, and she lords it over me because she has three."

Whit's eyes widened. Children? Shock hit him—

then warmth spread through him, and he had to take a deep breath. Jackie had filled his life to overflowing. She would give him sons and daughters. After all the years of wandering alone, with so little hope, he had a reason for being—a family.

Nada sensed that the two young people wanted to be alone. "I ate hours ago," she said, hanging her apron on a hook and grabbing up her bonnet. "I'm going to gather tomatoes for supper tonight. You two go ahead and eat—or," she said shrugging, "just sit there staring at each other like you're doing now."

When the door slammed behind Nada, Whit held out his arms, and Jackie rose from her chair and ran into them. Their lips met in a hungry kiss, and he pressed her to him.

"I couldn't sleep last night," he said, drawing a tortured breath and kissing her eyelids and then along her jawline. "You were just down the hallway from me, and I was thinking how you'd look all curled up on your bed. Tell me again you'll marry me."

Her arms slid around his shoulders, and she nestled against his chest. "If you want out of this, you'd better run now, because I intend to have you for my husband."

"You'd better make it soon. I'm a very impatient bridegroom." He pressed her against his body, and she could feel the evidence of his impatience.

"Will Saturday be soon enough for you?"

"No." He tilted her chin. "But I have waited a lifetime for you; a few more days won't hurt. Much."

"Whit. I love you."

His mouth curved into a smile. "You have changed the course of my life." He touched her pert little nose.

"You have tried my patience at times; like the time you went after the cougar single-handedly. I fear my life is about to get a whole lot more complicated just trying to keep you out of trouble."

"You should keep me in your bed—that would keep me out of trouble."

His eyes widened, and his body reacted to her suggestion. "You're a bold little baggage. What kind of woman am I marrying?" he asked.

Jackie frowned, thinking he was serious. "It's not that. I just promised myself that when I met the man I wanted to spend the rest of my life with, I would always be truthful with him—with you."

He let out his breath and crushed her to him. "I am the luckiest man alive."

"Yes, you are," she told him, with mischief dancing in her eyes. "I was considered the most marriageable woman in two counties."

He poised his mouth just above hers. "And I'm supposed to wait until Saturday to find out why?"

She laughed aloud. "You are the one who said I should learn about the love between a man and a woman in the marriage bed."

She actually looked as if she were enjoying torturing him. He stepped away from her.

"I think we'd better eat before you start something I can't finish."

She watched his golden eyes flame, and her body responded, aching for what those eyes promised.

"I'll eat now."

Chapter Twenty-nine

The clouds were slate gray at sunrise. By midmorning a light mist fell; by noon a strong wind from the gulf had whipped the clouds away, then gentled to a soft breeze, giving Jackie a golden day for her wedding.

Nada fastened the tiny seed-pearl buttons at the back of Jackie's wedding gown, while smiling at her granddaughter in the mirror. "I only had to take a few tucks at the waist, and your mother's gown is a perfect fit for you. You are even the same height as your mother was. And you have her beautiful hair."

For a moment Jackie felt a pang of sadness that Virginia wasn't there to share in her happiness. She became pensive, thinking about the two brides who had stood before this beautiful gilded mirror that had been shipped to Texas by her great-grandmother. "I can almost envision Mama standing where I now stand, wearing this gown. She must have been beautiful in it."

Nada turned Jackie toward her. "She was a happy bride the day she married your father. I couldn't have loved her more if she'd been my own daughter. She was a good wife to my son, so why wouldn't I love her? And," Nada added, "I'm glad I can be with you today." She handed her granddaughter a fragrant bouquet of violets that Whit had given her earlier— the handsome rascal had told her the flowers reminded him of the color of Jackie's eyes. And so they did.

"I have never been as happy as I am today, Gram. I'm going to try to help Whit get past all the sadness he's suffered because of his sisters' deaths, and because he can't find his brother, Drew. I want to make him as happy as I am."

Nada's eyes misted. "I have no doubts about this marriage. Whit is the answer to my prayers for you. I could not have wished you a better, more honorable man for your husband."

Jackie took a deep breath. "I was lucky the day he came into my life."

Nada chuckled. "As I recall, that day you weren't happy about meeting him in the least."

Jackie nodded. "That's because he confused me right from the beginning, and I didn't like the way he made me feel."

"I know—I saw that right away."

Jackie turned back to the mirror and nodded. "I'm ready."

Jackie stood on the porch beside her new husband, watching Reverend Witherspoon help her grandmother into his buggy. Whit's hand was warm against the small of her back, and the lazy way it glided toward her shoulder and then back again made her close her eyes.

"I'll be coming home Saturday next," Nada said, distracting her granddaughter. "Have Mort come to town to fetch me."

"I will," Jackie called out, her heart giving a leap as Whit's hand paused at the back of her gown, and he undid one of the buttons.

He grinned down at her and drew her close against him. "You don't really think she's going to the house in Copper Springs because she needs to paint the shutters, do you?"

Jackie waved to her grandmother as they drove away. "I know for a certainty she's not. The shutters were painted last spring."

"Your grandmother is a very wise woman. She knows I want you all to myself."

She shyly glanced up at Whit, remembering the short ceremony that had made her Whit's wife. He was handsome in his black suit, and the white shirt he wore called attention to his deep tan. Her grandmother had worn a gray lace gown, looking lovely with her hair swept into a chignon. Ortega and Luisa had stood behind Whit and Jackie, both smiling and happy. Mort had worn his only suit, a brown tweed several decades out of style. She smiled, recalling how he'd plastered his unruly hair into place.

Whit brushed his mouth against the top of her head. "You're mine now." His mouth curved in a sensuous smile. "But you were mine the first moment I laid eyes on you—we just made it legal today."

"You were pretty sure of yourself, weren't you?"

"Not at all." His warm breath touched her mouth

for a quick kiss, and she imagined the deeper kisses that would come later. "I had to fight for you, little redhead." He tilted her head up. "You aren't disappointed because of the simple ceremony, are you?" A frown furrowed his brow.

"Everything was just the way I wanted it. I'm wearing the gown my mother wore when she married my father." She glanced into his eyes. "And as you say, I belong to you now."

Jackie felt the pressure of Whit's hand when he drew her tighter against him. "Happy?"

"Mmm. This is the best day of my life."

His laughter was deep as he took her hand and raised it to his lips. "Let's just see if we can make it even better."

Her heart was thundering as he led her into the house. It seemed to Jackie that her whole life had been leading her to this moment. She loved and respected Whit more than any man she'd ever known, and she wished she could express those feelings to him—she felt so much, words failed her.

His lips touched hers lightly, and then his arms tightened about her as he kicked the door shut behind them. "Now," he said, tilting her chin, "I can kiss you properly, Mrs. Hawk."

She trembled as his mouth laid siege to hers, and she clung to him, because her knees went weak as he deepened the kiss. He brought her tightly against his body, and she could hardly catch her breath. His golden eyes flamed as he lifted her into his arms, his fingers already unbuttoning the back of her gown.

Jackie ached with need—she had wanted to be with him for so long, and now she was ready to truly be his wife, although she was somewhat uncertain. She didn't exactly know what she was supposed to do.

"Sweetheart," he asked in a husky voice, "do you know what I said to myself when I first saw you?"

His hand brushed against her cheek, and she caught it in hers. "I imagine that you were wondering why I was dancing without a partner." She hid her face against his shoulder. It still embarrassed her to remember that day.

"No. That's not what I felt at all." He tilted her chin and made her look at him. "I told myself you were going to belong to me."

Her eyes widened in surprise as she looked up at him. "You didn't."

"I can assure you I did. You have caused me no end of trouble, and I think it's time you paid the price."

She arched her brow, laughing. "And just what do you have in mind?"

They had reached her bedroom. She and her grandmother had transformed it into a room where a man would feel comfortable. He slid her to her feet, but kept his hand on her arm. "Do you know I can hardly think straight when you are near me?" He moved her against the wall, pressing his body against hers. "I have wanted you from the very beginning. You've caused me too many sleepless nights, and I think it's time I retaliated."

Warmth rushed through her. "You want to cause me a sleepless night?"

He laid his cheek against hers. "In the worst way." Even as he spoke, he was preoccupied with unbuttoning her gown.

Her heart was so full she had to swallow twice before she could speak. "I do love you so, Whit."

"Loving you has brought me peace." He closed his eyes and rested his chin on top of her head. "You have helped heal my soul."

His words swelled in her heart. She couldn't have spoken if her life depended on it.

By now he'd unbuttoned her gown to her waist, and the frilly creation swished about her feet. He held his hands out for her inspection. "Look how I tremble, Jackie. You do this to me."

She clasped his hands between both of hers. "I know—me too," she admitted as she stepped out of her crinoline.

He slid his arms out of his suit coat and loosened his tie. He pulled it off with a jerk of impatience; all the while his gaze was brushing across Jackie's body, which was now covered only by a thin chemise. Night shadows crept into the room, but neither bothered to light the lamp.

Jackie watched as Whit undressed, but dropped her gaze when he removed his trousers. Her shyness passed in a moment, and she reached out and touched his chest, rubbing her palm over the curly black hair. When she glanced into his eyes, she saw the flames of desire flickering there. Her hand swept down his rib cage past taut muscles. Her fingers moved upward, because her imagination and her gaze would go no lower. Not yet—everything was too new for her.

Determined not to rush her, and wanting to make her first time unforgettable, he tried to keep his own desire under control. He placed one hand on her shoulder and raised her chin with the other. "I like it when you touch me."

She went into his arms and laid her head against his chest, feeling the heat of his naked flesh against her. "Whit," was all she could manage to say.

His palm slid down her arm to her hand, where he laced his fingers with hers. "I know what you are feeling, Jackie, and there is no reason to be afraid. I will be patient, and go as slow as you want me to." His voice deepened as he felt her firm breasts pressed against his chest. "You are my life, Jackie. I can't think how I existed before I met you."

She kissed his skin just below his shoulder blade and felt him tremble. "I want to be everything to you, Whit."

Slowly he eased the straps of her chemise off her shoulders and allowed the garment to slide to the floor. He took a step back and gazed upon the most beautiful sight he'd ever seen. The setting sun touched her skin, turning it a golden color, and he swallowed a lump in his throat.

Jackie's shyness left her when she saw such gentleness in his eyes. His gaze started at her hair and traveled downward, and she almost felt as if he were caressing her. She felt like a wanton where he was concerned. Her gaze started with his eyes, went to his broad shoulders, then traveled down his chest to his narrow hips. Her mouth went dry when her gaze dropped lower.

"It's dangerous for you to look at me like that," he warned with a deep groan, gathering her in his arms. His lips found hers and he lowered her to the bed without breaking off the kiss. She felt the mattress shift under his weight, and her arms slid around his shoulders. She turned her head toward the window and bit her lip when his hand brushed against her breast.

He touched her as he'd wanted to for so long. He examined the rosy tips of her breasts, then placed a kiss on each one. His hand moved over her stomach, between her thighs, to the tangle of curly red hair that stood between him and paradise.

"Jackie," he said in a strangled voice.

With the last dying rays of the sun she stared into the face of the most beautiful man she'd ever known. She didn't know what luck had brought him into her life, or what chance had made him love her, but he did. "I love you, Whit. So very much."

He closed his eyes and drew in a quick breath when her hand brushed against his erection, and she quickly pulled her hand away, as if she'd done something wrong. She had been born and raised on a ranch; she knew about mating, but not when it applied to her. "What must I do?" she asked in confusion.

"Touch me," he told her. "I want you to know my body, and I want to know yours."

She wanted to touch all of him—she ached for the moment he would make love to her. Shyly at first, she slid her hand down across his hip; then she grew bolder, blood coursing through her body like wildfire.

With a growl, he eased her onto her back. "Sweetheart, I told you I would go slow, and I will if I'm able—but I'm not sure I can hold back if you keep looking at me like that, and touching me like you are," he said almost as an apology. One long finger stroked across her breast, then circled the nipple. "I'll try, though.

"No." She brought his head down to hers, her lips close to his. "I don't want you to treat me like a porcelain doll. I won't break, Whit." She took his hand and put it on her breast. "I was created for you—don't you feel that?"

Flames danced in his eyes as he waged the battle to keep from spreading her legs and driving into her. Her breath teased his mouth, and when she pressed her body against his, he almost lost the battle.

He spread her legs as he bent to claim his kiss. He examined the soft curve of her hips. Although she wasn't a tall woman, her legs were long and perfectly shaped. His hand slid down her leg to the arch of her foot, while every instinct urged him to make her his. With a strength he didn't know he had, he took his time, exploring, wooing, lovingly stroking her skin.

Jackie's virginal body was issuing him an invitation as her hips swiveled toward him. When he looked into her passion-bright eyes he knew what she was feeling. He smiled. "Just enjoy what I do to you."

Sudden uncertainty hit her, chasing every other thought from her mind. What if she was inadequate, and unable to do what was expected of her? "What if you don't like me after we . . . when you . . ."

Her innocent plea made him swell and harden even more. "I will only love you more, if that is possible." He took her hand and held it to his face. "Jackie, what is about to happen between us was inevitable from the start, and we both knew it." He kissed along her throat. "That's because we both recognized that we were meant for each other."

"This is probably the most important moment of my life," she said shakily, feeling his hardness pressing between her legs.

Whit's mouth swept downward, brushing the smooth curve of each breast, and when she threw back her head and groaned, he lost the battle completely. A strong urgency slammed into him, and he gripped her hips, gritting his teeth. He stroked her with his other hand, his finger sliding into her moistness. He suddenly froze: for the first time he was afraid he might hurt her. "I'm big, Jackie, and you're tight and small."

"No," she said, her voice trembling with need. "Don't think that you will hurt me."

His finger slid farther inside her. Silk. Heat. He was helpless against the feelings that rocked his body. No woman, not even the most experienced he'd been with, had made his body ache with such fierce need. He supposed that was how it was when a man found the woman he loved. If merely touching her as he was did this to him, what would it be like when he slid into her body?

He kissed her hungrily, the tip of his tongue sliding into her mouth as he poised himself above her, then slowly eased into her. His body trembled, his heart slammed against the wall of his chest, and his breathing stilled.

Jackie gasped at the invasion, her body aching and throbbing for something just out of reach, something that was about to happen. Whit filled the void inside her while he stroked past the barrier and took her virginity. She felt a sharp sting, but it didn't last long. She slammed her hips against his in a fevered state, and squirmed, inviting him farther inside her.

Whit slid his hands beneath her hips, raising her to receive more of him. His heart was thundering, his breath trapped tightly in his chest. His mouth plundered hers, but he kept his rhythm slow, introducing himself to her tenderly, letting her feel the pleasure of their joining flesh.

Whit was overcome by a feeling that hit him like a storm tide slamming against rock. He had found and claimed the perfect woman for him. "Jackie . . ." He breathed her name like a prayer.

She grabbed his waist, meeting his thrusts, needing release, experiencing a pleasure beyond anything she could have imagined. Tears gathered in her eyes as her body became his.

Whit kissed her closed eyes, tasting the saltiness of her tears, and his eyes closed as he experienced a similar emotion. Passions rose; whispered words passed between kisses. Whit struck hard and deep now, and Jackie felt her body tremble over and over, and she cried out with joy.

The climax hit hard as Whit's seed spilled inside Jackie. She felt her body clutch again and again as she clung to him. His mouth closed over hers, and he felt another sensation building—it had never happened to him before, but he wouldn't be telling his bride that as his warmth poured into her.

He rolled her over on her side, keeping her tightly against him.

Deep blue eyes stared into amber. "I never knew it would be like this," she admitted.

"Neither did I." He kissed her cheek, her eyelids, then along her neck. He rested his head against her breasts and closed his eyes, wanting to think about what had just happened between them. He felt her fingers slide into his hair and he had the sudden feeling that he had just come home.

"How often can we do this?"

His laugh was swift and deep. "As often as I'm able."

She cupped his head between her hands and gazed into his eyes. "I'm going to take care of you, Whit. In every way."

"I believe you just did, Mrs. Hawk."

Then he went quiet, thinking about his struggle to get to this time in his life. He'd never expected to have a normal life—never thought he deserved one—but he did now. "I love you." The admission was torn from his throat. Saying it out loud freed more of his tortured soul.

"I know you do." She moved back and propped her head on her hand. "I want you to understand that I know you will still want to search for your brother. If you have to leave for a while, I'll understand that as well."

He stroked his hand down the curve of her breast, then cupped it in his hand, lowering his head to place a kiss there. "I won't be leaving you, Jackie. Not if I can help it. I want you by my side for the rest of our lives."

She glanced into his eyes and saw renewed passion flaring there.

"Are you sore?" he asked, massaging gently between her legs.

327

His movement brought a groan from her, but it wasn't from being sore. "You can't hurt me with love, Whit."

He wondered if she knew how adorable she was with her honesty. "Come here, you," he said, flipping her onto her back.

They made love and talked most of the night. Jackie finally fell asleep with her head resting on Whit's arm. He gathered her close, thanking God for the day his horse had thrown a shoe—otherwise he would have ridden past the secluded meadow, and his path never would have crossed Jackie's.

Jackie.

Chapter Thirty

It was still two hours before sunup when Whit gently shook Jackie's shoulder. Her eyes slowly opened, and then she smiled lazily up at him.

"Is it time for me to make your breakfast?"

"Not yet. I have a surprise for you. Hurry. Get up and get dressed."

She leaned on an elbow, staring at him. He was already dressed. "Why?"

"Don't ask questions, just get dressed."

She was puzzled, but she smiled and slipped into the gown he tossed her.

"Don't bother with your shoes," he said when she reached for them. He lifted her in his arms and kissed her soundly. Then he carried her out of the room, through the kitchen, out the back door, and toward the barn.

"Whit," she said, snuggling in his arms, and looked into his liquid gold eyes. "What are you doing?"

"I'm going to make all your dreams come true."

She was still puzzled when he set her on her feet and

saddled his horse. Climbing into the saddle, he
reached down and swung her up in front of him, settling her across his thighs.

He nudged the horse forward, and they rode out of
the barn and across the pasture. He kissed her often,
touched her breasts, and nuzzled her neck. Happiness
burst through her heart when she realized where he
was taking her.

The meadow where he'd first seen her.

When they reached the exact spot where he'd found
her, he handed her down and dismounted. "Now," he
said, smiling. "what was that tune you were humming
the day I first heard your beautiful voice?"

" 'Greensleeves,' " she told him.

He took her hand in one of his and slid the other
around her waist just as rain started to fall. "Dance
with me," he said. "And sing with me."

Jackie's heart was so full she couldn't utter a word
at first. But Whit swung her around the meadow,
humming the tune in a deep baritone voice, and she
soon joined him.

She had trodden barefoot on this very ground, feeling alone and helpless at a time when her world had
been tumbling down around her. Then Whit entered
her life and made everything right.

They whirled and danced as the rain continued
to fall. Their voices blended sweetly, and in the falling rain, Jackie never knew that Whit had tears in
his eyes.

Ortega rode up the hill, looking for Lucifer, who had
crashed through a fence again in another bid for freedom. That crazy bull was more trouble than he was

worth. He'd been forced to drop everything to search for the devil, and in the rain, too, so it was hard to track the villain.

Ortega reined in his mount and stared at the sight in the meadow just beyond the cedar brush. Jackie and Whit were dancing in the rain. He felt like an intruder, so he quietly backed his horse up, turned it around, and rode back the way he'd come.

A smile creased Ortega's face. Jackie had been barefoot, and he'd heard the beautiful blending of their voices.

Whit's mouth touched Jackie's earlobe, then went on to explore her jawline, her eyes. He watched as her blue gaze ignited with aching need, the same urgency he was feeling.

"This is the second-best present you have given me since we were married," she told him breathlessly.

He swung her under his arm and caught her around the waist again. "And what was the first best?"

She laughed up at him. "When you take me back to the house, I'll show you."

Whit stopped, just holding her. He no longer felt lonely—he had a family. And he had all the love he could handle in this one little redhead looking at him now with a puzzled expression.

"Don't you want to know what the first-best present is?"

His mouth came down quickly and hungrily against hers, and after a long, drugging kiss that left her gasping, he said against her lips, "I already know. And I think I'll cut this dance short." His mouth swept across hers; then he settled for a lingering kiss.

331

He lifted her into his arms, saying thickly, "I'm taking you home right now."

Her head fell back on his shoulder as he mounted and turned the horse toward the house. She had danced in the meadow with him, the meadow where he had first stolen her heart.

"Mrs. Hawk?"

"Yes, Mr. Hawk?"

"Will you dance with me for the rest of our lives together?"

Joyous laughter burst from her lips. "I will dance with you, or I'll have no other partner."

Later, when Ortega sat at the kitchen table and Luisa placed his supper before him, he raised a spicy sausage to his mouth and paused to look at his wife. They had been married for thirty years, and although Luisa's dark hair was streaked with gray, she was as beautiful to him as she'd been the day he had first seen her.

Ortega thought of the sight he had witnessed in the meadow and asked, "Luisa, would you ever consider dancing barefoot in the rain with me?"

She looked at her husband as if he'd lost his mind, and said as much. "¿Tú estás loco en la cabeza?"

He laughed at her startled expression and settled back against his chair. "No. I am not crazy." He took a bite of his sausage and nodded his head. "Maybe they are so much in love they did not notice it was raining. It was that way with me when I had the fire in me for you." He thought for a moment. "The fire is still there," he said in amazement.

Her hands went to her hips, and she tapped her foot impatiently. "Of what are you speaking?"

"Nothing," he said, reaching for his second tortilla. He smiled. Everything was going to be all right for his little *chiquita*.

Epilogue

It had been raining hard all morning, but now only a light mist was falling. Jackie had been watching out the kitchen window for Whit to come home. She had turned away to take a cherry pie out of the oven when she heard his booted footsteps coming up the back steps.

When Whit opened the door, Jackie went flying into his arms. He held her against him, almost losing his balance and laughing hard as he tried to keep them both from toppling off the steps.

"Now that," he said, after he was sure of his footing, "is what I call a welcome."

"Dinner is ready."

He spun her around and kissed her soundly. "All this, and she can cook, too."

"I want to be everything to you, Whit."

He traced the outline of her face, knowing every beautiful part of her body. "You set me free and gave me a place to heal. That's everything to me, Jackie."

*   *   *

Simon walked through every room of his palatial home, looking at the expensive paintings on the walls, the plush rugs beneath his feet that cushioned his footsteps. He paused to glance up at the new gas crystal chandelier he'd just had installed. He'd come a long way from the dingy little two-room shack he'd lived in with his mother. His home was much grander than his father's place had been, and he had more money than he knew what to do with.

He should be happy, but he wasn't. Something was missing from his life, and he didn't know what it was. He was respected by his neighbors and revered by the city of Galveston—what more could a man ask for?

Why couldn't he find peace within his heart?

He thought of Whit Hawk, who'd come to Galveston with nothing but the clothes on his back; yet Whit had bested Simon at every turn. Hatred rose up in his throat like bile. He had heard that Hawk had married Miss Douglas and had settled on La Posada. No doubt they hoped to rebuild the ranch and raise a passel of kids.

Hope.

That was what was wrong with Simon—he had no hope. Every day was just like the one before, and the one before that. His wealth had been acquired at a high price—blood on his hands. Sometimes, like now, he still felt like the ragtag little boy who had cried out for his father's recognition.

He dabbed at his neck with a handkerchief. The constant humidity pressed in on him like a heavy hand. He shoved the plush velvet curtains aside and glanced at the sweeping lawn and flower beds planted with every variety of colorful flowers. He watched two gardeners toiling to keep the yard manicured.

There were dark clouds moving across the sky, and Simon watched the two gardeners run for shelter as the heavens opened up and rain fell heavily, pelting against the window.

He stalked into his office, unlocked the bottom drawer of his desk, and removed Harold Hawk's ring. He slipped it on his finger. The ring fit better now, because Simon had gained a little weight. He wanted the ring to belong to him—not because he'd taken it from a dead man, but because he'd earned the right to wear it.

He removed Harold Hawk's journal and stared at some of the passages he'd added. With anger driving his actions, Simon jerked up a pen and scribbled in bold script:

> *The father will not long precede the*
> *son in death. Whit Hawk must die!*

Simon removed the ring, dropped it back in the drawer, and replaced the journal, locking them away so no one could find them.

Jamming his hands in his pockets, he swore under his breath. His list of enemies was growing. Whit Hawk was at the top of that list. And because Chantalle had come down on Whit's side and loaned him the money to buy La Posada, she was now second on the list.

No one could escape Simon's wrath for long. He was a patient man. He would wait for just the right moment—bide his time—and then he would strike!

Don't miss the next installment
in the Hawk Crest Saga!

Hawk's Passion

Elaine Barbieri

a special preview

COMING AUGUST 2006!

Chapter One

Elizabeth Huntington entered the Easton Hotel and glanced around her in silent despair. Surely there was some mistake. Surely the carriage she had hired at the train station had brought her to the *wrong* Easton Hotel. Surely the dependable Thomas Biddlington, Esquire, her adoptive mother Ella's family attorney, could not have arranged for accommodations for her in this . . . *place!*

Elizabeth walked across the shabby hotel lobby toward the registration desk, a stiff semi-smile on her lips. She had been warned not to expect too much, that Galveston, Texas had suffered greatly during the war, both from a brief occupation by Union troops, and from a blockade that had held the port hostage after Union troops were driven out. She had been told that Galveston would probably be unlike any city she could remember—surely different from New York City where she had lived for the past eight years of her life with her adoptive parents, Ella and Wilbur Huntington; yet she had dismissed that concern as inconsequential. The death of her dear adoptive father two years earlier had triggered a return of the nightmares that had plagued her for as long as she could remember. Those frightening dreams had made it no longer bearable for the first years of her life to remain a mystery, and she had been more driven to put the mystery to rest. She had told herself that since Texas was the place where her adoptive parents had found her, Texas was most likely the place of her birth, and she could never feel uncomfortable there.

Wrong.

Elizabeth glanced around her. Galveston left her feeling as unsettled as the appearance it presented: Union soldiers freely walked streets where only months earlier the same uniforms had been scorned; buildings and thoroughfares damaged by cannon fire and neglect stood side-by-side with new construction that appeared hasty and haphazard at best. The hotel's deteriorated exterior had been a disturbing sight as she had approached it on a street still bearing the scars of cannon bombardment, yet the interior lobby left her stunned. Drab and gloomy, a step above a shambles with its mismatched furniture and worn carpeting, it had the look of a place long past its prime.

Disturbing her even more, however, were the occupants of the lobby. They were male, poorly dressed and unkempt, outfitted in all manner of western dress. They appeared to be either indolently passing the time of day relaxing with a smoke, or leaning against a bar visible through an open doorway nearby with half-empty glasses in their hands. They made no attempt to hide their interest in her appearance, and were even bold enough to follow her progress across the room with snickers and whispered comments that left no doubt as to their opinion of a woman who would be registering at that hotel by herself.

For the first time, Elizabeth regretted bidding good-bye to her traveling companion, Agatha Potter, the sour-faced, cynical, middle-aged woman hired by her mother's attorney to travel with her in her adoptive mother's absence. Mrs. Potter had not been shy about voicing her opinion of the journey *after* leaving New York. She had said that Elizabeth was "borrowing trouble" with the hopeless dream she was pursuing, and that the sizable sum she was being paid to accompany Elizabeth barely made the journey palatable. The abrasive woman had declared more often and with more vehemence than Elizabeth had been able to abide that she would be only too happy to leave the "lawless state of Texas and return home to the civilized city of New York," and Elizabeth had taken the first opportunity to accommodate her.

She could now see that had been a mistake.

"Can I help you, ma'am?"

The hotel clerk's question was polite, even if his gaze, as it assessed her from the top of her sensible brown hat to the tip of her equally sensible leather shoes, caused her to stammer, "Yes . . . well, I believe . . . I think you have a reservation in my name?"

"You must be Miss Elizabeth Huntington then. I figure you have to be her because there ain't nobody else who would bother with a reservation for a room here." The fellow did not wait for her reply as his toothless grin flashed and he continued, "But you was supposed to share a room with another lady."

"Mrs. Potter won't be coming."

"You're paid up for two weeks in advance. The draft came with your reservation, and your room is ready, so that's all right with me. If them's your bags over there, I'll have a fella carry them upstairs for you."

Uncertain how to react to the clerk's statements, Elizabeth said simply, "Yes, those are my bags."

"Hey, Charlie!" Startling Elizabeth, the clerk called out sharply, "Where are you, old man?"

"I'm right here, and I'm a step ahead of you."

Elizabeth turned to stand eye-to-eye with the scruffy, white-haired man who appeared at her side with her bags in hand. His back curved with age, his hair sparse, and his legs bowed, he said gruffly, "Follow me, lady."

When she did not immediately react, the old man said harshly, "Did you hear me? I'll lead the way."

The buzz of comments in the lobby heightened as Elizabeth started up the stairs behind the grizzled old fellow. She attempted to discount the heated gazes that followed her, and she raised her chin higher. She told herself that it didn't matter how poor her present accommodations had turned out to be, or what any one of those men thought, she was a woman with a mission and she wasn't about to leave Texas until she had accomplished it.

Jason Dodd stood near the doorway of the Easton Hotel. He watched as the young woman climbed the worn staircase to the second floor, aware that he was one of many watching the sway of her narrow hips. It also occurred to him that watching her was probably exactly what she wanted. Unfortunately, he'd seen too many of her kind since the blockade had been lifted. They had arrived in increasing numbers, along with Yankee speculators hoping for a quick profit at the expense of Galveston residents. Women like her usually fit into one of the following categories: Yankee women hoping for an alliance with one of the wealthy speculators; southern "ladies" raised in a genteel manner—women who had lost everything but had learned nothing about the changes war had brought to their way of life; or women who had had no loyalty to either side and who were as willing as some of their male counterparts to profit from the suffering of those less fortunate. All were women willing to trade on their physical assets or by doing whatever they must to support a lifestyle they felt they deserved.

Jason admitted to himself a moment's regret when the young woman disappeared from sight. This woman was particularly clever. She hadn't arrived dressed to attract attention; the sober brown traveling outfit she wore modestly covered her curves. She appeared to be smart enough to realize that there was no need to embellish the simple beauty of honey brown hair that shone with a glow of its own, of dark brows complementing incredibly long fans of lashes framing wide hazel eyes, or a faultless complexion set off to perfection by small, delicate features. The picture she presented was that of a demure, unworldly young woman on her own for the first time in her life—a young woman in desperate need of a protector strong enough and wealthy enough to keep her safe.

The only problem was that if she had come to this particular hotel hoping to strike that kind of a liaison, she had come to the wrong place.

It was true that the Easton Hotel's reputation had been sterling many years before the war. Like other locations in Galveston, however, it had suffered greatly since it was built, and even more greatly during the war. In short, it was no longer a meeting place of the affluent.

The only thing the Easton Hotel now had to recommend it was its proximity to the rail yards. As a result, it was now the choice of an occasional businessman, but more often of stragglers representing the city's current mix—men desperately hoping to improve their situation, those who were uncertain which way to turn, and those who had given up trying.

Jason glanced at the clock on the lobby wall and frowned. He was only too aware that he fit into one of those categories somewhere—actually one of the former determined never to become one of the latter. For that reason he had come directly to the hotel after long days on the trail with the knowledge that he was already late for a meeting. He could not afford to sacrifice timeliness to either comfort or convention. He was equally aware that his appearance was lacking. His dark hair curled in an unsightly manner at the collar of his sweat-stained shirt, his firm chin was covered with three days' growth of beard, and his strong features were marked with lines of strain. His clothing also showed the effects of long days spent in the saddle, from a hat and bandanna still layered with dust, to pants and boots liberally spattered with dried mud—but all that mattered very little to him at present.

Approaching the registration desk with a long, fluid stride that bespoke cool resolve, and with a powerful stretch of shoulders denoting years of physical labor, Jason halted to tower over the squinting desk clerk. "A man by the name of William Brent should have arrived sometime late yesterday or early today. I'm supposed to meet him here."

"Mr. Brent . . . yes . . ." The clerk assessed his appearance for long moments, leaving Jason uncertain whether he would be forced to state his case more strongly before the fellow continued abruptly, "Mr. Brent arrived this morning. He said he was expecting somebody, only I figured maybe that somebody would be female, more like the woman who just registered. I guess I was wrong."

"I guess you were."

"He said to send his visitor right up."

Jason waited.

"Mr. Brent looked like he might be a railroad man. I figured he was here on some kind of business." The clerk winked. "I ain't the kind to talk about what kind of business that might be—legal or otherwise. I figure that's none of my affair."

Jason glared at the nosy clerk. He was tired and irritable. He knew he looked less than professional, but he didn't like the fellow's assumption that he had come on business that would be considered shady—or the fact that the clerk appeared only too happy to tolerate it.

His patience short, Jason responded coldly, "That's right, it's none of your business—and Mr. Brent's room number is . . . ?" When there was no immediate response, he added more forcefully, "Or do you want me to pound on every door in this *establishment* until I find the right one?"

"No, sir!" The clerk took a spontaneous backward step. "That would be room number eight up them stairs. Like I said, he's probably expecting you."

Jason turned in the direction indicated. With a last, deadening glance at the clerk, he headed up the stairs.

Elizabeth stood stock still inside the doorway of her hotel room. Her bags on the floor beside her, she stared around her with dismay. The room was small and spare. A single window covered by a lopsided shade and limp curtains overlooked the street; faded wallpaper hung tenuously from the smoke-darkened walls; and a threadbare rug that had long since lost any hint of its original color covered the floor. Crammed into the space between door and outer wall was a bed, a nightstand sporting an oil lamp, a dresser with a mottled mirror, and a crooked wooden chair with one leg obviously shorter than the others. She hadn't expected much as she had followed the old man carrying her suitcases down a hallway of nicked and stained doors bearing numbers that appeared to follow no particular sequence, with discolored walls marked by years of wear and deliberate abuse; yet she supposed she had hoped for more.

She was spoiled, that was the problem. Her dear adoptive mother and father had given her the best they could afford from the day they had rescued her. The best included a speedy trip home to their Park Avenue mansion in New York City, medical treatment guided by their personal physician at the best hospitals the great city could offer, and recuperation in a

large, airy, sun-filled room that she was able to call her own.

Elizabeth sighed as she recalled those days. She had been protected from everything with her new parents—everything but her own, nameless fear. That fear had nagged at her during endless nights while nightmares of a raging fire assaulted her; while terrifying images within the flames awakened her time and again to the darkness of her room.

The shifting shadows in the night had then worked to accelerate a fear that rose to the point of hysteria in her mind, only to be controlled at last by a faint echo ringing in the back of her mind:

Fear is an enemy. Don't let it win.

Strangely enough, she had been told time and again as an adult that she was fearless. There was no task she would not tackle, no question she would not challenge, no individual too big or too brash for her to confront. She was proud of that facet of her personality, and she'd been forced to exercise it occasionally within her adoptive family.

There was an aunt who took every opportunity to attempt to discredit her in her adoptive parents' eyes. Firm in her rebuff of all Aunt Sylvia's unfair insinuations, Elizabeth was always civil to her, but she had long since given up trying to change the situation. It was a mystery to her how Aunt Sylvia could possibly have given life to a son as gentle and kind as Trevor, who often suffered abuse from his mother in his cousin's defense. Although at first concerned by Aunt Sylvia's concealed animosity, she no longer gave it much thought because she knew her adoptive parents were proud of her and of the way she had handled things.

It was her silent humiliation, however, known only to herself and her dear adoptive mother, Ella, that as fearless as she was in most aspects of her life, she had not yet totally conquered her fear of the dark. Instead, she had learned to control her fear, and she had told herself that would have to do.

Still standing inside the doorway of her room, Elizabeth silently berated herself for her reaction to the austere quarters. She walked a few steps further and scrutinized the bed linens as she folded them back. They were spotlessly clean and fresh. She then noted that the oil lamp sparkled with cleanliness, the rug on the floor had obviously been swept, not a trace of dust marked any visible surface in the room, and resting on the dresser was a small glass in which a few wildflowers, obviously freshly picked, had been artlessly placed.

Elizabeth swallowed hard against the lump that rose unexpectedly to her throat. Someone had made an obvious effort to present the room in the best possible manner.

It was equally obvious that someone had memories of a time when the Easton Hotel had been more than it presently was—and she envied that person. Memory was a gift . . . a treasure to hold forever in one's mind. Her own limited memories had been tenderly cultivated by her adoptive parents—yet she was haunted by the void in her past where memory had been consumed by the same fire that had almost taken her life.

Almost overwhelmed by a familiar sadness, Elizabeth sat on the side of the double bed. She reached into the neckline of her traveling dress and withdrew a delicate oval pendant emblazoned with an elaborate crest. She had no idea how she had gotten the pendant or what it meant. It was all that remained of a past buried somewhere in the shadowed reaches of her mind—yet she was certain it was the key to the *who* and *why* of all she had forgotten.

She studied it, caressing its raised surface with her slender thumb. It was beautiful. Daintily wrought on a gold base in subtle shades of blue enamel, it pictured a sailing ship on a sea of white-crested waves. The image of a hawk in flight was outlined by a red, rising sun. Below the ship, on a banner garlanded with a vine of orchids, were the Latin words *Quattuor mundum do;* and on the bow of the ship, in miniscule letters that had been almost too small for her to identify, was inscribed the name *Sarah Jane*.

She had no idea how an orphaned child had come to possess what appeared to be a meaningful symbol of the past. She only knew that her adoptive mother told her she was wearing the pendant underneath her torn and scorched dress when she escaped the fire; that she had stirred from the pained semi-consciousness of the days following the fire only when someone inadvertently touched the pendant; and that the pendant was—for a reason Elizabeth could not quite define—her most cherished possession.

After Elizabeth's subsequent recovery from her injuries in New York, her adoptive mother attempted to discover more about her origins, but the fire had done its work too well. Ella had learned by having the Latin translated that *Quattuor mundum do* meant,

Elaine Barbieri

"To four I give the world"; yet Elizabeth's perspicacity was responsible for deciphering the miniscule letters that formed the name *Sarah Jane* on the bow of the ship. A relentless search of ships' registries in the time following revealed several ships named *Sarah Jane,* but only one registered in Texas—in Galveston. That was when the idea of making her present journey was born.

Tears briefly clouded Elizabeth's vision. Years had passed since that moment of discovery. Her adoptive mother and she had intended to make the journey of discovery together, but her adoptive father's unexpected illness and his three-year struggle to survive had put it on hold. Her adoptive father finally slipped away, but his extended illness had already affected her adoptive mother's health adversely. When Ella Huntington suffered a stroke, Elizabeth knew she had no choice but to remain by the side of the dear woman who was the only mother she could remember.

The mystery of her past was never forgotten, however. It interfered with the progress of her life. Aaron Meese, a handsome, sincere young man who was heir to his father's fortune, loved her—but she had been unable to make a commitment. Another sought-after bachelor, Gerald Connors, made similar intentions known, but her answer was the same, that she could not commit to the future while her past was shrouded in darkness.

Helpless against nightmares that grew in frequency as time passed, Elizabeth had no choice but to agree when her adoptive mother insisted that she delay her search no longer. She knew Ella would be disturbed when Agatha Potter returned prematurely and she realized Elizabeth was alone in her search. She suspected Aunt Sylvia would do her best to place harsh blame on her for Agatha's return, but Elizabeth also knew she could not allow either thought to hinder her. She was in Texas, the place of her birth, she hoped. This was her last chance to unearth the mystery of her past and to halt the nightmares that plagued her. She knew—

Elizabeth's pensive moment ended abruptly at the sound of a knock on her door. Uncertain, she approached it slowly and asked, "Who is it?"

"It's me, ma'am. I figure you was waiting for me."

Waiting for him . . . ?

Had someone recognized her? Could her search have ended successfully and so quickly?

With a shaky smile on her lips and her heart pounding, Elizabeth pulled open the door—then went stock still at the sight of the bearded, grinning cowpoke swaying in her doorway. She took a backward step as the smell of whiskey and stale perspiration reached her nostrils. She said stiffly, "I think you made an error when you knocked on my door, sir. Perhaps you should try another room."

"No siree, you're the one I was looking for." The man's grin widened, allowing a broader view of uneven, yellowed teeth. Elizabeth suppressed a grimace when he reached into his pocket with hands that were less than clean and pulled out a wad of greenbacks as he said, "I got the money to pay for a good time, and you're the one I want to spend it with."

As he attempted to enter the room, sudden fear closed Elizabeth's throat. Reacting spontaneously, she shoved hard at his chest, knocking him a few steps

backward, but she was not quick enough to halt the
hand that grasped the door as she attempted to slam
it. She was still struggling to force the door closed
when the cowpoke pushed it open with a sudden
thrust and said harshly, "Think you're too good for
me, huh? Well, you ain't, and it looks like I'm going to
have to prove it to you."

Elizabeth responded in as firm a tone as she could
manage, "You've made a mistake and I'm asking you
to leave. If you don't leave, I'll call the manager of this
establishment and have you thrown out."

"The *manager?*"

The cowpoke's burst of laughter was halted abruptly
by a deep voice from behind him saying, "You heard
the lady, partner. You made a mistake, so put your
money back in your pocket and go back where you
came from."

Elizabeth restrained a gasp when she looked at the
big man standing behind the drunken cowpoke.
Bearded, disheveled, and decidedly unclean, he was a
much larger version of the man he was displacing.

Making contact with the hard, dark-eyed gaze that
turned briefly in her direction, Elizabeth swallowed.
No, she was wrong. This man wasn't drunk—and unless she was wrong, he wasn't someone who would be
turned away easily, either.

What had she gotten herself into?

The big man's gaze did not falter as he stared at the
shorter fellow and pressed, "Did you hear what I
said?"

The drunk looked up at the man standing behind
him. His expression hardened a moment, but then he
appeared to reconsider, saying abruptly, "All right, I

ain't so drunk that I can't see you're bigger than I am and steadier on your feet—so you win. She's all yours. As far as I'm concerned, she ain't worth the trouble she'd cost me, not when I can go to Miss Sadie's place and get me a woman who's more willing."

"That's good thinking. Miss Sadie's is the right place for you today."

The drunk was staggering back down the hallway when the big man turned toward Elizabeth and said unexpectedly, "I hope you learned a lesson here today, *lady.*"

"I beg your pardon!" Insulted by his tone, Elizabeth continued, "If you're insinuating—"

She took a step backward as the big man closed the distance between them, stopping so near that she could feel the brush of his surprisingly sweet breath against her cheek as he said softly, "I'm not insinuating anything. I'm *telling* you. You're not going to find the kind of *protector* you're looking for in this hotel. My advice would be to take yourself down to the Seamont Hotel where you can find a man with better manners and a fatter wallet." His dark eyes drilled into hers as he added, "You're wasting yourself here."

"How dare you insinuate—"

"I told you, I'm not insinuating. I'm telling you. Galveston survived a blockade that cost it dearly, and the people here are celebrating their freedom any way they can. If you don't want the same kind of fella knocking at your door again, get yourself out of here so you won't be a temptation to men who have suffered much and have little resistance to your kind of allure. There might not be somebody around to help you out next time."

"Help me out? Is that what you think you did?" Elizabeth was incensed. "I'll have you know that I could've handled that fellow on my own. I didn't need your interference, and neither will I ever need it again! And for your information, my room here has been paid up two weeks in advance, and I don't expect to lose any part of that sum, your *advice* notwithstanding!"

"Suit yourself."

"I will do exactly that!"

The big man's dark eyes drilled into hers a moment longer before he dismissed her without a word and headed on down the hallway.

Catching herself staring after the fellow—at the self-possessed way he walked with his head high and his broad shoulders squared, as if he knew where he was heading and no one was going to stop him— Elizabeth strode back into her room and slammed the door closed behind her. She was breathing heavily when she turned back to twist the key in the lock. She glimpsed her face unexpectedly in the mottled mirror. *Her kind of allure?* What was it about her that had made either of them assume—?

Preferring not to finish that thought, Elizabeth picked up her suitcase and placed it on the bed. So she should go to the Seamont Hotel where she could find a protector with better manners and a fatter wallet, huh? She gave a short laugh. Better manners, maybe, but she didn't need a fatter wallet *or* a protector.

Elizabeth withdrew a small derringer from her suitcase and slipped it into her handbag. She had made a mistake packing away the small weapon that her adoptive mother had insisted she carry—but the truth was, she hadn't thought she'd need it. But then, neither had she thought lessons on the small gun's care and usage were necessary when her adoptive father had insisted on them years earlier.

Wrong twice.

But she *had* learned a lesson a few minutes earlier, even if it wasn't the one the dark-eyed derelict had intended. She would never be caught unawares again.

The face of her unlikely savior returned unexpectedly to mind, and Elizabeth frowned. He had been angry when he left and had looked as if he regretted having halted the advances of the fellow who had appeared at her door. His advice to her had been caustic and his obvious assumptions were insulting. In addition, the intense heat of his dark eyes when he had looked at her had made her uneasy in ways she could not clearly define.

The conclusion was apparent. She needed to avoid him—and she would. She had more important things to do.

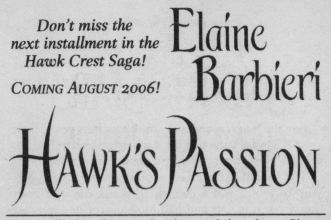

THE MOON
AND THE STARS
CONSTANCE O'BANYON

Caroline Richmond started running on her wedding day—the same day her husband died. Her solitary life is filled with fear of her malicious brother-in-law always one step behind her. She thought she'd found a shred of peace in Texas. But when a mysterious bounty hunter comes to town, she knows the wrath in his amber eyes is meant only for her. He finds a way to be everywhere she is, making her nerves hum in a way she thought she'd conquered.

Wade Renault came out of retirement for one reason: to see a deceptive murderess brought to justice. But when he meets the accused woman, he senses more panic than treachery. She lives too simply, she seems too honest and scared. Someone had deceived him, but he will wait to get her right where he wants her, beneath...*The Moon and the Stars.*
